PRELUDE TO A KISS

Vivian didn't understand it. Why were she and Glenda sitting in her apartment, dateless in front of the television on New Year's Eve? They were young, reasonably attractive, had good jobs, used breath mints regularly and watched their weight.

"Maybe we're too old," Vivian said, thinking aloud.

"What?" Glenda's voice was muffled because she had a mouthful of pizza.

Vivian responded by picking up the remote control and turning off the television.

"All right. What is it?"

She paused for dramatic effect. "This is the year we're going to meet our Mr. Rights."

Glenda made a face. "Puh-leeze. I've known you for what, four years? Both of us were looking even before then, and nothing's changed. Face it, Viv. If it's not fated, it ain't gonna happen."

"Well, maybe fate needs a helping hand. . . ."

BOOK YOUR PLACE ON OUR WEBSITE AND MAKE THE ARABESQUE ROMANCE CONNECTION!

We've created a customized website just for our very special Arabesque readers, where you can get the inside scoop on everything that's going on with Arabesque romance novels.

When you come online, you'll have the exciting opportunity to:

- View covers of upcoming books

- Learn about our future publishing schedule (listed by publication month and author)

- Find out when your favorite authors will be visiting a city near you

- Search for and order backlist books

- Check out author bios and background information

- Send e-mail to your favorite authors

- Join us in weekly chats with authors, readers and other guests

- Get writing guidelines

- AND MUCH MORE!

Visit our website at
http://www.arabesquebooks.com

PRELUDE TO A KISS

Bettye Griffin

BET Publications, LLC
http://www.bet.com
http://www.arabesquebooks.com

For my sister, Beverly Griffin Love

ARABESQUE BOOKS are published by

BET Publications, LLC
c/o BET BOOKS
One BET Plaza
1900 W Place NE
Washington, D.C. 20018-1211

All Kensington Titles, Imprints, and Distributed Lines are available at special quantity discounts for bulk purchases for sales promotions, premiums, fund-raising, and educational or institutional use. Special book excerpts or customized printings can also be created to fit specific needs. For details, write or phone the office of the Kensington special sales manager: Kensington Publishing Corp., 850 Third Avenue, New York, NY 10022, attn: Special Sales Department, Phone: 1-800-221-2647.

First Printing: December 2001
10 9 8 7 6 5 4 3 2 1

Printed in the United States of America

ACKNOWLEDGMENTS

To my husband, Bernard Underwood; brother Gary A. Griffin; brother-in-law Thomas J. Love and stepson Timothy Underwood for agreeing to go along with my little joke. It was not possible to get an okay from my brothers Peter and Gordon, who are deceased . . . But if I get hit by a falling object while walking down the street, I'll know they didn't think much of the idea!

Bernard, because of what you've taught me about computers I was able to resurrect Chapter Eight all by myself.

To Cheryl Ferguson, Marcia King-Gamble, and Gwen McGee, for knowing exactly what I mean . . . You know what I mean?

To Irene Umstead for providing authenticity to the ski slope scenes (try saying that one five times fast). I'm an itty-bitty baby slope person myself.

To Zandra Bryant, Felice Franklin, Ava Gardner, Clennon King, Maureen King, Linnel Little, Naseema Maat of Nefertiti Books & Gifts, Kimberly Van Allen, Cynthia White, and Betty Williams for being so wonderfully supportive and just plain nice.

To Glenda Blau, who had the misfortune of calling me just as I was trying to decide on a name for a minor character in my book A LOVE OF HER OWN. The character is a woman who stole, abused drugs, neglected her children, and was incarcerated. Ouch. I hope I've redeemed myself in this tale by giving your first name to someone more honorable.

To my critique group, The Bard Group (as in no holds barred, folks), including Jeffrey, Steve, Lee, Beth, Larry, and Heidi, and, of course our esteemed leader, Frank.

Prologue:
The Date from Hades

The only thing she intended to serve was what could fit on his plate.

Vivian had high hopes for what might happen between her and Thomas Joseph. They had met the previous weekend on a setup with her friends Beverly and Michael White. The four of them had gone to dinner, and she and Thomas hit it off to the point where she was disappointed to learn he was going to Texas on business the following Wednesday and would be gone for a week and a half. She'd invited him over for dinner at her apartment, but it was important he understand there were no ulterior motives. Well, actually there was *one*. She didn't want him to forget her while he was gone.

"It was really nice of you to invite me over," Thomas said.

"I thought you might enjoy a home-cooked meal, since you'll be eating out a lot while you're in Texas. It'll have to be an early night, though."

"That's fine. I've got a morning flight. Can I help you out?"

"No, but you can keep me company."

The tiny kitchen was really too small to hold two people, but Thomas stood in the doorway. She felt his eyes on her as she turned on the burner and poured some peanut oil into the wok. She then opened the refrigerator and removed the package of pork strips from the top shelf, the healthy, pinkish-white color attesting to the pork's freshness. The look on his face told her he liked what he saw. Maybe there was a nice compliment forthcoming . . .

Or so she thought.

"You know," he said, "it's really best to keep your meats on the bottom shelf of your fridge. That'll keep the juice from dripping down onto other foods and contaminating them. Juice from rare meat is just as dangerous as rare meat itself."

"Gee, I never thought of that. I always thought meat should be kept on the top shelf where it's supposed to be coldest."

"Actually, the bottom is where it's the coldest. It's closer to the motor."

"You're kidding! I didn't know that." Vivian mentally filed this new information in the remote area of her brain where she stored useful facts. Thomas knew what he was talking about. He was a professor of microbiology at New York University, which was certainly a first for her. She could just hear her mother bragging to everybody in New London, Connecticut, that her daughter was dating a microbiologist. At dinner last week with Bev and Michael, he'd amused them all with a story about being reported to the police when a patron at an upscale Greenwich Village restaurant saw him crouching in a men's room stall. He'd actually been testing for bacteria, but when he explained that to the officer the reply was a caustic, "Yeah, right. I arrested another one like you three days ago." Only an endorsement on his behalf from the maître d' saved him from being issued a summons.

Vivian turned on the faucet and, leaving it running, sprinkled a few drops of water into the wok. It sizzled but quickly died out, indicating the oil wasn't hot enough for cooking. She put the stopper in the sink and poured in a quick stream of dishwashing liquid, which quickly formed soapy pockets around the pot and spoon she'd used to make rice earlier, as well as around the plastic cutting board she'd used to cut strips of onion, and red, green, and yellow pepper. By the time the sink filled up, the wok was ready, so she dumped the meat in first, keeping it moving with a long-handled flat spoon.

Once she started, the process went very quickly. She removed the meat, added the vegetables, the rice, and then the meat again, mixing the ingredients with stir-fry sauce. "Voila!" she said proudly, tilting the wok and inviting him to look at her culinary creation.

"Smells great. Makes me reluctant to spend a week in some river town in South Texas. I'll probably live on Stouffer's microwaveable dinners."

"Nowhere to eat there, huh?"

"Nowhere I'd want to go. Just little coffee shops, maybe a diner. I actually eat out very little unless I'm able to inspect the kitchen."

"Do people actually let you do that?" she asked as she moved the wok to a cold burner. She was beginning to feel a bit uneasy, considering that maybe his offer to help was borne of a desire to inspect *her* kitchen.

"If they don't have anything to hide, they do.

But if I think they might kick up a fuss, I just order fried chicken. It's a good bet that at least it'll be thoroughly cooked."

That's what he'd had Saturday night, she remembered.

"Much safer than hamburger. Did you know that meat is often ground together, even when it comes from different distributors? That means if there's a breakout of *E. coli* anywhere in the United States you're at risk, since the meat used in a single hamburger can come from literally hundreds of cows. There's no such thing as a local outbreak."

"Wow," Vivian said with more interest than she felt. She'd heard all about the danger of eating any meats rare, but she preferred her burgers and steaks well-done anyway.

"Anyway, being invited to work on this study is a wonderful opportunity for me. I'll manage, even though the restaurant situation leaves something to be desired. It's a town, not a city, and there's only one hotel, one of those midrange places. That concerns me, too. I've found that the more expensive the room, the fewer bacteria it has."

"I guess that's true. I've always been suspicious of those bedspreads. I mean, how often do you suppose they really clean them?" Without waiting for an answer, she took two plates from the cupboard and handed one to him. "I'm going to let you fix your own plate. There's plenty; take as much as you want. It'll just take a minute for the egg rolls to heat up in the microwave." She busied herself by adding empty bowls and spoons to the dishwater.

"You know, you really shouldn't leave dishes soaking like that. Warm water and food is the perfect setting for food-borne germs like Salmonella or Campylobacter to breed."

"Oh. I didn't know. It seems to make them easier to wash after dinner."

"You'd be surprised how quickly food particles come off, probably just in the time it takes to fill up the sink."

While she appreciated the information, at the same time she was feeling the tiniest twinges of irritation. This was supposed to be a fun and light-hearted evening, but it was turning into a lecture on how to avoid germs.

They took their plates and glasses and sat at the table opposite the kitchen. The ordinary thirty-six-inch round butcher block, for which she'd forsaken standard dinette chairs in favor of a pair of more exotic fan-back wicker chairs, had an especially cozy look to it now that she'd put a crocheted overlay on top of the tablecloth and had lit candles.

"Where's your bathroom?" Thomas asked as he put his plate on the table, instantly killing the mood she'd worked so hard to create.

"Right around the corner." She knew he wanted to wash his hands; someone in his position would never sit down to a meal without doing that. Hell, she was surprised he'd fixed his plate already. She felt perfectly wholesome herself, having washed her hands thoroughly just before starting to cook. Still, he could have done that in the kitchen. There was a container of liquid soap—fortunately it was antibacterial—clearly visible in the corner by the sink, as well as a roll of paper towels on a holder. Now she found herself worrying whether or not he would think her bathroom was clean enough. Of course, she'd given it a thorough wipedown with a sponge wet with a mixture of water and lemon-scented Mr. Clean while she was preparing the apartment for entertaining, but she didn't have time to mop the floor. It was, after all, a Tuesday night, and she'd worked all day. She remembered what he said about the bathroom in the restaurant and wondered if he carried a bacteriometer or something in his hip pocket.

She sipped her wine and took a few bites, unable to sit there and merely breathe in the appealing aroma of the meat and onions while she waited for him to return. It seemed like he was gone a long time. How long did it take him to wash his hands, anyway? Was he scrubbing under his fingernails? How dirty could his fingernails be, given his obvious tendency toward fastidiousness? Howard Hughes probably hadn't been this obsessed about germs.

Finally, he returned and began to eat. "Delicious," he said after swallowing. "Did you make the egg rolls, too?"

"No, those came from the deli at the supermarket. I just heated them up. I'm glad you're enjoying it."

"You know," he said as he swallowed, "in your bathroom I couldn't help noticing that you keep your toothbrush in the built-in rack on the wall."

"That makes sense, doesn't it? I mean, that's what it's for."

"It would, except that the rack is awfully close to the toilet. I did an experiment once where I put three sterile petri dishes around the bathroom and then flushed the toilet. Afterward, I tested and there were bacteria in each dish—even the ones three and four feet away! It has to do with an aerosol cloud. . . ."

At that point Vivian gave up any thoughts that this could be the beginning of anything memorable and just vowed to get through dinner. If he called when he returned from his trip she just wouldn't answer the phone. *Thank heaven for caller ID,* she thought as she took a long gulp of wine.

By the time he left she had learned all kinds of tidbits, most of them unappetizing. She tried not to gag when he told her that most people's toilets are cleaner than their kitchen drains; that sponges, dishcloths, and dishtowels are havens for staphylococcus and enterococcus; that doorknobs are usually filthy; and that the cleanest stalls in public rest rooms are often the ones at the far ends, possibly because they are the least used. Then he actually had the nerve to ask why she wasn't eating. The man didn't have a clue.

When he finally kissed her good night and left, she imagined the first thing he would do when he got to his car would be to wash out his mouth with alcohol-based mouthwash to protect himself, since he'd also graciously pointed out—during dinner, no less—that a dog's mouth is likely to have fewer germs than that of another human. The whole episode made her want to gag.

Chapter 1: Another Auld Lang Syne

Vivian didn't understand it. Why were she and Glenda sitting in her apartment, dateless, in front of the television on New Year's Eve? They were young, reasonably attractive, had good jobs, used breath mints regularly, and watched their weight.

She bowed her head, knowing she wasn't being totally honest. It was true that they looked good and their breath was fresh. They had well-paying positions at the same chemical manufacturer— Glenda ran the payroll department and she was an administrator in human resources. Her fibbing was in regard to their weight and ages. It was true they were watching their waistlines, and it was getting easier to see them every week. The loaded pizza with sauce-filled crust they were munching on certainly wasn't doing anything to combat calories. Both of them had picked up about ten or fifteen pounds over the last year. Weight had never stuck like that before. It probably had something to do with getting older. At this point they could only be called young if the person doing the calling was over sixty. They were both thirty-four . . . and thirty-five was just around the corner, especially for Glenda, whose birthday was on January twenty-third.

"Maybe we're too old," Vivian said, thinking out loud. Now she knew how Demi Moore must feel. One minute she's the twelve-million-dollar woman, and the next she hasn't made a picture in three years, and there's a younger brunette on the scene. It can happen quicker than you can say Catherine Zeta-Jones.

"What?" Glenda's voice was muffled because she had a mouthful of pizza.

Vivian responded by picking up the remote control and clicking off the television.

"What'd you do that for? They're about to show the good part."

"It's cable, Glenda. You've seen it a million times before." She made her voice sound flat and duncelike, imitating the line from the eighties comedy *Night Shift* she knew her friend was waiting for. " 'Barney Rubble. What an actor.' This is important," she added, speaking normally.

"All right. What is it?"

She paused for dramatic effect. "This is the year we're going to meet our Mr. Rights."

Glenda made a face. "Puh-leeze. I've known you for what, four years? Both of us were looking even before then, and nothing's changed. Face it, Viv. If it's not fated, it ain't gonna happen."

"Well, maybe fate needs a helping hand."

"So what do you plan to do about it?"

"Prospective husbands aren't going to come ringing our doorbells. We have to get out and find them. And I mean 'get out.' We're going to travel."

"Travel how?"

"There are organizations all over the country that sponsor social events. We're going to go. Whether it's a winter ski trip, a summer cruise, those music festivals they have every year in New Orleans and the Caribbean . . . we're going."

"Are you crazy? That'll cost a fortune!"

"We both got bonuses last week. The company made a bundle last year with those new products they introduced. We've never gotten so much."

"Especially you," Glenda pointed out. "Remember, I'm just a lowly payroll supervisor. You're the big-shot human resources administrator, giving people their walking papers."

"I know how much you make, Glenda. Don't put on a poor mouth with me." Glenda had been with the company considerably longer, and because of her seniority her salary was actually slightly higher than Vivian's. It was only because Vivian's position had a higher profile that she had been awarded a larger bonus.

"And I was going to invest mine."

"You *always* invest yours. Spend it this time." She shook her head. Sometimes her friend could be tighter than Mariah Carey's dresses. "It's not like you don't put away anything from your regular paychecks."

"What about you? Are you going to be able to afford to do all this traveling plus that safari you're going on? Your bonus wasn't *that* big."

"Most of the money for my safari is coming from my putting off buying a new car. You know I've always wanted to take this trip." When Vivian and her childhood friend Lauren Walters booked the trip she had invited Glenda to join them, but her friend didn't find the idea of sleeping under the stars appealing. "Take me to the nearest Holiday Inn," she had said with a wave of dismissal.

"It won't cost us anything to go to the open house tomorrow," Glenda said now.

"Yes, but everything else will have a price tag, so find a money market with a nice rate to park it in. You'll need a good return. Chances are you'll spend every penny of it, and then some."

"I'll say. What you're proposing will take all of this year's bonus plus last year's, too." Glenda took another bite of pizza. "This better not backfire," she said after she swallowed. "If I spend all that money traveling to New Orleans and the Caribbean, only to meet my soul mate and find out he lives in Texas or California someplace, I'm telling you now, I'm gonna be hot."

"Life's a chance, Glenda. All I know is that after my last attempt at dating I've got to do something."

"I guess I can understand why you'd feel that way. I think of your experience with that microbiology dude every time I disinfect my drain."

Vivian laughed. "I do mine regularly now, too. Those pointers he gave me did come in handy, but it would have been nice not to have learned about them on our first date." She wrinkled her nose. "That's why it was also our last."

"Just think, Viv. You could've had a doctor, if you'd let Desirée give him your number."

It was true that Vivian's former neighbor Desirée Mack, who lived in Colorado but had spent an extended period in New York the year before, had wanted to introduce her to a single physician who was her boyfriend's close friend. The two men owned the building Vivian lived in, and she had looked forward to the meeting, but it had never panned out. Whenever Vivian was available, the doctor wasn't, and vice versa. "I don't like the idea of giving my phone number to total strangers. Besides, Thomas was a doctor, and he was a jerk, so there's no guarantee."

"Thomas doesn't count, Viv. He wasn't a people doctor."

"No, but he's a Ph.D. Don't make it sound like he was a vet."

The New Year's open house was being held at a loft in the Chelsea section of Manhattan: West Twentieth Street. Glenda had met Ivy Smith at a closed-circuit screening of a heavyweight boxing match she had attended at someone's apartment with a date. When they were introduced Glenda noted that her *last* name was Ivey. They determined that they used different spellings, and they ended up chatting while the fellows watched the fight. Ivy invited Glenda to the open house, which she was giving with four friends. The object was for each woman to invite five men and three women, with hopes that their friends would meet interesting people in a setting where the men outnumbered the women.

It took forever to find a place to park, the standard for Manhattan, which Vivian regarded as a nice place to live if you could afford taxi fare every time you went out after dark. After getting their hopes up at what always turned out to be a fire hydrant or commercial driveway, they found a spot on Seventeenth. The minute Glenda turned off the engine they pulled down their respective sun visors to take a last look in the mirrors on the backs.

"Oh, my. Do you see what I see?" Glenda asked as they approached the building. Three men were approaching from the other side, along with a woman, who was obviously the date of the man her arm was linked with.

"Yes. Let's hurry so we can meet up."

The parties got to the front of the building simultaneously. "Hello," Vivian said to the others. "Are you ringing loft four?"

Someone said yes, and the door was held open for them when the buzzer sounded. "Thank you," Glenda said graciously.

The six of them loaded the elevator. It was only one flight, but by the time the doors opened on the second floor they had all exchanged names. Vivian noticed that the man named Bobby seemed to stick close to Glenda, and that from the beauty contestant smile on Glenda's face, she didn't mind.

The scene inside the loft was even more promising. There were men everywhere, most of whose attentions were focused on the big-screen TV in the huge, bright living room—the windows were easily six feet tall—which was broadcasting a college football game.

"Happy New Year!" Glenda said as she hugged a strikingly attractive woman who was wearing a V-neck bouclé sweater and wide-legged slacks. "Ivy, this is my good friend, Vivian St. James. Vivian, Ivy Smith."

"Hello, Ivy. Happy New Year."

"Happy New Year to you, Vivian."

"Thanks for inviting me." Vivian's eyes scanned the mostly male crowd and tried not to salivate, but she felt like a half-starved person at a smorgasbord. The men came in different varieties: Thirty-

ish, fortyish, short, tall, bearded, clean-shaven, and
a few shaved heads.

"Happy New Year. I'm glad you could make it,"
Ivy replied with a hint of a British accent. "We're
putting coats in the first room on the right. The
bar is in the corner. It's self service, and if you like
your eggnog with a kick you'll have to spike it yourself; we left it nonalcoholic for those who prefer it
plain. The buffet table is across from the bar, by
the kitchen." She pointed with a discreet index finger. "The powder room is in the hall, the first door
on the left. There are ashtrays all around if you
want to smoke. That's it, I guess. Go ahead and
introduce yourselves. I don't know half the people
here, anyway."

"We will," Glenda said. "This is a beautiful place,
Ivy. Is it yours?"

"Don't I wish. It's owned by a family friend. He's
on extended assignment in Europe. I'm just water-
ing the plants, walking the dog, dusting . . . stuff
like that."

"Ah, house-sitting. Nice work if you can get it."

Glenda and Ivy went into a conversation about
the advantages of taking care of someone else's
home, but Vivian wasn't paying attention. Her eyes
had connected with those of a man sitting in one
of the leather director's chairs in the living room.
He had a rather large head in proportion to his
body and a receding hairline, but regardless of that
there was a blatant sexiness about him. She slipped
out of her coat and handed it to Glenda. "Would
you be a sweetheart and put this away for me? I'm
really thirsty. I'm going to fix myself a drink."

At the bar she poured herself a glass of white
wine. They were using real glasses, too, not those
annoying Styrofoam cups that were more suited for

children's parties. Her intuition told her she would not be alone for long, and when she heard a deep voice say "Happy New Year" she knew who would be standing there before she looked up.

"The same to you," she said. She wasn't disappointed. His mustache and beard were laced with gray, but curiously there was none in his hair.

"I'm Gary Allen."

"Vivian St. James."

"Are you a friend of Bethany's?"

His lips, surrounded on all sides by facial hair, fascinated her. She always thought there was something incredibly sexy about a bearded man's mouth. "No, I don't know her. I'm a friend of Ivy's, or rather the friend of a friend of Ivy's."

"Ah, yes. It all gets rather tricky, with so many hostesses. Five of them, I believe. But it's always nice to meet new people. Tell me, are you a football fan?"

"No, not particularly, but I guess I can shout out when you do."

He responded by holding out his arm, which she took. As he escorted her to the seating area of the living room she looked around for Glenda, finally spotting her fixing a plate at the buffet table with Bobby and looking quite content.

It was apparently an exciting game being played in this year's Rose Bowl. There was a lot of shouting, sometimes so loud she thought they might be able to hear it all the way in California. Most of the women wore the same I-don't-get-it look that was on her own face, except for one show-off who was making comments like, "Great run" and "What a hit," clearly understanding everything the fellows were saying. Vivian disliked her immediately.

The boisterous setting gave her and Gary little time to really talk beyond exchanging the standard where-do-you-lives and the utmost important what-do-you-dos, but it was fun. Besides, there was no reason to think this wouldn't be continued as a one-on-one on Friday or Saturday night, which wasn't a bad way to kick off the new year, especially considering that just last night there wasn't a single prospect in sight. In the meantime she enjoyed the sight of his lips moving whenever he talked.

· When she went to the buffet table after about half an hour she noticed Glenda was still talking to Bobby in a quiet corner. The buffet was laid out on a rectangular table; appetizers, entrees, breads, and desserts surrounding a large punch bowl filled with eggnog. She helped herself to some lasagna, ignoring the strain her thickened middle was putting on the waistband of her slacks, passed on the chicken wings in favor of the pinwheel sandwiches—it would be embarrassing to smile at Gary with a piece of chicken between her teeth—and added some raw vegetables, silently congratulating herself on eating sensibly. If she kept this up the next time she wore these pants they wouldn't leave indentation marks on the skin of her waist.

She glanced at the television area when the crowd got particularly loud and noticed circles of smoke near the twelve-foot ceiling. If there was anything she found more annoying than telemarketers who called at dinnertime, it was a room filled with people lighting up. She was allergic to tobacco, but she felt none of the usual effects of her nose running or her nasal passages getting clogged. Those high ceilings must make the difference.

The game was almost over when Glenda ap-

peared, taking a seat on a nearby floor pillow.
"Hi!"

"Hi. What happened to Bobby?"

"He left. The couple he rode down with only
had a baby sitter for a few hours."

"Where does he live?"

"Somewhere in Queens. Springfield Gardens, I
think."

"Kind of far from Riverdale, isn't it?"

"It's only geography. Plus seven dollars in tolls."

When the game ended they decided it was time
to leave themselves. Gary offered to walk them to
their car. Vivian was grateful, since it was now dark
and she didn't know how many people would be
on the streets in this part of Manhattan. "We'll just
need a minute to get our coats."

"This is a gorgeous place, isn't it?" Glenda commented as they searched for their coats on the
king-size brass bed in the spacious master bedroom.
Space was at a premium in New York, so much so
that it was not unusual for families of five or six
to squeeze into three-room apartments; and it was
refreshing to see that some people had living
rooms large enough to play ball in. Whomever Ivy
Smith was house sitting for had beaucoup bucks.

"It sure is. Did you see the master bath? It has
a huge sunken tub with Jacuzzi. It's sharp."

"I saw it. Here we go." Glenda pulled out her
winter-white coat as well as Vivian's brown-and-
white herringbone. "They were close to the bottom. They probably got tossed to the side by the
people who left before us."

Vivian glanced around to make sure they were
alone. "So how'd you make out?"

"I'll tell you in the car."

Coats on, they returned to the living room,

where Gary waited, still wearing a tan crew-neck sweater. "Aren't you wearing a coat?" Vivian asked Gary.

"I put it on the rack by the door so I wouldn't have to dig through a pile of coats on a bed."

Glenda was saying good-bye to Ivy, and Gary and Vivian did the same. Gary, the arms of his pullover sweater pushed up to his elbows, removed his leather jacket from the rack and swung his left arm into it, but when he swung his right arm he made a strange sound, like he'd been stung by an insect or something. He lowered his arm, and it was covered with blood.

They all gasped at the sight of his bloody arm. "I'll get a towel," Ivy said.

"What happened?" Vivian asked, dumbfounded.

"The damndest thing. I went to get my arm into my jacket. I guess I was too close to the rack and one of those hooks got me. Damn, it stings."

"It looks awfully deep from the way it's bleeding," Glenda said. "It's long, too. You'll probably need stitches to close it up."

Ivy returned with a clean dishtowel, which she immediately wrapped around Gary's forearm. "I'm sorry," she said when he winced. "I know it's painful."

"I'm bleeding all over your floor."

"It's all right. I'll take care of it in a minute." Ivy peeled back the towel, part of which was soaked red. There was still too much blood to actually see the wound. "You'll have to go to a hospital. Did you come with anyone?"

"No."

"Glenda and I can take you," Vivian offered.

"That's awfully nice of you. We can go to Hudson, in Washington Heights."

"But that's all the way uptown!"

"I know, but it's close to where I live. It's not too far from you, either. I need to be able to drive myself home afterward. Besides, it's not like I'm in danger of bleeding to death. It's not quite that bad."

He had told Vivian he lived on upper Riverside Drive, making Hudson Hospital an ideal choice. Near the mammoth Columbia-Presbyterian complex, it was a much smaller hospital and probably had a less busy ER. After he was repaired it would be an easy ride home for him . . . and just a slightly longer one for her and Glenda.

She fixed Gary's jacket around his shoulder. "How far away did you park?"

"I got lucky. I'm right on the next block."

"All right. Why don't we go to your car first, then we'll drive Glenda to hers, then head for the hospital."

"Sounds like a plan. Let's go." Gary turned to Ivy. "I'm sorry about your towel, and your floor."

"Don't worry about it. The towel is replaceable, and I'm going to mop up the floor right now. You just get yourself fixed up."

On the brief walk to the next block Vivian found herself curious about what he drove. From their conversation she learned he was an art director for an advertising agency headquartered in midtown. Did he have one of those cute foreign numbers that only seated two? That would be great, even if she and Glenda had to squeeze into one seat. They could manage for a couple of blocks. Or maybe he had a rugged SUV.

She could barely conceal her shock when he stopped in front of a weathered beige Volvo that looked like it was at least ten years old, although with a Volvo it was hard to tell; before they modified that boxy shape a few years back the car had changed little in thirty years. "I'll drive," she offered.

"I forgot to tell you, it's a stick. But I should be able to hold the wheel with my left hand."

"I can drive a stick, Gary." She experienced a twinge of what felt like resentment at his assumption that she couldn't, but she chased it away. "It's been a long time since I have, so it might be a little jerky ride at first, but once I get to the highway I'll be fine."

They got in, Glenda in the back, and Vivian drove to where Glenda had parked.

"Hudson Hospital, right? Where exactly is that? I'm not sure," Glenda said.

Vivian paid close attention as Gary instructed her; if he dozed off during the ride she didn't want to wake him to ask for directions.

The ER at the hospital wasn't crowded. There were only a few people in the waiting room, none of whom appeared to be in discomfort. Perhaps they were waiting for patients and not for treatment. It wasn't what Vivian expected to see on New Year's Day. She supposed all the rabble-rousers had gone to Presbyterian.

The triage nurse checked Gary in and inspected his arm. The blood flow had stopped, and a gash about three inches long could clearly be seen, as well as the inner top layer of his skin. "Ooh, that's nasty," the nurse said, wrinkling his nose in a gesture more typical of a civilian than a health-care professional. Vivian could remember the days when she could distinguish doctors from nurses strictly by gender. No more. This man had horn-rimmed glasses and graying hair. He even wore sea-green scrubs. He might look like a surgeon straight out of the OR, but he was an RN relegated to desk duty, collecting unexciting information about patients' symptoms, medical histories, and allergies.

The very thought of most nursing duties made Vivian queasy, but she believed in dressing to be taken seriously, whatever your profession. There was certainly nothing wrong with being mistaken for a doctor. She'd take someone dressed this way over the ones who wore scrubs printed with drawings of singing stethoscopes or dancing thermostats any day.

An ER nurse showed up for Gary within minutes. "Can she come with me?" he asked her, gesturing to Vivian.

"Sure."

She accompanied Gary to a curtained-off cubicle, where she felt trapped by the antiseptic smell so typical of hospitals. It offended her nostrils and made her wish she could go outside and breathe in a great gulp of filthy city air. She fully intended to provide moral support for Gary, who appeared as uneasy as she did about being in an emergency room, but when the nurse began cleaning the wound she became squeamish and felt like she had to get out of there. She hastily excused herself and wandered off. Glenda should be here by now and was probably looking for them.

She walked around the department, trying to find the way out. The scene in this ER wasn't anything like the frantic atmosphere portrayed on the television show with the same name. Some of the curtains were partially open, and she could see an occasional patient wearing an oxygen mask or sitting on a stretcher with an Ace wrap around an ankle or wrist. One man was snoring loudly. She decided he'd had too much celebration and was simply sleeping it off.

"Hello."

She turned and looked into the face of what had to be the best-looking man she'd ever seen. His skin was the color of dark honey, his near-black hair close-cropped, and in a strange but not unpleasant contrast, his eyes were electric blue. "You startled me," she said, realizing her mouth had dropped open.

"I'm sorry. But you look lost."

"I'm actually trying to find the way out."

"Have you been released?"

"Oh, I'm not a patient. I'm here with a friend who was hurt."

"Is it serious?"

"No, just a rather unpleasant cut on the arm."

"I see. Well, if you make a right at the next hallway it'll lead you to the waiting room."

"Thanks." She wanted to say something else, but couldn't think of anything. This man was just too fine to be real. He left her speechless.

"You're very welcome."

Zack Warner watched as the woman made her way down the hall and disappeared around the corner. She was a real looker. Her dark skin had a glow about it, and her thick but neatly shaped eyebrows topping luminous brown eyes reminded him of a young Audrey Hepburn in that movie that was a favorite of his cousin Sydney's, the one in which she played a chauffeur's daughter. Her figure was concealed by her kneelength coat, but it didn't look like there was anything there that would diminish his interest.

"Dr. Warner, would you check on Kevin? He's all set and awaiting clearance." One of the nurses was speaking to him.

"Sure."

Zack released his patient, a thirteen-year-old who had sprained his ankle while ice skating. Then he checked the patient board. There was a male patient in curtain three being treated for an arm laceration. The wound had been cleaned but not yet sutured. "Why don't you let me take this one," he offered to his colleague Jeff Hertz. He might as well find out as much information about the woman as possible. He already knew she wasn't married; "a friend," she had mentioned.

"Sure, go ahead."

"Hello there," Zack greeted. "I'm Dr. Warner."

"Gary Allen."

"I see you've had a little mishap."

"A freak accident. I cut my arm on a hook from a coat rack while I was putting on my jacket."

"Ouch. Let's take a look at it."

"Lousy way to end a party," Gary remarked as Zack inspected his arm.

"I hope it was nice otherwise."

"It was great. Met a lovely young lady who was nice enough to bring me up here."

So they'd just met. The word "friend" was probably too strong; they were merely acquaintances. Good. "I'm going to numb the area and then stitch it up for you."

"Please. It stings bad."

"I wouldn't recommend you drive after taking pain medication, anyway."

"I don't have very far to go. I was way downtown when this happened."

"Well, that was certainly nice of your lady friend to bring you all the way up here."

"Yes, it was. Fortunately, she lives in Mount Vernon, so she won't have too far to go."

Zack's expression was impassive, but he was pleased with the information he had managed to glean from Gary. It was rare for him to be this interested in what his patients had to say; usually he just tried to soothe and reassure them. He finished suturing Gary's arm. "I want you to sit tight for just a few minutes. I'd like to do a quick recheck before I authorize you to leave."

"It looks fine to me, Doc."

"It's just a precaution."

"I'm really in a hurry to get home. The anesthetic is going to wear off, and then my arm will start throbbing again. Besides, not only is my friend waiting, but a friend of hers is with her, too. I don't want to hold them up."

"I promise I'll be back in five minutes."

"All right."

Zack headed for the waiting room. The attractive woman he'd offered assistance to was sitting with another female. They both looked like they wished they were somewhere else, but then, most people didn't enjoy hospital waiting rooms.

"Hello again," he said. "I'm Dr. Warner."

"I'm Vivian St. James, and this is Glenda Ivey."

"I just treated your friend."

"I didn't know you were a doctor—I mean, his doctor," Vivian said.

"So, Doctor, will he live?" Glenda asked.

Zack laughed. "I just finished suturing his arm. I expect to release him as soon as I check him and give him some instructions. Will either of you ladies be taking care of him at home?" he asked innocently.

"No," Vivian answered. "We just met him a few hours ago. We were going his way . . . he really shouldn't have had to drive with his arm bleeding like that."

"I agree. The pressure could have re-started the blood flow. Do you live near here?"

"In Westchester," Vivian said.

"In Riverdale," Glenda said simultaneously.

They all chuckled, then the answers were repeated one at a time.

Zack was running out of time, and he knew it. He couldn't think of a single thing to say. It wasn't every day that women who looked as good as Vivian St. James walked into the ER, but how could he possibly let her know he'd like to see her again? She wore no ring, and she had just met Gary. She probably wouldn't refuse. "Well, ladies, come back anytime. I'm at your service," he said with a smile that vanished the moment his back was turned. *You wimp*, he said to himself as he returned to Gary.

"What a hunk," Glenda drawled.

"Did I fall over myself or what?"

"What was that you said about not knowing he was a doctor? Did you see him before?"

"In the back. I thought he was an orderly or a nurse or something. The guy who checked Gary in had that doctor look, but he was just a nurse. These days you just can't tell. Did I fall over myself when I said that?"

"I noticed you seemed a little excited about him being a doctor, but I don't think he did. Did you notice his eyes?"

"Right away. They're so bright; it's like he's got X-ray vision."

"I'm glad I wore matching underwear," Glenda remarked. "And speaking of eyes, I saw you cut yours at me."

"Well, I did see him first. I was afraid you might have forgotten that."

"So what are you gonna do about it?"

Vivian's forehead wrinkled. "What do you mean?"

"About the doctor. You know, the one you saw first. I think he likes you."

"What makes you say that, him saying to come back anytime? He was making a joke, Glenda. This is an emergency room!"

"I don't know. Something I saw in his eyes. The vibes. His sticking around and making small talk. I just have a feeling he was attracted to you."

"Shh. Here comes Gary."

"Then again," Glenda continued, "maybe he was attracted to *me.*"

Vivian gave her a "Say What?" look, but quickly turned her attention to Gary. He made an attempt at smiling, but it was obvious he was in discomfort.

"How's the arm?" Glenda asked.

"All stitched up and still numb, but probably not for long. The doctor gave me a pain pill for tonight and said tomorrow it shouldn't hurt as bad. Right now I just want to go home." He reached for Vivian's hand with his uninjured left hand. "Ladies, I can't tell you how much I appreciate your bringing me here."

"I'm glad we could help," Vivian said.

She and Glenda went outside with him, and after bidding them good-bye—she also received a kiss on the cheek and a promise that he would call her soon—and watched as he drove off. "All right," Glenda said the minute his Volvo disappeared around the corner, "back to what we were talking about."

"What do you suggest I do, Glenda? Sprain my wrist? Give myself a first degree burn so I can show up for treatment? Forget it. I'm looking for my Mr. Right, but I'm not desperate."

Later, after dropping Glenda at her apartment and getting her own car, Vivian considered the irony. Her friend Desirée had wanted to introduce her to a doctor over a year ago, but they could never coordinate their schedules, and then Desirée returned to Colorado. Now it looked like she'd missed out on another M.D. Like Glenda said, if it wasn't fated, it wouldn't happen.

Maybe there was a nice lawyer out there waiting for her, or even an Indian chief.

Chapter 2:
Manic Monday through Stingy Saturday

The phone lines in human resources were busier than usual, even for a Monday morning. Vivian didn't understand it. The company's upcoming merger with another, larger manufacturer hadn't even been announced yet. How did everyone know about it?

There was a knock on her office door, and the head bookkeeper of accounts payable asked in that nasal tone that gave New Yorkers a bad rep. "Is it true we've been bought out?"

"Wherever did you hear that?"

"It's what everybody's saying. They say they're going to downsize because they don't need two of each department, or that some of us will have to go to their offices in New York. I only have three years left before I retire. I don't want to start commuting into the city, Vivian."

She could easily understand why. Eloise Sherman lived fifteen minutes away from their offices and could barely manage to find her way to work now.

"But I would consider early retirement if they made me a good enough offer," Eloise added with a meaningful look.

Vivian marveled at Eloise's swift change in demeanor from whiny to crafty. She was privy to advance knowledge of early retirement packages, but she refused to be baited into spilling any confidential information. "I honestly don't know what's going on, but I'm sure it'll all be cleared up this morning."

Eloise had barely left when the senior secretary in research and development showed up. "Vivian, what's this I hear about us being bought out and moving to the city? Why would they want to do something like that? I thought the company was doing so well."

If there was anything that made her more uncomfortable than trying to diplomatically get rid of people who dropped by without calling, it was having to lie. She had a highly ethical character; she hadn't even told Glenda about the company's plans.

She managed to get rid of the secretary with a noncommittal response and then dashed down the hall to the director's office. Connie's desk in the reception area was vacant, so she went directly to Lisa Mahoney's office and knocked on the open door. "Lisa, we've got a problem." She had just finished explaining how the announcement, which was not due to become public until later in the week, had gotten out prematurely, when Harriet, the clerical assistant who sat outside her own office, buzzed. "Lisa, is Vivian in there?"

"Here I am."

"Glenda is on two for you. She says it's urgent."

Lisa picked up the receiver and handed it over.

"What is it, Glenda? They did *what?* No! Oh, hell. Okay. Thanks a lot."

She gave the phone back to Lisa, who hung it up. "You're not going to believe this. Apparently the original copy of the memo about the merger was left in the machine in the copy center. Someone found it this morning, made copies, and passed it out."

Lisa's face reddened. "Who made those copies?"

"Glenda wasn't able to find out exactly who, and whoever did it will never admit to it. The whole company probably knows about it by now."

"Thank you. Would you ask Connie to come in, please?"

"Sure."

She found Connie near her own office with Harriet, the two of them talking in hushed voices. The fearful look on Connie's face said it all; she was the unfortunate party who'd left the memo in the copier. "Lisa wants to see you," she said to Connie softly. This was a terrible situation. Senior management would get wind of what had happened, which meant that Lisa would be under the gun; and of course she would hold Connie responsible.

Connie sullenly went off toward Lisa's office. "What a shame," Harriet remarked.

Vivian had always liked Harriet Simmons. In her late fifties, she had been with the company nearly thirty years, working in various departments over that time. "That was such a mean thing to do, copying that memo and distributing it instead of bringing it back here."

"It was obviously a major announcement. Some people always have to be the first ones to break big news and be in the know, especially the ones in the copy center."

"Connie came in Saturday specifically to do the photocopying while no one was around. The alternative was to have the job done on the outside, and now I'm sorry Lisa didn't do it that way. It was such an honest mistake. It could have happened to anyone. I tell you, those women are vicious." One of the extensions began to ring. "There they go again. I'll get it."

Vivian was working when she looked up and noticed someone standing near Harriet's desk. Harriet was there, but she was helping someone on the phone. "Can I help you?" she offered.

The very tall form of Peter Arnold filled her doorway. He was a chemist relatively new to the company. Rumor had it that he was brilliant. His build—he was about six-five and on the thin side—was actually more suggestive of a retired basketball player. He had the longest fingers she had ever seen. Out of habit she always checked out a man's hands, whether she was interested in him or not, both to look for a wedding band and because she found long, slim digits more appealing than short, stubby ones. She felt she did it subtly, not like some men who talked to her with their eyes fastened to her chest.

"Hi, Vivian," Peter said. "I wanted to know if I was eligible to join the 401(k) plan. December twenty-seventh was my six-month anniversary."

"Yes, you can join. You're actually a little late; most of the people starting up got their paperwork turned in before Christmas."

"It's not too late, is it?"

"You might have to offer Glenda a bribe, but since we haven't had a payday yet this year I'm sure it'll be okay." She wanted to put in a plug for her friend, whom she knew thought Pete was "kinda cute."

"Quite a lot of excitement around here this morning, isn't there?" he remarked.

"Yes. It's regrettable." She handed him some printed forms. "This is what you need to fill out. I would suggest you complete it as soon as possible and give it to Glenda."

She saw Pete again that day as she hand-delivered an envelope of employee change forms to the payroll department for Glenda to process. He was walking ahead of her down the hall, and she gasped when he walked into what she knew was a closet. He came out within seconds and immediately looked around to see if anyone had witnessed his blunder. "I'm still having a little trouble finding my way around this place," he said sheepishly before disappearing into the men's room next door.

She merely gave him a smile, not trusting her voice to betray her with laughter, which she knew would be cruel. Still, she couldn't help thinking, *The man's been here six months and doesn't know the closet from the men's room?*

She and Glenda laughed heartily over the incident in the relative privacy of the payroll office, which Glenda shared with the two clerks she supervised. The confidential nature of the work they both did spared them from being assigned to those portable-walled cubicles so popular in offices nowadays. "So what if he's a little confused," Glenda said. "He's a scientist. They always say they're a little ditsy. It's part of their intelligence."

"Yeah, right. I'll bet George Washington Carver was always walking into closets."

Glenda rolled her eyes. "How's Gary's arm?"

"He says it's much better. It's a little sore, but it's not throbbing like it was when he first cut it. He'll have the stitches taken out before the weekend."

"Maybe you should offer to go with him to have them removed. You might get to see that fine Dr. Warner again."

"I'm sure he'll have the stitches taken out by his own doctor. There's no need to go to the emergency room for something so minor, unless he doesn't have a family doctor."

"It was just a thought." Glenda lowered her voice. "So are they going to get rid of me or what?"

"I admit I did know about the merger; Lisa told us last week. She swore me to secrecy. I hope you're not mad that I didn't tell you."

"I understand that, but do you know about the future of my department? Carol and her husband just bought a house, and she's a little frantic."

"Well, the letter said no changes are expected right away."

"All that means is that everybody's probably safe for the next six months or so. I'm interested in the long term."

"I honestly don't know, Glenda. I guess nobody's job is safe." That wasn't exactly the truth, either. Lisa told them that Human Resources would remain untouched. She would be commuting between the two locations, since the other company did not have a director, only a manager. When Harriet pointed out that they didn't have a manager, only a director, Lisa had smiled and said Vivian would be in charge of the department in her absence. Not only would she keep her job, but there might be a promotion in it for her from administrator to manager.

"Well, if they decide to pink-slip me I'm going to take the money and run right out of New York. I'll go someplace where the odds of finding my soul mate are better. And a warmer climate won't hurt, either."

"I think the odds of finding your Mr. Right are going to be the same anywhere. Besides, anyplace in the Sunbelt is going to pay you maybe half of what you're getting now, maybe sixty percent, tops."

"That's all right. From what I hear you can live better, even on less money, because everything's cheaper. I can buy some property instead of making my landlord rich every month. And speaking of money, am I allowed to buy a new outfit to wear to dinner out of my bonus money?"

"Not really. That money should be earmarked for travel expenses, not for outfits or getting your hair done. Oops." She had forgotten that Glenda had given up on getting her long, thick hair relaxed every seven weeks, wearing it pulled back or pinned up in its natural kinky state instead of loose. "When the operators at the hairdresser start arguing over whose turn it is to do your head, it's time to go off and live nappily ever after," she had said at the time.

Now she said, "Well, it *should* count. It's all part of the process. I've caught Bobby. Now I want to reel him in." She pantomimed the act of fishing.

"You haven't exactly caught him yet. This is only your first date."

"Trust me. He's as good as gone."

* * *

Glenda's enthusiasm carried through the phone line on Sunday morning. "We had a great time. He let me pick the restaurant, and I chose seafood. We went into the city and ate at the latest hot spot on Columbus Avenue, this place that everybody's raving about now, but'll be gone in a year when they forget about it and start going someplace else. After dinner we took a long walk down the street, stopped to get some ice cream and ended up at a jazz club. The music was fabulous." She sighed romantically, and Vivian could picture the dreamy look on her face. "I must say it was a nice evening. And I like Bobby, too."

Vivian drew in her breath. "That's wonderful, Glenda! Sounds like you might have accomplished your goal."

"Well, I wouldn't mail the invitations just yet. Relationships are always good when they're fresh. It generally takes a while before you start getting on each other's nerves."

"Yes, but the goal was to *meet* our Mr. Rights. The ceremony can come later, like next year. There'll still be plenty of time to have a baby before forty."

"You're so sweet. And I don't mean to hog the conversation. Tell me all about your date with Gary."

Vivian made a face, even though there was no one in the room to see it. "Let me put it this way: It sucked."

She could hear Glenda made a choking sound, and then there were gulping noises as she took a long swig of whatever it was she was drinking to clear her throat. "I just got Sprite coming out of my nostrils. You caught me off guard. I don't think I've ever heard you use that expression before."

"I've never been on such a miserable date before. This man makes Thomas look like a great catch. Hmph. If he's a catch, I'm throwing him back."

"What went wrong?"

"Everything. You wouldn't believe where he took me for dinner. One of those family style steak houses. It was maybe two steps removed from a McDonald's. Bright lights, screaming kids, clanging silverware, and no booze. Not even any beer or wine. It was terrible."

"I won't ask about the food. But at least you got a movie out of it."

"Yeah, at five-thirty in the afternoon."

"Why so early?"

"We went to the half-price twilight show. The man is cheap with a capital C, Glenda."

"I don't get it. Isn't he a commercial artist?"

"Unless he lied, but he's a little old to be working in the mail room."

"Does he have a lot of child support to pay or something?"

"He told me he's never been married and doesn't have any kids."

"Well, what's his problem?"

"I told you: He's cheap. Cheap, cheap, cheap." If there was anything she found more irritating than seeing houses still lit up with Christmas lights in mid-January, it was a skinflint. "I guess I should have gotten my first clue when I saw that broken-down car he drives. Did you notice he has the glove compartment held together with string?"

"I didn't notice."

"It's a '78, and he bragged about having the engine rebuilt twice. I know that everybody isn't into that 'you are what you drive' attitude. I'm sure not;

my Mazda is seven years old, and as soon as I get back from the safari I'll have to get a new one. I was thinking maybe he had a really nice apartment or a summer house or a boat or something, and maybe he does, but he also doesn't want to open his wallet unless absolutely necessary."

"He ought to be ashamed of himself, the miser."

"Live and learn, I guess. Even Thomas, bless his germloving heart, sprung for dinner at an upscale restaurant, the type of place where I could wear a cocktail dress and not look overdone. So it's on to the next conquest, I guess. Whoever he is."

"Vivian, go down to Hudson Hospital. Look up Dr. Warner. Invite him to lunch."

"I am not going to chase after that man, Glenda!" She didn't mean to sound harsh, but she was still smarting from last night's disappointment. She had felt foolish and overdressed in her skirt and boots, going to a movie before dark and then to a noisy, bright restaurant. And when it was over Gary had the nerve to ask if he could stay the night with her. She declined his offer sweetly, controlling the urge to hit him over his leonine head with a two-by-four. It was true that she would love to see the handsome Dr. Warner again, but it was a lost opportunity. But what could she have done? He knew she was there with Gary. That would have looked really bad, flirting with another man while her so-called date lay bleeding just a few yards away. Okay, she wasn't his date, she was just being a Good Samaritan, but she didn't want Zack to think she was a hussy. Sometimes it was better to simply make a graceful exit.

"Well, it could be worse," Glenda said.

"Yeah, how?"

"Your mother might know you missed the opportunity to be fixed up with one doctor, rebuffed another, and blew the chance to get to know a third."

Vivian pictured her mother standing with the Macaulay Culkin expression of distress, palms flanking her jaws, her mouth wide open, and her eyes wide with panic. It wasn't pretty. "Amen to that."

Chapter 3:
Break a Leg

"Looks like a nice crowd," Glenda commented.

"Wow, they've got three buses. I'm feeling optimistic." Vivian hoped she would meet someone special on the ski trip, which was being sponsored by a group called NBP, which stood for Nothing But a Pastime. "Why didn't we know about these people before?"

"Just be glad we found out about them now."

Vivian had to agree. It was February already. Glenda and Bobby were doing fine, but it didn't look like *she* would be having a valentine.

Gary had called her several times. At first she gave tactful excuses, saying she was swamped with the work brought by the company's upcoming plans on existing personnel, but when he didn't seem to get the message, she had to come right out and say the same thing she told Thomas Joseph, that she felt they lacked chemistry, and continuing to see each other wouldn't really be fair to either of them. It was an out-and-out lie—there had been chemistry between them from the beginning, but his frugality was too much of a turnoff for her. She was glad to step aside and let some other unlucky woman be the recipient of his Saturday-night-for-twenty-five-bucks-or-less plan.

The buses were leaving from the parking lot of a major shopping center early on Sunday morning for the ride to the Berkshires for a day of skiing. NBP sponsored all kinds of activities: Cruises, train rides, dances, picnics, even bowling tournaments, attracting singles and couples from Massachusetts to Maryland. Vivian was an experienced skier, but Glenda had never gone before and would be taking a lesson.

They remained in their respective cars, parked next to each other with the windows rolled down to allow for talking, watching as the buses were boarded. There was no need for either of them to acknowledge that they were doing this to make sure they chose a bus with a good crowd, as in lots of men.

"It's a toss-up between the one in the middle and the last one," Glenda said.

"The last one looks best to me. The middle one has too many kids on it." The ski trip was a family affair for some, with a fair abundance of children in the seven-to-twelve range.

As it turned out it really didn't matter much, for the bus ride was rather quiet. It was still very early, and many riders fell asleep, including both Glenda and Vivian. The atmosphere perked up as they approached the mountains, after everyone had a chance to rest.

When the riders disembarked they were divided into groups. Glenda went for her lesson and Vivian introduced herself to other experienced skiers, most of whom, she was happy to see, were men.

"Do you ski often?" she heard a male voice ask.

"Not as often as I'd like to. Once a year, maybe twice, I get together with some friends I grew up with. But it's much nicer going in a large group like this."

"You'll have to let them know about our group, especially if they're as lovely as you are."

"Well, thank you." She didn't think it appropriate to mention that most of her childhood friends were not African-American.

He took a seat next to where Vivian was putting on her ski boots. "I'm Gordon Wilson."

"Vivian St. James."

"Nice to meet you, Vivian."

"Same here." Gordon Wilson was brown-skinned, with thick wavy hair, a mustache and glasses. He was on the short side, but at least he was taller than she was. *You could do worse,* she told herself.

She straightened after finishing with her boots. "Well, I guess I'm ready to hit the slopes." She flashed Gordon a brilliant smile. "Will you join me?"

"I'd love to."

Skis on their feet and poles in hand, they clumsily walked over to the lift for the ride to the slope. Vivian loved the feeling of zooming down a steep hill, the white-covered world passing by in a blur. It was exhilarating.

She and Gordon took the lift back to the top. During their ride she learned he lived in White Plains and was an accounting director. Funny. When they got off the lift he seemed a mite taller than he had before. . . .

They had lunch together in the restaurant, but Vivian insisted on paying for her own. She was ravenous and didn't want him to think she was being gluttonous because she wasn't paying.

"You ski pretty well," Gordon said. "How long have you been doing it?"

"When I was about ten my parents started taking us on winter vacations. My brother and I took lessons. A couple of times we even spent Christmas in the mountains."

"That explains why you're so good. And that's pretty impressive. Back then you didn't see a whole lot of black people on the ski slopes."

Vivian smiled. "No, there weren't a whole lot, but it's not like we were the only ones, so we never felt out of place." She scanned the room, which was peppered with brown faces. "But never this many. This is great. I almost expect to see James Brown and the Famous Flames come out in their ski sweaters and do a number, like they did in some old movie I saw on TV."

"Yeah, I remember that movie! *Ski Party*, or something like that."

"So where did you learn to ski?"

"With the club. I've been a member for about three years. I took lessons with them, and I guess I had a little bit of an affinity for it." Gordon chuckled. "Me, a city kid whose prior athletic experience consisted of mostly roller skating, basketball, and swimming in the Long Island Sound."

"I grew up on the other side of the Sound. New London, Connecticut. Not that we could swim there; the shore is full of rocks."

"Ah, so you didn't have very far to go to get to the mountains."

"I wouldn't say that. I seem to remember it took hours, whether we were going to the Berkshires or the Poconos. It was a lot quicker to get to Cape Cod in the summertime."

"I guess you've figured out geography isn't my

strong suit. I don't know too much about Connecticut, although I do remember going out to visit cousins in Old Saybrook."

"New London is further out. It's close to the Rhode Island line." With her peripheral vision she saw someone waving, and when she focused fully she saw Glenda waving to her and returned the wave. Her friend was apparently lunching with others in her ski class.

"That was good," Gordon said, pushing his plate toward the center of the table. "Now it's time to burn off those calories. Are you game?"

"I'm ready."

When they got back to the slope Vivian was the first to push off, but Gordon quickly zoomed past her. It was probably his male ego trying to show her he felt as comfortable on skis as she did. She hoped it didn't bother him too much that she was more experienced. Some men were sensitive about everything, from how much money a woman made to how much education she had and everything in between, and felt the ideal woman was one who had never experienced anything he hadn't. It wasn't the type of observation she could make to him; it was too awkward. Still, she hoped he wouldn't make too big a deal of trying to outski her. Heaven forbid he should run into a tree or sustain another type of injury.

She no sooner had that thought when Gordon, still ahead of her, suddenly tumbled in the snow. She steered herself toward where he lay. "Gordon, are you hurt?"

He managed to shift to a sitting position, but he grimaced in pain. "My ankle. These damn skis got all twisted up when I fell. It hurts something awful, and now this boot feels like it weighs fifty pounds."

She carefully moved into a sitting position. "Here, I'll help you get the ski off."

As she unhooked Gordon's right ski she looked at the descending skiers. He would require assistance getting back to the top, and she didn't see the patrol anywhere.

A man came to a stop a few feet away. "What happened?" he asked.

He definitely wasn't with NBP. He was white, his cheeks flushed from the cold.

"I fell," Gordon said. "I did something to my ankle. I hope it's just a sprain."

"I'll take the lift up and get the patrol to help you," the man offered.

Vivian and Gordon thanked him, and he took off down to the lift.

"It shouldn't be too long until the patrol gets here. Then the EMTs will look at you," she said.

"Emergency medical technicians?"

"Yes."

"That won't be too much help. My ankle needs to be x-rayed."

"Hey, what's going on?"

"Danny, hey." Gordon gave his friend a high-five from where he sat. "I'm on the injured list. One of the skiers went for help. They'll get me up to the lodge."

"You know, one of the guys with NBP is a doctor."

"How'd you know that?"

"At lunch. He was at the next table and had a couple of girls hanging around him. The word kinda filtered out."

"What's his specialty?"

"I don't know, Gordy." Danny smiled at Vivian.

"Excuse my buddy; his pain makes him forget his manners. Danny Lee."

"Hi, Danny; I'm Vivian. Did you two come together?"

"Yes. I'll be able to get him home . . . or to the emergency room. In the meantime I guess I'd better see if I can dig up this doctor."

Vivian didn't reply. Hearing about an emergency room made her think of Dr. Warner. If they had been in New York instead of on a mountain in western Massachusetts she would have brought Gordon to Hudson Hospital. . . .

By the time the staff got Gordon to the lodge Danny was waiting. "They're getting the doctor."

"Did you ever find out if he's an orthopedist?"

"No."

Gordon rolled his eyes. "Watch him be a doggone obstetrician."

"If he is we'll just call the EMTs. At least they're trained for these type of injuries. It'll be okay, Gordon," Vivian said, rubbing his shoulder reassuringly.

"You must be the patient."

"Are you the doctor?"

"Yes, I am."

Vivian, accustomed to seeing medical professionals wearing shirt, tie, and lab coat, almost laughed out loud at the sight of this man in a ski cap, sunglasses, nylon jacket, gloves, and ski boots, and carrying skis and poles. She was glad her own sunglasses hid her eyes; she didn't want Gordon to think she made light of his pain, but she knew her eyes would betray the amusement she felt.

"Are you an orthopedist?" Gordon was asking nervously.

"I'm a little bit of everything. My specialty is emergency medicine."

Vivian looked at him with interest. He leaned his equipment against the table and then removed his sunglasses, revealing brilliant blue eyes, and she stiffened in surprise, knowing what surname he would give.

"Zack Warner," he said.

Gordon stated his name, and they shook hands. "This is Danny Lee and Vivian St. James," Gordon added.

"Vivian St. . . .Wait a minute. Weren't you in my ER last month? Hudson Hospital?"

She peeled off her cap and removed her sunglasses. "Yes, that was me. Nice to see you again, Dr. Warner."

"Call me Zack. Now, let's see what we've got here." He began an inspection of Gordon's ankle.

It was the second time he had given his first name, but this time something in Vivian's brain clicked.

Zack? Vivian thought wildly. *Zack* Warner? Could this Zack be the same fellow Desirée wanted to introduce her to? Austin's friend, the doctor? Her *landlord?*

Zack's face was impassive as his trained fingers felt Gordon's anklebones. He'd thought of Vivian St. James several times since their brief encounter in the ER, each time telling himself how foolish he was for spending his time that way. He was certain he'd never see her again, but here she was. That was life for you, he thought. He had to come all the way to the Berkshires to find her. She'd probably been on the next bus with NBP.

"I think it's just a sprain," he said to Gordon.
"I'm sure I can get some wrap for it at the lodge
office. You'll need to see your own doctor tomorrow and get an X ray, just in case there is a hairline
fracture; and in the meantime stay off it." Zack
turned to Vivian. "Will you see that he gets home
all right?"

"I'm here with a friend," Gordon said. "He'll
get me home. Vivian, I don't want to ruin your
afternoon. I'll be fine here."

"Are you sure you don't need anything?"

"Nah, I'm good. I'll see you before it's time to
leave."

"You stay off that foot, now," Zack cautioned.
"Use your poles as crutches."

"I'll do that. Thanks, Doc."

Vivian and Zack fell into step together as they
left the building. She could hardly believe he was
here beside her. What a wonderful opportunity. It
had to be fated. "Tell me," he asked, "is this standard for you?"

"Is what standard for me?"

"Do your dates frequently end up in need of urgent medical care?"

She tensed. "Wait a minute. Are you suggesting
I'm a jinx?"

"No, of course not."

She wasn't convinced. "Let me tell you a few
things," she said, stopping and turning to face him.
"First of all, I'm not a jinx. Second of all, neither
of these men were dates. In both cases we had just
met. So what if one cut his arm? People have freak
accidents like that all the time. It was pretty mild
as those things go. And people also get hurt skiing

all the time. A twisted ankle isn't a serious injury. The way Gordon was tangled up in his skis he's lucky he didn't break his leg. These two incidents are nothing more than unfortunate coincidences, and I think you've got a lot of nerve suggesting otherwise."

"I didn't mean anything by it. You're right, it's just coincidence. And just to prove I don't think you're a jinx, let's hit the slopes together."

"Only if you promise to run into a tree," she snapped, beginning to walk again.

Zack put his hand over his heart and looked wounded. "Ouch."

Vivian really didn't wish anything bad to happen to Zack, she was just still smarting from his inferring she was bad luck. She remembered how Gordon twisted his ankle and hoped Zack wouldn't feel he had to outdo her.

As it turned out that was an unnecessary concern. Zack was an excellent skier, zigzagging down the hill with true agility and gliding to a smooth stop at the bottom. It was all she could do to keep up with him.

"Hey, you're really good," she said to him as they rode the lift. "You've been at this for a while, haven't you?"

"Only a few years. NBP is big on skiing. I went to Switzerland with them last winter and practically lived on the slopes the whole time I was there. What about you?"

Vivian recounted her background in the sport.

"Ah, so you were one of those privileged Negroes from the suburbs."

"Why, where did you grow up?"

"I'm a city kid from St. Nicholas Avenue, where

we played on the sidewalks and any grass around was for viewing only and was cordoned off."

"New London was a nice place to grow up. I guess maybe I was a little privileged. But does that have to be dirty word?"

"No, of course not. It's really what you make of yourself, not what your family has. And our generation had a lot of opportunities our parents, aunts, and uncles didn't."

"That's very true. I'm sure your family is proud of you. Where did you go to school?"

"Howard."

"What made you choose emergency medicine?"

"I know this sounds corny, but I wanted to help people. Believe me, there's no difference in the length of time it takes to be an ER doctor than there is in being an ophthalmologist."

"That's true. But it probably requires a lot more practice."

"All right. Now that I've told you all about me don't you think it's your turn?"

"All right. You know where I'm from. I went to U. Mass, and I'm a human resources administrator."

"You're the one who summons the unsuspecting to your office on Friday afternoons and ruins their lives, huh?"

"No, but I conduct their exit interviews. We leave the firing to the individual managers, although a couple of the bigwigs have occasionally been too cowardly to let their secretaries go. That's fallen to my manager, not to me."

"Do I detect a bit of wistfulness?"

"I guess you do. I love my job, Zack, but I'm ready to be a manager myself."

"So you can fire executive secretaries?"

"No, silly. I just want to be a manager. I'm qualified. I've been working in human resources ever since I finished college. My goal is to become a vice president, but I need a manager's position first, then a director's position, before I can even think about becoming an officer."

"Ah, the pitfalls of corporate America."

"It's not so bad. There are perks."

"Yes, I know. My buddy owns his own company, and every year he and his partner give themselves nice, fat bonuses."

Vivian almost said, "Austin," but she caught herself. Once upon a time she had had an eye—all right, both her eyes—on the stealthily handsome Austin Hughes, whose parents lived downstairs from her, but then she met and became friendly with Desirée and learned she held the keys to his heart, so that was the end of that. Still, there was little doubt of whom he was referring to.

Meanwhile, if anything progressed between she and Zack he would learn about her connection to Desirée and Austin and that he was her landlord, but a sixth sense told her to keep mum for now.

"That'll never happen working for a hospital," Zack concluded.

"It could if you were in private practice. I know you practice emergency medicine, but there are private clinics, acute care centers, whatever name they go by, all over the place."

"Don't think I haven't thought of it. I'd like to do that someday, but not in New York. Maybe some out-of-the-way place on Long Island or up in Westchester. Where do you live, anyway?" He already knew from Gary Allen that she lived in Mount Vernon, where he owned property; but that day she had only told him she lived in Westchester.

He was glad she didn't still live in Connecticut; that was awfully far.

"I'm in Mount Vernon." At least he didn't ask where she *stayed,* a form of speech that was right up there with people driving the wrong way down one-way parking lot rows on her personal vexation scale.

She waited for him to say he owned an apartment building there, but he only said, "Oh, yes. Convenient location."

Maybe he felt it was best if she didn't know about his real-estate holdings. She couldn't blame him. It would be difficult to make even a casual statement along those lines and not sound like he was bragging. "It is convenient," she agreed. "Where do you live?"

"Harlem. You know what they say. You can take the boy out of the city, but you can't take the city out of the boy. So are you going to join NBP?"

"Oh, I don't know. I'll have to find out what the benefits are. All their events are open to the public, aren't they?"

"Yes. They give a discount on admission or travel if you're a member. That's the main benefit."

The rest of the afternoon went by in a maze of trying different slopes and talking while riding the lift. Before she knew it, it was time to board the bus for the trip home. "What bus were you on, Zack?" she asked.

"The last one. You?"

She hid her disappointment. "Number two." Gordon, too, was on the last bus. Neither man had asked about seeing her again, and while she found Zack infinitely more attractive she wasn't ready to rule out Gordon. But time was running out. She wouldn't see either of them again if they didn't have any way to contact her.

"I'm going to turn in my skis. Vivian, it was a lot of fun skiing with you. I hope we'll get to do it again."

She forced herself to sound light and unruffled. "Likewise. You take care, now."

As she looked around the crowded lodge for Glenda she suddenly felt very tired. She hadn't expected husband hunting to be this exhausting. She had thought things were going well between her and Zack, in spite of the rocky start. Why hadn't he asked for her number? Had she turned him off in some way? Did the mints she consumed after lunch not cover the fact that she'd had onions added to her hamburger? Had her deodorant failed? Maybe she should have told him about knowing his friend, Austin, and Austin's girlfriend, Desirée, after all; it would have provided a link . . . plus he'd know where to find her.

She saw Gordon waving her way and went over to where he sat, knowing that walking was difficult for him after his fall. "I'm glad I saw you before I got on the bus. I'd like to see you again. May I call you?"

"I'd like that." She had to force the enthusiasm in her voice. If she had her choice of just one of them, it would be Zack who asked for her number and Gordon who gave her a polite kiss-off.

She scribbled her home number on the back of one of her business cards and handed it to him. "How's the ankle?"

"Now that my foot is elevated it doesn't hurt as much. Danny is turning in my equipment."

"I've got to find my friend myself. I've barely seen her all day. Take care of your foot, Gordon."

"I will. Thanks for your help. I'll call you soon."

Vivian gave up looking for Glenda in the lodge and went out to where the buses were parked, where Glenda stood waiting. "I was looking for you. I thought you'd be in the lodge."

"You know, I was just about to go in there, since I didn't see you out here. It's warmer, for one thing."

They climbed on the bus and took seats. "Ooh, my legs are sore," Vivian complained. "Those ski boots must weigh ten pounds apiece."

"I'm afraid I'm not much for skiing. I probably need to stick to water sports." Glenda lowered her voice to a whisper. "You seemed to have a nice time. Every time I saw you, you were in the company of a man."

"Well, let's see. One of them twisted his ankle on the slope. Fortunately, there was a doctor who Ace wrapped it for him."

"A doctor? Was he with our group?"

"Yes. It was Dr. Warner."

"No!" Glenda exclaimed loudly.

Vivian scowled and waved her hand, gesturing Glenda to talk more quietly. "He's a member of NBP. And there's more than that. He's the same guy Desirée wanted to introduce me to. Can you believe that?"

"How'd you find that out?"

"By his first name. It's Zack. The only thing I knew about him other than him being a doctor was his first name. When we were talking about working in corporate versus the health care industry and he said something about a friend of his who owned his own company I knew it had to be him. He was talking about Austin."

"You didn't ask him if he knew Desirée?"

"No. Maybe I should have. I think it came as too much of a shock. This man is my landlord, Glenda. He and Austin own the building I live in."

"So what happened?"

"We went skiing. Gordon encouraged me to go ahead, since he was out of commission."

"And you're going to see him again, of course."

"No."

"What do you mean, no?" Glenda hissed. "This is the answer to a prayer!"

"Glenda, he wasn't interested in seeing me again. He didn't ask for my number or anything. The only thing he did was ask if I was going to join NBP."

"We'll have to make sure we go to their next event. It's a dance, next month. He'll probably be there."

"No. To me that's the same as my going to the hospital looking for him. I wouldn't do that, and I'm not going to do this, either."

"Don't be stubborn, Viv. It's not the same thing. There are interesting people at these events. You did meet someone else today, didn't you?"

"Yes."

"Well, then."

Vivian had to admit that Glenda had a point. All she would accomplish by staying home was missing out. It was better to go out and have a good time than sit home alone.

The other skiers were a raucous bunch during the ride back to New York, but Zack didn't have much to contribute. His mind was elsewhere. He'd seen Vivian St. James again, and, once again, he didn't give the slightest indication that he was interested. Instead, he'd put his foot in his mouth with his comment about her male friends having accidents, which had been innocent in nature, but with the wisdom of hindsight he realized could easily be taken the wrong way. Vivian was about as mad as a theater patron would be if Erykah Badu sat in front of them wearing one of those mile-high head wraps.

After that fiasco, he thought it best to try to patch things up so they could part on pleasant terms when it was time. It shouldn't be too long before he saw her again. His bet was that she would show up at next month's dance at a Westchester country club. If she didn't, he'd find her, even if he had to resort to using one of those "We Find Anyone" services on the Internet. Seeing her again had convinced him that their meeting was not meant to be a one-time, brief, impersonal encounter in a hospital emergency room. He wanted everything to be perfect, and he didn't want to rush and botch it. He'd antagonized her once, but from now on he was going to take it slow and easy.

Vivian St. James was special.

Chapter 4:
Scoundrel in a Red Jacket

"Vivian, it's Desirée."

"Hi! Are you in town?"

"No, I'm in Colorado. I wanted to call and let you know . . . Austin and I are getting married."

Vivian covered the receiver and shrieked.

"He proposed on Valentine's Day, and I said yes."

"Of course you did! Desirée, I'm so happy for you!"

"I know you are. You were there for me during the tough times in the beginning."

"Did you get a ring already or are you going shopping for one?"

"He gave it to me when he proposed. Pretty sure of himself, that Ozzie." Desirée giggled.

"So, it looks like I'm going to a wedding. Hey, where's it going to be, there or here?"

"We're still talking, but I'm leaning toward having it here. It's hard when the families are in two cities so far from each other."

"Maybe you can compromise and hold it somewhere in between, like Chicago."

"No, I don't think that'll work either. Then *every-*

one will have to travel, and I'd prefer to be in the same city so I can meet with caterers and florists face-to-face."

"Have you set a date?"

"We're still deciding. I like September, but I can't help thinking that it would be just my luck for us to get hit with a surprise early snowstorm, which none of the out-of-towners will be prepared for. My mother thinks July would be better, but finding a place that's not booked up will probably be a challenge. If not, we'll have to wait until next spring at the earliest. I don't really want a year-plus engagement, but I might not have a choice."

"But, Desirée, you might have a hard time getting everything planned so quickly. July is less than six months away."

"Are you kidding? My mother has a collection of business cards from bands and caterers from every affair she's been to. She's already gotten on the phone to find out what they can do for us."

Vivian laughed. "Yes, I've forgotten about how mothers can be. Mine probably has amassed a similar collection she's not telling me about until the far-off day I announce my engagement, at which point she'll break them out, all yellowed and curling with age. But you will tell me the date as soon as you decide?"

"I promise. I want to give people who have to travel as much time as possible to plan."

"Thanks. In the meantime all my plans for that general time frame will be considered tentative." Vivian drew in her breath, suddenly remembering something she wanted to tell her friend. "You'll never believe this, Desirée. I ran into Zack."

"You did? Was he visiting Ozzie's parents or something?"

"No. The first time was for professional services."

"The first time? How many times have you seen him?"

"Twice, but the second was more social, although his medical know-how was needed then, also." Vivian recounted the mishaps involving Gary and Gordon. "I don't mind telling you I was very disappointed that he didn't seem interested in seeing me again. I thought things were going pretty well."

"Did you tell him you were my friend, the one I had wanted to introduce him to?"

"No. I thought about it but decided to let things progress on their own, which, of course, I know now was a mistake."

"I'm so sorry it didn't work out. One thing I can say about Zack, he does tend to enjoy female attention . . . and he gets plenty of it. I'm afraid it's swelled his ego just a little. He's a bit of a scoundrel, but he's so charming about it he manages to be loveable."

Something else had occurred to Vivian as she considered the reasons for Zack's lack of interest in her, and she knew Desirée would understand. "Do you suppose . . . Well, is he one of those men who go for the Halle Berry type?"

Desirée chuckled. "I haven't met a man yet who wouldn't go for someone who looks like Halle Berry. The girl is gorgeous."

"You know what I mean, Desirée."

"I do, and the answer is no. Zack likes all women, all shades." Desirée did not add that she had asked Zack this herself before suggesting he meet her new friend. She and Vivian were both of a darker hue, and just like some white men preferred blondes, some black men wouldn't look twice at a brown-skinned sister. "Maybe he thought he would see you when the buses arrived back in New York."

"If he did that wasn't too bright an idea. It was dark by the time we got back to the parking lot we left from, and everyone was exhausted and anxious to get in their cars and go home. It was a Sunday, and there was work for most of us the next day. But the club is holding a Valentine's dance tomorrow night. I hope he'll be there. He mentioned that his shift rotates."

"But Valentine's Day is over, Vivian."

"I guess scheduling is hard when it falls during the week, even though I would have thought they would hold it the week before rather than the week after. Maybe the price to rent the country club went down."

"Well, please call and let me know what happens. Hopefully you'll see him again. And I hope no one gets hurt." Desirée chuckled.

"I will. And congratulations to both you and Austin. I know you'll be happy together for the rest of your lives."

Vivian was pleased with the way she looked. Since she had a number of dressy outfits in her closet, most of which she had only worn once, she decided against buying a new one for the occasion. Besides, she wanted to reserve her cash for the travel and activity expenses she would have in her quest for a mate.

She had left work an hour early and gone to a local salon, where her short hair had been washed and styled, then brushed back from her face with a few waves, courtesy of skillfully applied gel. She'd also had her naturally thick eyebrows shaped. Eyebrows had a way of growing unruly when you weren't looking, but when they were shaped they opened up her entire face. She wore minimal eye makeup; her brows said it all.

Instead of a dress, she wore a black tunic with shirred shoulders, sleeveless, with a gentle drape and cinched waist over matching loosely draped slacks. The tunic had no sleeves, but she wore long black gloves that would warm her arms and be compatible with the required semiformal dress, as well as hide the fact that she hadn't had time to do anything to her nails. Her jewelry was her best small ruby drop earrings with a matching necklace and bracelet worn on the outside of her gloves. She figured most of the women would be wearing dresses, and red ones at that, given the Valentine's Day holiday.

The phone began to ring, and, as it had become her habit over the last few weeks, she checked the caller ID first. When she saw Gordon Wilson's name, she didn't answer. The creep had made a dinner date with her and then stood her up. He'd been calling ever since, but as far as she was concerned, he was too late. Unfortunately, she had written her home number on the back of her business card, and he had been calling her at work, also, where she couldn't screen him. "We have nothing to say to each other," she had told him in an even, unemotional tone when he caught her at her desk.

"I'm really sorry about what happened. I had an emergency."

"You could have called me, Gordon. You didn't. Let's say I'm just following your lead." She had hung up, but he continued to call her every few days, usually at home. He was probably calling to find out if she was going to the dance. Well, he could eat his heart out. When he saw how good she looked he'd truly regret being so careless. Even if someone had died, he could have called . . . and she wouldn't have felt so humiliated, getting dressed and made up to wait for a knock that never came.

Vivian was pleased to see that the parking lot held a respectable number of cars. The event had begun at seven-thirty, but it was now nearly ten o'clock. She didn't believe in getting to this type of function too early. She supposed someone had to be the first to arrive, but on the other hand she didn't believe in going in unless she knew it would be worth her while.

Once she was parked, she reached under the armrest and pulled out her cell phone. She had the number to Glenda's phone installed in memory and held down the assigned digit. Within seconds the line was ringing.

"What took you so long?" she asked when Glenda picked up on the fourth ring.

"I had to feel for the phone. I couldn't take my eyes off the road; this exit ramp is curvy."

"Oh, so you're just getting off the highway. That means you'll be here in ten minutes."

"How's the crowd?"

"It's good, from the looks of the parking lot. I just hope they're not all females. Listen, it's too cold for me to wait for you out here. I'm going in to check my coat. I'll meet you in the powder room."

"You bet."

It only took a minute or two for Vivian to ensure

that she looked her best. The chilly temperature of the February night kept her makeup fresh, and the hair stylist had applied so much spray to her short tresses that it would take a fifty-mile-per-hour wind to budge them.

After her time at the mirror she sat at one end of the flowered sofa in the powder room, drumming her fingers impatiently on the rolled arms. Ten minutes could be a long time to wait with nothing to do, and she became bored. Every woman who entered the lounge was with a friend, giving credence to the sentiment that grown women rarely went to the restroom alone, and she felt like an oddball. Besides, sitting in here where no one could see her was a waste of her efforts. Doggone it, she looked too good to be hidden away.

She suppressed a smile, thinking of a catchy ditty used by an auto manufacturer in which the car's alter ego sang that it was too sexy for mundane things like the groceries, the drivethrough, and the dry cleaning. She was humming the jingle as she left the lounge. It wouldn't hurt to check out what was going on in the ballroom and get herself a drink. She'd still be able to spot Glenda when she arrived.

"Vivian! I was hoping I'd see you."

She frowned. She had had a feeling she might see Gordon tonight, but her hunch didn't make the reality any more pleasant. His sprain had had plenty of time to heal, and by now he was probably ready to dance till dawn. He'd have to find somebody else to play Ginger to his Fred; she wasn't interested.

"Hello, Gordon." She lowered her voice. "I don't want to make a scene, so let's just leave it at that. It was nice seeing you. Good-bye."

"Vivian, I wish you'd listen to me."

"I already made myself clear," she hissed. "No one stands me up and gets another chance. Now, please excuse me." She walked over to the bar, which had been set up against the wall about halfway down the length of the room. "Vodka and grapefruit juice, please," she ordered when she had the bartender's attention. Usually she drank wine, but Gordon's persistence was wearing on her nerves, and she preferred something a little stronger.

"Wow. Sounds like someone's driving you to drink. Is there trouble in paradise?"

The words were spoken softly, so close to her right ear that she felt them reverberate. She knew it was Zack even before she turned around. The man had a way of knowing just what to say to get the muscles of her jaw to tighten up. Maybe she should have ordered a double and nursed it all night. All she knew was that she was getting more and more tense, and she'd only been here five minutes.

She turned to give him what she hoped was a withering look, but it wilted like day-old salad greens when he filled her line of vision. Most of the men present wore dark suits. A smaller number wore tuxedos, but Zack looked striking in a red blazer, navy shirt and slacks, and a tie and matching handkerchief printed with red curvy lines and polka dots on a navy background. Vivian always appreciated a well-dressed man, and Zack could be on a cover for *GQ*. One look and her resolve went the way of most New Year's resolutions.

He reached for her gloved hand. "What's the matter, Vivling?" he asked in a gentle tone.

She willed her hand not to tremble in his and

was grateful for the gloves. "My name is Vivian," she managed to say. It came out just a little louder than a whisper.

The bartender set a drink down on a napkin in front of her. She opened her purse. Her hand was barely on a bill inside when a red-sleeved arm reached out and handed the bartender currency. Then the same arm linked itself in hers and led her away, barely giving her time to grab her drink.

"Okay, Vivling, tell me all about it," he said when they were well away from the bar and approaching the floor-to-ceiling windows overlooking the gardens.

She glanced to her left, where the arm that had just been next to hers was now around her shoulder. It had been such a smooth movement she hadn't noticed it until after the deed was done.

"I thought your specialty was emergency medicine. You're behaving more like a psychiatrist." She didn't bother to tell him again not to call her Vivling; something told her it would be no use.

"If there was a couch here I'd suggest you lie down." He looked embarrassed at the cynical look on her face. "Oops. I think I just put my foot in my mouth. Again."

Her smile was mischievous. "You do that a lot, don't you?"

"With you I seem to. I'm not sure why."

"Why don't we sit for a few minutes?" She took advantage of the opportunity when her back was turned and treated herself to an ear-to-ear smile. Zack had seemed so vulnerable just now, like a thirteen-year-old with a crush on a classmate.

There were two chairs flanking a small glass table between the windows, and they took those. "You look real good," he said.

"You're trying hard to say something nice, aren't you?"

"What? That wasn't nice?"

She laughed, already feeling more relaxed. "It was very nice. Thank you." Then she saw Glenda and waved. She was wearing a cream-colored silk jacquard dress, her natural hair crinkled and pinned at the crown of her head. "Oh, shucks. She doesn't see me." She hated to leave Zack when things were going so well, but to continue to sit with him wasn't fair to Glenda.

"Will you excuse me? The friend I'm meeting is here."

"Sure. I'll catch you later."

Zack watched as she walked away from him. She was so elegant. His instincts had been right. She made every other woman present look ordinary. He wanted to ask her to dance, but not to the finger-snapping kind of music they were playing now. He would wait until they played something slow and dreamy, where he could hold her in his arms.

Vivian and Glenda were both asked to dance at the start of the very next song the deejay played. From that time on they seldom had time to sit. After an hour Vivian began to develop a thirst. She was about to go to the bar for a plain grapefruit juice when another man approached her. "Would you like to dance?"

"Sure," she said, deciding the bar would still be there when she was ready for it.

They joined the other dancers in the center of the room. His movements struck her as being on the stiff side, but he was kind of cute, tall with curly black hair, a goatee, and glasses.

The deejay played a succession of some of her favorite songs, but after the third Vivian found she was getting sluggish and gestured to her partner that she wished to stop.

He escorted her off the dance floor and thanked her. "May I buy you a drink?"

She hesitated. This was tricky. It was a nice gesture, but a lot of men felt that the purchase of a single drink for a woman entitled them to monopolize her company for the rest of the evening. She wouldn't be willing to exchange her freedom for the price of a Rémy Martin, much less a simple grapefruit juice. Still, he seemed like a nice enough fellow, and she wouldn't mind talking with him, at least for a little while. If he didn't seem willing to let her go, she would manage to tactfully get away. "Thank you, yes."

They walked over to the bar.

"What would you like?"

"Just grapefruit juice, please."

He gave the order to the bartender, requesting a rum and coke for himself, then introduced himself as Bernard Williams. In turn she gave her name, and they carried their drinks to the reception area where it was quiet enough to talk. Vivian learned he was a stockbroker for a major firm in the New York Financial District and that he lived in Riverdale. In return, she shared with him the same basic information about herself: where she lived and what she did.

She glanced at her watch. She had been talking with Bernard for forty-five minutes, and she was beginning to feel a little restless. But when the deejay slowed his pace Bernard stood and held out his hand, and she took it.

The crowd on the dance floor typically thinned out when the slow jams were played. She wasn't sure why this was. Maybe the fellows just didn't feel like getting that close. As she stepped into Bernard's arms she wondered where Zack was. A glance around at the other couples on the floor did not reveal that he was among them, and in that red jacket he would be easy to spot. Wherever he was, she hoped he saw her with Bernard, who, while not the best-looking man in the place—that honor would ultimately go to Zack—was no slouch in the looks department. He looked every inch the successful businessman in a navy blue suit that seemed perfectly tailored to his tall, thin body. If there was anything that irked her more than seeing women incorporate those dyed fabric shoes—obviously left over from days of always being a bridesmaid—into their everyday wardrobes, it was a man whose clothes didn't fit properly.

Zack was standing with a number of other men near the door. He stood slightly behind them so that Vivian would not be able to see him. If she didn't see him, she wouldn't know that he knew she was in the arms of another man. He had received compliments on his ensemble from men and women alike, but now he felt like his red blazer stood out like a fire engine among a group of black limousines.

He had felt a vague sensuous light flickering between them when they talked earlier. It was like there was no one else in the building but the two of them . . . until she had spotted her friend, and then the magic moment passed.

He'd danced and socialized since then, but all the while kept an eye on where Vivian was and whom she was with. Some undernourished-looking dude had latched on to her, and, from the looks of it, wasn't ready to let go.

"Hi!"

He turned his head in a lackadaisical manner. He was getting tired of bold females approaching him.

But it wasn't another brazen husband-hunter who stood before him; it was Vivian's girlfriend, the one who had been with her at the hospital and whose name he couldn't remember. "Hello. You're Vivian's friend, aren't you?" He hoped she would furnish her name.

"Yes. Glenda. How've you been, Doc?"

"I'm well. Call me Zack."

"I understand you were on the ski trip."

"You were there, too?"

"Yes. I'm not an experienced skier like you and Viv. That's why you didn't see me. I was with the novices who had to take a lesson on a little baby slope."

He nodded. "One lesson makes it hard to get into, unless you're there for a few days and have the time to really get into it."

"I guess that explains why I didn't care for it much." Glenda scanned the couples dancing. "Oh, there's Viv. I was wondering where she was." She turned to Zack. "I'm afraid she might be trapped."

"What do you mean, trapped?"

"I think she might be having trouble shaking this guy she's talking to. She signaled to me a few minutes ago, just before they started dancing. After they finish I'll make an excuse to go and get her. We do this type of thing for each other all the time." She patted his upper arm. "I just wanted to say hello. See you later."

"Good seeing you, Glenda." Zack looked at Vivian again. She appeared to be enjoying herself, but he wasn't fazed. Glenda had just provided him with valuable information, and he had news for her. *He* was going to be the one to get Vivian away from her dance partner. Maybe it wasn't in the same league as rescuing her from a burning building, but he was sure she would be grateful just the same.

He walked over to where Vivian and the stranger were dancing and tapped him on the shoulder. "Excuse me. May I cut in?"

The man, as he expected, looked stunned. It certainly wasn't a request one heard at every function, but he quickly recovered and acquiesced, with a parting smile Vivian's way.

"This is a surprise," Vivian said as she and Zack fell into step. His timing couldn't have been better. It was almost as if he knew she was scheming up a way to make a graceful break from Bernard, not because she disliked him, but just so she could do a little more socializing. There was no reason why she couldn't meet two new men in a single evening. This was only February, but her average so far was zero, and she needed to double up; it would increase her odds of meeting her goal of getting the life partner she sought. Could it be that Zack was interested in being a contender after all?

She loved being so close to him. He had a delicious, musky scent, and the fabric of his blazer—it felt like a wool blend to her palms—was so soft and welcoming. How wonderful it would be to be able to claim this man as her own.

By the time they had made a single revolution of the dance floor, she became aware that the eyes of various women standing or moving about on the sidelines were fixed on her and Zack. They probably all knew him from NBP, but, of course, she was new to the group. Some of the stares were more obvious than others, and while some were curious, others were outright hostile. That meant she and Zack must make an attractive couple.

"I hope you didn't mind my breaking in," he said.

"I thought it was very sweet. I'm flattered."

The music began to fade out, to Vivian's colossal disappointment. That meant the slow jams were over and the dance music was about to return, and she and Zack had barely had a chance to say two words to each other.

The strains of the next song began as the music they were dancing to grew fainter. "Oh, no, you're not going anywhere yet," Zack said when she broke away from him with the intent of going to the sidelines. "This is a great tune."

She had to agree. The deejay favored what was generally referred to as classic R&B, music that had been at the top of the charts about twenty years before, but sounded as good to her ears and her sense of rhythm at thirty-four as it had at fourteen. Apparently, she wasn't the only one who felt that way. The crowd around them became thick, but their space wasn't reduced. The nice thing about having an event in a banquet room at a hotel or country club was that there was plenty of room in the center of the floor, unlike nightclubs with parquet dance floors measuring perhaps twelve-by-twelve feet, with more than a hundred people trying to squeeze on.

Zack was a wonderful dancer whose moves seemed effortless. Vivian found herself working hard to keep up with him. She had been moving conservatively while dancing previously, conscious of her outfit. Certain moves, while perfectly appropriate in a T-shirt and jeans, one just didn't make when all gussied up. Ordering a beer was one of them, even though a cold beer was a great thirst quencher. Getting down on the dance floor was another. She wanted her movements to be smooth, not jerky.

"Had enough?" Zack asked after about ten minutes.

She nodded and began to lead the way out of the dancers surrounding them. They had barely made it to the sidelines when, with her peripheral vision, she saw a flash of red zoom in toward Zack.

"Zack, I've been waiting for you to dance with me all night. Let's do it now."

Vivian turned sharply to see who this interloper was. The woman's dress was belted at the waist and the skirt had a scalloped hemline. Curiously, the bodice was long-sleeved on one side and cut into a halter style on the other. In spite of three-inch red pumps she barely stood five-four, but she was perfectly proportioned. She took hold of his arm, and, for such a petite woman, demonstrated remarkable strength pulling him back into the crowd.

It all happened so quickly that Vivian was left alone. Her mouth dropped open in shock, and she quickly shut it. What had happened just now?

She quickly realized she couldn't just stand there

like an abandoned child, so she moved forward, toward the sidelines. She heard someone call her name. A look in the direction of the voice revealed that it was Bernard.

"I want to introduce you to my buddy," he said, gesturing to a balding brown-skinned man. "Vivian St. James, this is Terry Terrell."

"Terry Terrell?" she repeated uncertainly as she shook his hand.

"My real first name is something I keep secret from my own mother," Terry said with a smile.

"I'll bet you don't tell her how old you are, either."

The three of them laughed, and Bernard asked if she wanted another drink.

"I'd love one," Vivian replied without hesitation. She decided Zack was a lost cause. She resolved to simply enjoy the evening and Bernard's company.

She walked with them over to the bar. Glenda was leaving it, a fresh drink in her hand. Her eyes met Vivian's in obvious confusion, and Vivian knew she was trying to figure out how she had gone from dancing with Zack to talking with Bernard once more.

"Oh, there you are," Vivian said. She introduced Glenda to both Bernard and Terry, and noticed that Terry immediately perked up. From the terrified look in Glenda's eyes, Vivian knew she had noticed, too. What with his receding hairline, prominent teeth, and slightly rounded belly, Terry was not exactly their idea of what their Mr. Rights would look like.

Vivian watched helplessly as Terry struck up a conversation with her friend. "Are you a member of NBP?" he asked her.

Bernard turned to Vivian. "It looks like those two are hitting it off."

"Well, actually, Glenda is seeing someone. She came tonight as a favor to me. I didn't know anyone else who could make it, and I didn't want to come alone."

At a little after two A.M. Glenda suggested to Vivian that they leave, and Vivian agreed. The function would go on until four, but they had both gone to work that day and were tired. Even if it was a Saturday, they would leave early. Neither one of them liked the idea of sticking around until the lights were turned on full force and they were ready to close the doors.

Bernard and Terry were disappointed at their decision to leave. "I guess we'll be going, too, in a little while." Bernard said. "It's been a long day, and I'm not feeling that hot, to tell you the truth."

Vivian, remembering the mishaps that occurred with Gary and Gordon, felt her muscles tense. "You're not feeling well?"

"Oh, I'm sure it's nothing to worry about. Probably just working too hard. I'll call you tomorrow, all right?"

"All right. Good night, Bernard."

The two friends were able to speak frankly once they were in the parking lot. "You either did a fabulous acting job or you were really having a nice time with Terry," Vivian said.

"You know, he's very nice. Charming, funny, intelligent. What more could a girl ask for?"

"Good looks would be nice."

"All right, so he's starting to look a little middle-aged. But sometimes people put too much emphasis on looks. He's not ugly, he's just an average Joe."

Vivian personally thought Terry had more teeth than Louis Armstrong, a thought she knew was best kept to herself. "What about Bobby?" she asked instead.

"Let's say I've become disenchanted. He's very unsophisticated, Viv."

"What does that mean? Does he eat with his fingers or talk with his mouth full or something?"

"No. He's boring, I guess. He's lived in Long Island City all his life, and he seems content to stay there the rest of his life. He seems content with everything as it is. He's never eaten lobster. He's never even been on an airplane."

"Why is that, I wonder? He makes good money, doesn't he?"

"Yes, but from what he's told me I don't think he did much when he was a kid, never went anywhere, never saw anything but Queens and Manhattan. Maybe because of that he never developed any curiosity or interest in the outside world or how people live in other places."

"No wonder he's not married. Nobody wants his butt."

"Anyway, since I'm not about to spend my life living in a cramped apartment in Long Island City, I think I'd better cut him loose. Hey, did Zack look good or what? I tell you, it's not every man who can get away with wearing a red jacket. What happened to him, anyway? The last I saw, you two were dancing together."

"I got sidetracked by Wilma Flintstone," Vivian replied dryly. "I didn't see him after that. I didn't see her, either, and in that ridiculous dress she would be easy to spot. Maybe they left together."

"I know who you're talking about. Zigzaggy hemline, one shoulder out. Did she actually cut in while you were dancing?"

"No, but she must have been waiting for us to stop, because she grabbed him right away." Vivian sighed. "But Bernard is nice. He's a stockbrocker; lives in Riverdale."

"Terry has one of those in-law apartments in a private house in White Plains. He's a systems analyst. He asked me to lunch, since our offices aren't too far from each other. We're going on Tuesday."

"You're doing real good, Glenda. First Bobby, now Terry."

"You sound like you haven't been busy yourself, or were Gary and Gordon figments of your imagination?"

"At least you and Bobby got somewhere—before you found out he wasn't interested in going anywhere. Gary and Gordon were duds from the beginning. You're way ahead of me."

"Don't sweat it. I'm six months older, remember?"

Chapter 5:
Kind Hearts and
Kidney Stones

Three weeks later Vivian and Glenda attended an off-Broadway revue, an outing sponsored by Glenda's church. Two buses had been chartered for this event, all consisting of groups of women and couples. Neither Vivian nor Glenda had expected this to be a venue to meet men; they both just wanted to see the show.

Prior to that, Vivian had begun dating Bernard, while Glenda dumped Bobby in favor of Bernard's friend Terry Terrell, whose real first name, she learned, was Grover.

Relations between both couples seemed to be going relatively well, except Vivian found Bernard's occasional complaints of belly pain unnerving. Zack Warner's offhand remark about her bringing bad health to the men she dated had wounded her more deeply than she'd originally thought. Could she carry some kind of hex? But Bernard repeatedly insisted his discomfort wasn't anything serious.

"So how's Terry?" she asked Glenda.

"He's good. You know, I think he was actually relieved to learn that you and I were going out tonight. It'll give him and Bernard a chance to chew the fat over a couple of beers."

"They're awfully tight," Vivian said.

"Maybe too tight."

"What do you mean?"

"As far as I can tell they talk every day."

"So do we."

"We work together, Vivian; it would be hard for us not to. Often on weekends we don't talk unless we're going somewhere together. But those two seem closer than Montgomery and Ward. Do you ever get the feeling that Bernard shares everything that goes on between the two of you with Terry, and vice versa?"

Vivian shrugged. "It's not like there's anything juicy going on, but I *would* like to feel I have some privacy."

"There's nothing sexually happening with Terry and me, either. I've stuck to my guns about keeping that out of the picture unless me and the man in my life are absolutely mad about each other."

"You didn't two years ago."

Glenda rolled her eyes. "David wasn't serious, but it was steady. Besides, I didn't want to miss my peak. Can I help it if I wasn't in love then, like you were? I was leading a lonely, shallow, and meaningless life. When I was with David it was just shallow and meaningless. No harm done."

Vivian averted her eyes. It was true that she'd had strong feelings for Douglas Mathis, and he for her, but she had ultimately decided that his alcohol intake was more than she felt comfortable with. He was a mail sorter at the post office, a well-paying, but rather boring, occupation in which people had been known to go berserk in the past. She was afraid that only trouble lay ahead and in her heart she'd always known the breakup had been for the best. She never regretted it; Douglas simply wasn't her Mr. Right.

She felt Glenda's elbow gently poke her side and stopped thinking about her old flame.

"Talk about an audience full of females," Glenda hissed. "Any woman with a man is over fifty and has probably been married to him for twenty years."

Vivian scanned the spectators in front of them, from left to right. "Not that couple." She pointed to the right with her chin.

"Hmm. Interesting. I'm glad somebody out there has managed to snare a date. Maybe there's hope for us yet, eh?"

They both found their attention held by the couple. They could only see the backs of their heads and the sides of their faces. They were deeply engrossed in conversation and seemed oblivious of their surroundings.

A slight commotion having to do with someone being in the wrong seat just a few rows ahead of where she and Glenda were captured Vivian's attention, and then she noticed that the couple was looking in that direction as well. The man looked even more handsome now that she saw his entire face, but she gasped when she got a closer look at the woman. To say she was not attractive was being kind. There were spaces between her upper teeth large enough to drive a Harley-Davidson through, suggesting advanced periodontal disease like in those scary posters at the dentist's office. The obviously dyed reddish-gold chignon hairstyle which looked so fashionable from the rear was badly in need of a touch-up. Dark roots at least half-an-inch long were clearly visible in the front. A thick layer of make-up failed to disguise the fact that she had bad skin.

"Did you *see* that?" Glenda whispered.

"Yes. Listen, I don't like to begrudge anyone their good fortune, but there must be two dozen unescorted women in our group alone, and every one of them is better looking than she is."

"She must be paying."

"Maybe. But it's depressing all the same."

A warm front hit New York the next week, a hint of the spring that was still over a month away. Usually such unseasonable weather was reserved for work days, but New Yorkers awoke Friday morning to temperatures in the high forties that would reach the mid-sixties by the afternoon. The television meteorologists were promising it would last until Monday.

Bernard called Vivian at work that afternoon. "I hear it's going to be real warm this weekend. Let's plan on doing something outside."

"Sounds good to me."

They spent Saturday afternoon in Central Park and walked down the most fashionable part of Fifth Avenue. On Sunday they went to a deli and bought sandwiches, fruit, cheese and wine and had a picnic in one of the pullover areas on the West Side Highway overlooking the Hudson River, just north of the Seventy-Ninth Street Boat Basin. It was rather noisy, with southbound traffic whizzing past at sixty miles an hour, but somehow it was relaxing at the same time, just cooling out knowing that they had nowhere in particular to go.

"I always wanted to have a boat," Bernard said. "I'll bet it costs a fortune to keep one here."

Vivian was lying down with her head resting on his thigh. She followed his gaze to the boats docked in the basin. "I think most of those people live on their boats."

"Well, that's a thought. It beats paying rent, I'm sure." He made a strange sound, almost like a whimper.

She immediately sat up. "You all right?"

"Well, actually I'm not feeling that great. Do you mind if we wrap up a little early?"

"Of course not. I'll even drive." She got up right away and began gathering the contents of their outing, including the bag they had used for trash.

"You know, Bernard, you really should make an appointment to see a doctor," she said when they were settled in his cream-colored SUV, Vivian behind the wheel, waiting for a break in traffic so she could pull out.

"I know. I'll definitely make the call tomorrow. It's become pretty apparent that whatever this is, it isn't going to go away by itself. Do you mind if I put my seat back?"

"No, go ahead. I'm fine."

Vivian took the first exit, then got back on heading north. She was glad the toll was on the southbound side; she wanted to get Bernard home as quickly as possible.

It only took fifteen minutes to get to Bernard's co-op in Riverdale, but in that brief time he had fallen asleep. She gently shook him awake. "Yeah, I'm up," he said unconvincingly.

"I'm coming upstairs with you. I'm not leaving until I know you're all right."

"I need to bring you home."

"If you're not up to it I'll just take your car to go home in. If you feel better later I'll bring it back to you, and you can bring me home then. Even if you don't feel up to it later, we can do it tomorrow. You take the train to work, anyway, and the car will be safe on my street."

On his floor she stopped at the incinerator closet to toss the trash bag from their outing. "Leave the door open," she called. She opened the incinerator chute, stuffed the bag inside and did a quick reflex action to make sure it had actually gone down. She then rushed down the hall to Bernard's apartment. The door was ajar, held open by the deadbolt lock in the locked position. She wondered if she would get a look at his bedroom. She wasn't in the least concerned that he might try for sex; that look on his face reflected genuine pain. In the meantime she could learn more about his personality, like if the neat appearance of the front of his apartment was real or just for show.

The television was on in the living room. Perhaps out of habit he had turned it on to watch the afternoon's basketball games.

"Bernard?" she called haltingly as she entered the living room. She drew in her breath when she saw him laying on the floor between the coffee table and the sofa, facing the sofa. Good Lord, he must have passed out. There was blood on the edge of the coffee table. She also noticed blood on the area rug underneath the table.

She was afraid to look at his face, but she had to determine if he was still breathing. She knelt in front of him and tried to roll him over, without much success. For such a thin man he felt awfully heavy. His forehead was covered with blood. "Bernard. What happened?"

He mumbled something unintelligible.

"Wait. I'm going to call for help." She reached for the phone and dialed nine-one-one, then went to get a cloth to wipe away all the blood.

Vivian drove Bernard's SUV to the hospital instead of riding in the ambulance; that way she would be sure to have a way to get home. The ambulance brought Bernard to Hudson Hospital. It was in Manhattan and there were plenty of hospitals in the Bronx, but it was a ten-minute drive from Riverdale, right off the Henry Hudson Parkway. She really didn't think about the possibility of seeing Zack until she pulled into the parking lot. She could only imagine what he would have to say at her accompanying yet another ailing male friend. If she was lucky, he wouldn't be on duty today.

The nurse at the triage desk interviewed her, but she was unable to provide most of the answers to the information they sought. "I don't know him very well," she added, feeling she needed to explain to the harried nurse, whose expression clearly conveyed that she felt Vivian was worthless. "When you're getting to know someone you generally don't exchange information like what medical problems or operations they've had."

When the nurse was done Vivian decided to notify Bernard's family. Of course, she had no idea of how to reach them, but she knew who would.

* * *

"Hello?"

"Glenda, it's Vivian. I need to get in touch with Terry."

"He's right here. We just got in from playing some miniature golf. Is everything all right?"

"No. I'm at the hospital with Bernard. He passed out in his apartment."

"Oh, my goodness! Is he okay?"

"They haven't told me anything yet. He seemed conscious when EMS came to pick him up, but he was talking gibberish."

"I hope he didn't have a stroke. He's young for that, but he does hold a high-stress job."

"At this point, all I can do is wait. But I do think his parents should know about this. Besides, they can answer a lot of questions I'm not able to, like if he has any medication allergies."

"Oh, sure. Hold on. I'll tell him to pick up." There was a pause, as if she was putting down the phone, but then Glenda spoke again. "Wait a minute. What hospital are you at?"

Vivian chuckled. "Where else but my favorite ER?"

A rushing sound flooded the receiver as Glenda inhaled. "Hudson! Did you see him?"

"No," Vivian replied flatly.

"Well, you don't have to sound so defensive."

"I am *not* being defensive, Glenda. This is a serious matter. Bernard was *unconscious*. You just said yourself that maybe he had a stroke. Zack Warner is the last person I'm thinking about. This is not part of our little husband-hunting expedition."

"Now you're making me feel guilty. Hold on; here's Terry."

* * *

Vivian sat in the waiting area, alternating between reading the "Arts and Leisure" section of the *New York Times* that someone had apparently left behind, and glancing up at the entry, wanting to see if anyone new had arrived. Terry had immediately offered to call Bernard's parents and let them know their son was at the hospital. "I'm sure they'll rush right over," he said.

Vivian expected as much. It had been a very long time since she'd met the parents of a man she was dating, and these circumstances were far from ideal. Terry had also told her that he and Glenda would be over right after they got something to eat. She found herself hoping that they would arrive before the Williamses; it would make the situation less uncomfortable.

As it turned out the next voice she heard was one that was becoming familiar.

"Hey. That you, Vivling?"

"Hello, Zack," she said knowingly before she even turned her head to visually confirm his presence.

"What brings you here this afternoon? No, don't tell me. You're here with the fellow with the ulcer."

"Bernard has an ulcer?"

"That's about my best guess until his labs come back. Test results will confirm." Zack took the vacant seat next to her, pulled a gleaming red apple out of his lab coat pocket and took a bite.

She was actually glad to see him. His familiar face soothed her nerves.

"Is he conscious?"

"Yes. I'd like to hear your version of what happened?"

"Didn't he tell you?"

"He doesn't remember. That's not unusual in a

situation like this." Zack held out his hand, palm up, gesturing for her to continue.

"Well, I wasn't in the room when it happened. I found him on the floor. He hit his head on the coffee table."

"And you don't know anything about his medical history?"

"I barely know him, Zack. But I believe his parents are on the way. They should be able to tell you whatever you need to know."

"That must have been a difficult call to make."

"Actually, I didn't make the call. Someone made it for me." Suddenly Zack's impassive expression was too much for her. "Why don't you just go ahead and say it?"

"Say what?"

"I know you're just dying to make some comment about coming to the rescue of the men I date."

"I was thinking no such thing, my little angel of the accident-prone."

"Are you through?"

"I don't know why you're insulted. It's not like I called you the angel of death."

"I guess since you're joking around like this, you think Bernard will be okay."

"He's got a nasty gash from his head connecting with that coffee table, which we've already cleaned and stitched up. His ulcer looks like it might be pretty bad, but I hardly think it's life-threatening. We've requested a GI consult to determine if surgery is needed, and he'll be admitted as soon as we can get someone to do it." He stood up. "I'll come out again in a few minutes. Maybe the family will be here by then. In the meantime I need to speak with another family." He returned the apple to his pocket.

Vivian was about to acknowledge his statement when a small, wiry man approached him. "Dr. Warner, any news on my daughter?"

"Ah, Mr. Mosely. I was just looking for you." He turned to Vivian. "Excuse me."

She nodded.

The men moved away before they began to talk. Vivian couldn't hear what Zack said, but the man's response was spoken quite loudly.

"Plastic surgery!" he exclaimed.

Zack continued to speak in the same calm tone.

"But I can't afford a plastic surgeon's fee. Why can't *you* sew up the cut?"

This time Vivian could hear Zack's response. "If it was her arm or leg that was lacerated I think that would be fine, Mr. Mosely. But it wasn't. It's her face. Surely you don't want your daughter to be scarred."

"No, of course not; but I can't afford to pay a plastic surgeon. I want you to do it."

Zack lowered his voice, but from his body language Vivian could tell he was trying to convince the man that this was the best route to take. She could also tell from the way his shoulders slumped that he was not successful. He left the room wearing defeat like a hand-me-down suit.

Vivian was still looking at the door he had disappeared behind when the Williamses arrived. "Miss St. James?"

She turned and immediately knew the identity of this sixtyish couple. "Yes," she said, smiling. "You must be Bernard's parents."

"I'm Levi Williams and this is my wife, Ceola."

Vivian shook their hands. Mr. Williams's grip was

strong, but his wife's felt like a mass of cooked pasta. "I'm so sorry we had to meet under such unpleasant circumstances."

"I am, too. Has there been any word on Bernard's condition?" Mr. Williams asked.

"Actually, the doctor was just here. He said he would come out again in a few minutes and see if you had arrived."

"What did he say?" This from Mrs. Williams.

"He said Bernard's injuries weren't life-threatening."

"Injuries?" his mother interrupted. "I thought he fainted. Was he attacked?"

Vivian didn't like the accusatory tone in her voice, but she chalked it up to a combination of being upset and uninformed. "He passed out in his own living room and banged his head on the coffee table," she said evenly. "The doctor suspects an ulcer. They're waiting for a GI specialist to determine if he needs surgery."

"It's all that stress at his job," Mrs. Williams said. She turned to her husband. "I *told* him to become an accountant instead of a stockbroker."

"All right, Ceola. Let's wait for the doctor."

"But he might need surgery!"

"We'll cross that bridge when we get to it. Let's just sit down."

Vivian regretted having mentioned the possibility of surgery. Mrs. Williams was clearly the theatrical type, and she had just provided her with ammunition.

"At least he wasn't attacked. Even Riverdale is getting bad these days," Mrs. Williams was saying as they took seats. "You know," she said, turning to Vivian, "Pelham is really much safer than the city. I don't understand why he felt he had to leave home. He came and went as he pleased, and I made dinner for him every night."

Vivian smiled politely, not letting on that she was thinking, *Does the word "suffocation" mean anything to you?* The way Bernard's mother was talking, she and her husband lived in a crime-free area. No such place existed, unless you counted Antarctica.

"Where do you live, Vivian?" Mrs. Williams asked.

"In Mount Vernon. You might say we're neighbors, since we share a border." The town of Pelham was sandwiched between the southern Westchester cities of Mount Vernon and New Rochelle.

"Oh, but people are always getting mugged and even worse in Mount Vernon. You might as well live in New York."

Her husband intervened. "Ceola, I think you've said enough."

That makes two of us. Vivian turned her head so the Williamses wouldn't see her rolling her eyes.

Zack reappeared ten minutes later. "Mr. and Mrs. Williams, I'm Dr. Warner."

Vivian sat nearby as Zack filled in the Williamses on Bernard's condition. There was nothing more to report other than what he had already told her.

Mrs. Williams gasped and clutched her husband's arm when he mentioned the possibility of surgery. "Can we see him?" she inquired.

"Yes, but only two at a time, and just briefly."

"Come on, Levi." Mrs. Williams moved forward, her hand still clamped on her husband's arm.

Zack turned to the man at the information desk. "Lou, I've got two going back." Then he turned toward the Williamses, who stood impatiently in front of the locked door. "He's behind curtain four. It'll be on your right."

The entry to the patient area swung open, and Bernard's parents hurried through it. Zack turned his gaze to Vivian. His eyes looked darker than usual, and they reflected anguish. Surely, it had to be the case of the child he had discussed earlier.

"I couldn't help overhearing your discussion with the father of one of your patients. Did he change his mind about getting a plastic surgeon?" she asked.

"I'm afraid not, not even after the head of the department spoke with him about it. It's out of our hands now. I did everything I could. This is one of the things I like the least about my work. There are cases where parents are pleading with us to do everything we can for their kids, and sometimes we aren't able to. Here's a case where we actually can do something but aren't allowed to because the father is too concerned about not being able to pay the bill."

"Don't they have insurance?"

"No. That's the problem; he's a self-pay. Still, there are some things worth going into debt for."

"I agree. What happened to the child? I mean, how was she injured?"

"They were in a car accident. She's got deep lacerations across her forehead and diagonally; and a jagged one on her cheek from all the glass."

"Oh, how awful! Where's her mother? I'm sure she wouldn't want her daughter's face to be scarred."

"She's in surgery. She took the brunt of the impact. The daughter was sitting behind her on the passenger-side. The father was able to walk away unhurt, although he might develop some muscle aches by tomorrow." Zack shook his head. "Vivian, this girl is only nine years old. You know how cruel kids can be at that age?"

"I have a feeling that as soon as her mother learns what's going on she might insist the girl have her lacerations repaired by a plastic surgeon. It can be done at a later time, can't it, even if you fix it now?"

"It can, but it's probably best to have it repaired correctly the first time. It'll be less traumatic for her, and the result will probably be better." He scratched the nape of his neck and shut his eyes.

"I hope none of your other patients are too difficult."

"Not really. I've got a woman who's a regular customer. She's five months pregnant and is hoping frequent ER visits will convince her doctor to put her on disability until her baby is born."

"She actually *told* you that?"

"No, but when repeated tests fail to show anything wrong, I don't see any other conclusion I can come to."

"I don't think you're being fair. It's not like you know anything about having a baby."

"No, but I passed a kidney stone once."

She cast him a cynical glance.

"All right. Anyway, your friend's parents seem like nice people."

"Yes, but I think Mrs. Williams missed her calling. She should have gone into the theater or the movies. I think she would have done what Dorothy Dandridge, Cicely Tyson, and Angela Bassett weren't able to do . . . get the Academy Award for Best Actress."

He looked at her curiously. "Sounds like trouble in paradise."

"I probably shouldn't have said that." Opening up to him seemed perfectly natural after he shared his own pain with her, but she'd better become less personal. "I really can't blame her for being distraught. He's her only child."

"You can go in to see him when the parents come out, you know."

"Thank you. I'd like to." She glanced at her watch.

"You got a hot date?"

Vivian looked at him in exasperation. He was flashing his trademark devilish smile. It was nice to see it again, actually. She must be getting used to Zack's sometimes twisted sense of humor. Then, again, she had witnessed his vulnerable side just moments ago. She supposed that subconsciously she hadn't believed such a side to him existed, in spite of his having a profession that often required the utmost sensitivity and compassion. But it was confusing, the way he could be kindhearted one minute and a smart-ass the next. "No, silly. I'm actually waiting for Glenda to get here."

"Is she your ride home?"

"No. I drove Bernard's car here. It's just that Glenda thought it would be easier for me if she was here. She doesn't live far from here."

The double doors opened, and Mr. and Mrs. Williams emerged, Mrs. Williams dabbing at her eyes with a white hankie.

Vivian frowned. There were few things she could think of that were more unpleasant than fat men in Speedos, but the drama-ridden lament of an overprotective mother came awfully close. She was really laying it on thick.

"Mr. and Mrs. Williams," Zack began. "I know

Bernard looks ill, but there's no reason why he shouldn't make a full recovery."

"But he looks so pale," Mrs. Williams wailed.

"He doesn't look well, Doctor," her husband added calmly, his arm draped around his wife's shoulder.

"He's had a nasty fall. I know that bandage on his forehead is frightening. He's also not feeling very well because of the ulcer, but I hate for you to be upset. We'll have him feeling better in a few days."

"Dr. Warner to curtain five." The female voice paging Zack had a slight Caribbean accent.

"I'm sorry to be abrupt, but I have to see one of my patients. I'll be here until eleven P.M. Please feel free to call me with any questions you may have or for an update," Zack offered.

The Williamses thanked him, and Vivian said, "I guess it's my turn to see Bernard."

"I think maybe you should let him get some rest," Mrs. Williams said quickly. "The nurse asked us to leave after only a few minutes."

"They won't let anyone stay more than a few minutes," Zack said. "Don't worry, Mrs. Williams. It'll be all right." He turned to Vivian. "Come on; you can get in with me."

"Please excuse me," Vivian said to Bernard's parents.

As she waited with Zack at the entrance to the patient area while he gestured to the man at the information desk to buzz them in, she overheard Mrs. Williams, making no effort to speak in a low voice, saying, "It isn't right to tire him out this way. She should just go home now." She shook her head and sucked her teeth in annoyance.

While Vivian was leaving Bernard's bedside, an

announcement came over the PA. "Dr. Warner,
telephone call." Probably tonight's date calling to
find out what time he was picking her up.

When she got back to the waiting room she was
relieved to see that Terry and Glenda had arrived.
Thank God she wouldn't have to deal with Bernard's parents alone. Terry was patting Mrs. Williams's hand, who looked at Vivian so intently she
wanted to ask if she had a booger in her nose or
something.

"How is he?" the older woman asked.

"He looks better than he did right after he
passed out."

"What was he doing when he fainted? Had the
two of you been up all hours, or something?" Mrs.
Williams persisted.

"He was sitting in his living room. I believe I
already told you that." Vivian knew her words
sounded curt, but she couldn't help it. It was clear
Bernard's mother was trying to hold her responsible for Bernard's illness, and she wasn't about to
stand here and be accused.

"I think we should go now, Ceola," Mr. Williams
said. "There's nothing else we can do. He's in good
hands. We can call Dr. Warner in a little while to see
what the specialist says." He turned to Vivian. "We
want to thank you for getting our boy to the hospital."

"You're very welcome, Mr. Williams. I was glad I
could help." Mrs. Williams was conspicuously silent,
she noticed.

Vivian turned to Terry when the senior Williamses had gone. "Is that normal behavior for her?"

"Yes, Terry replied, "but she's harmless."

"I don't know about all that. I can't think of a
person who has annoyed me more in such a short
time."

***

Zack picked up the receiver at the nurses' station. "Dr. Warner here."

It was the answering service of the building management company. "We have an emergency, Dr. Warner."

"What happened?"

"One of the tenants has been found dead in his apartment."

"Oh, no! Who was it? And what happened? It wasn't a murder, was it?"

"No. It was Mr. Ellis in 3-B. The coroner said there weren't any outward signs of foul play, maybe a heart attack, or something."

Zack took a moment to be grateful that no one would have grounds to sue him and Austin, as the building's owners, then said a brief prayer for Mr. Ellis. "He was an old man. He probably died of natural causes. I'll be by tomorrow to survey the apartment for damages. Get John to air it out, will you?"

"He's doing it now. I didn't stay too long; it smelled too bad. Mr. Ellis's son in Ohio is being notified. I'll expect to hear from him soon."

"All right. Thanks for letting me know. I'll see you tomorrow."

He replaced the receiver, a thoughtful frown on his face. Mr. Ellis continued to live alone long after his declining health warranted supervision. The last time he'd seen the old man his gray hair fell past his shoulders, and he wore a filthy coat. It wasn't surprising that death had claimed him, but it was sad nevertheless. If Zack had his way, no one would die alone.

He wondered how Mr. Ellis's son would react to

news of his father's demise. He couldn't imagine
living so far away and, by accounts, never visiting,
but of course not every father and son had the
loving relationship he shared with his dad.

Zack's parents now lived in the Bronx. He
wished he was in the financial position to buy a
home for them. While he knew they were proud
of him and they lived in relative comfort—they
had declined a reduced-rent apartment in the
building he and Austin owned—he wished he
could have done more for them. He found it
amusing that so many people seemed impressed
when he told them his profession, but the fact was
that ER medicine simply didn't pay at the same
scale as other specialties, like cardiology or surgery.
He was still paying off his student loans. Sometimes women seemed downright disappointed to
learn he drove an ordinary Ford Taurus instead of
a Benz or a Jaguar. It was probably hard for some to
believe, but he had gone into medicine because he
truly liked the idea of aiding the sick and the injured, not because he expected to become wealthy.
It hurt his heart to witness an incident like the one
he'd seen earlier, where economic fear of a plastic
surgeon meant a real cutie-pie would be marked
for life.

It had been a stressful day, and now there was
the matter of a vacant apartment. He knew it would
rent quickly, but there would be a delay in getting
Mr. Ellis's belongings out. Something told Zack the
man's son wasn't going to be much help. His rent
was paid up through the end of the month, and
ideally he'd like to have it rented by the time the
one-month security deposit expired at the end of
the following month.

After the unit was empty it had to be painted,

the parquet floors waxed, and a general clean-up done. He hoped the damages weren't significant; Mr. Ellis's unkempt appearance wasn't one of someone concerned with keeping an orderly apartment.

He chuckled. With all this on his mind he might not even have a chance to think about the lovely Vivian St. James, who kept coming into his life courtesy of the jokers she was dating. In his opinion, they were either clumsy or just plain unlucky. When he was able to stop thinking about her, she'd show up again, looking even better than he remembered. She'd seemed so caring about little Kelly Mosely, and, at that moment, he knew he was going to have to put himself in the running for Vivian's affections. He didn't have the slightest idea of where to find her, and to rely on the pattern of her male acquaintances suffering mishaps or becoming ill was foolhardy, but he was sure he would run into her again before too long. When it came to black, single professionals, the New York metropolitan area really wasn't all that big. He saw at least a few familiar faces at just about every event he attended, and with Vivian attending NBP events, the odds were even higher.

He was practically whistling when he sought out Bernard's parents and Vivian with an update. He didn't see the senior Williamses, but Vivian's friend Glenda had arrived. There was a man with them as well. He looked familiar. . . .

"Hi. Are Bernard's parents still here?" he asked Vivian when he got closer to them.

"They left. I told them I would call with Bernard's room number."

"I see. Hello, Glenda."

"Hi, Doc. Oh, this is Terry Terrell. Terry, Dr. Zack Warner."

The men shook hands, and Zack realized Glenda's companion was the dude who had been with Bernard at the Valentine's dance. Apparently the two friends had become a pleasant foursome. That certainly was cozy, just like the Kramdens and the Nortons.

"We're going to be admitting Bernard to the ICU, but probably just until his results are back. There can be dozens of reasons for syncope."

"What's syncope?" Glenda asked. "It sounds like a musical beat."

Zack smiled. "It's when a person blacks out."

Vivian couldn't remember the last time she had been so happy to see the building where she lived. For reasons she had never understood, on-street parking had always been relatively simple here, unlike other Westchester locations. Most of the buildings on her street were small apartment houses; others were duplexes, with a few private homes, most of which had no garages or driveways.

The two Harris boys, Miles and Mason, were playing outside and ran to her as she approached. She could see excitement in their faces. What was going on?

"Oh, Miss Vivian! Did you hear?"

"Did I hear what?"

Miles spoke first . . . or maybe it was Mason, the younger of the two by less than a year. They were practically the same size, and Vivian usually found it difficult to differentiate between the two. "They found Mr. Ellis dead in his apartment this afternoon."

"Dead! How did it happen, does anyone know?"

"It was real exciting!" Mason said. "The cops were here, and the people who take away dead bodies."

"It's called the coroner, silly." Eleven-year-old Miles had obviously been listening to adults in the neighborhood talk.

"Yes, that's right," Vivian agreed. "But does anyone know how he died?"

"They don't think anybody killed him or anything," Miles said. "They think he just sat down and died."

"He was *real* old," Mason added.

"Yes, well, sometimes things like that happen to people who are very old. Thank you, boys, for telling me. I've been gone all day. I think I'll stop in at Santos's and see what he knows." Santos—she didn't know his first name and doubted anyone else did either other than his wife and daughter—was the building's resident superintendent.

Once inside the building, she hesitated. Mr. and Mrs. Paul Hughes, Austin's parents, lived on the ground floor, next door to the Santos family. She wondered if she should ask Mrs. Hughes, who usually knew everything that went on in the building, but she decided that the super would be the most knowledgeable of anyone. Mr. Ellis lived directly upstairs from her, and she was less than enthused about there having been a dead body so close. She wondered how long he had been dead before anyone discovered him, since he lived alone and never seemed to have visitors.

She knocked on the door, using the metal knocker. The door was answered almost immediately by the Santos's pretty teenage daughter, whom Vivian noted with a twinge of envy was about a size five. The girl had a cordless phone to her ear, which she lowered to her side.

"Hi! I just got home and heard about what happened. Is your dad here?"

"Yes, just a minute, please." The girl turned and called out, "Daddy! There's somebody here to see you."

The girl resumed her conversation and stood there until her father appeared, then promptly disappeared.

Santos was a small, wiry man of about fifty with olive skin and curly gray hair. He nodded knowingly upon seeing her. "I knocked on your door this afternoon. I guess you weren't home. I wanted to let you know about Mr. Ellis. Mrs. Harris complained of a bad odor coming from his apartment."

Vivian's upper lip curled in distaste. Apparently Mr. Ellis had been dead for days. Why did people use words like "bad," "unpleasant," or "foul-smelling" to describe an odor, she wondered. The very word itself suggested something offensive to the nostrils.

"I've got it airing out up there. It's not bad, believe me. Lucky for us, Mrs. Harris has a sensitive nose . . . or else the situation could have gotten really ugly."

"Is there anything else I need to be aware of? The Harris boys told me outside that they think he died of natural causes."

"Yeah. That kind of thing happens all the time. I meant to check on him. I realized after the fact that I hadn't seen him probably since Wednesday or Thursday. I've been real busy lately, painting the basement. One more day and the mailman probably would have mentioned it. That's what happens most of the time when I'm too busy to notice; the mailman tells me. You don't gotta do nothin'. His son is supposed to be comin' in on Tuesday. You just go on up and don't worry about nothin'. In another month or two you'll have a nice new neighbor."

Chapter 6:
A Real Mother For Ya

"Hi, Mom. Listen, you know I would never blow you off, but can I call you back? I was just on my way out the door."

"You sound in a real hurry for a Monday night."

"Well, I need to get to the hospital to visit a friend, and they only allow a few minutes in the ICU."

"Good heavens, who's in the hospital?"

Vivian glanced at her watch. Her mother was incredible. How had she even known she was home? She had ducked out of work a half-hour early so she could get down to Washington Heights and back home again before it got too late, and it looked like all her efforts were going to be for naught. Only her mother could proceed to carry on a conversation after being told she didn't have time to talk. Vivian loved her mother dearly, but she was already regretting having answered the phone.

"It's Bernard. You don't know him," she answered, hoping that would be that, but doubting it would be.

"Is he the one you've been seeing the past few weeks?"

For a split second Vivian considered fibbing—no, make that telling an outright lie—and saying he wasn't. Surely her mother wouldn't feel the matter worth pursuing if this was a one-time Joe. But then she realized that wouldn't work. What if things became serious between her and Bernard? She would eventually have to bring him to Connecticut to meet her family, and her mother had a memory encased in cast iron.

"Yes, we've been getting together on the weekends," she replied as casually as she could.

"Do you go to nice places?"

Vivian was well acquainted with the special meanings behind her mother's words. What Caroline St. James was really asking was, *Does he spend money on you or is he tight?*

"Yes, Mom."

"Where is he from?" *Is his family well-off?*

"Pelham. That's a town between Mount Vernon and New Rochelle."

"Where does he live?" *Is he well-off?*

"Riverdale. That's the northwest corner of the Bronx."

"Oh, yes. I've heard of that. It's one of those areas that can make you forget it's part of New York City. What does he do?" *How much does he make?*

"He's a stockbroker." Vivian could feel the good vibes travel through the wires. Her ears actually tingled from her mother's approval.

"And what's his full name?" *Is he a Black Muslim named Muhammed, or a radical who's adopted some crazy-sounding African name?*

"Bernard Williams. I don't know his middle name."

"Very ordinary, isn't it? There must be millions of people named Williams."

"Mom, you were a Johnson before you married Daddy, remember? Listen, I really have to go. I'll call you the minute I get back." Without waiting for a reply she hung up. She was gone before her mother could press the redial button.

Zack saw a car pulling out of a space as he approached the building. He pulled up alongside the car in front of the space and backed into it with ease.

A look at the open blinds and neat, light colored curtains in the window on the front right reminded him he would have to stop in and say hello to Austin's parents before he left. He and Austin had been buddies since second grade. His own parents regarded Austin as a third son, after his younger brother; and the Hugheses treated him like one of their family. He knew they missed Austin terribly since his move to Colorado, even though they were thrilled about his engagement to Desirée Mack. He felt pretty good about their impending marriage himself. Desirée had made Ozzie happier than he'd ever seen him.

He let himself in the locked entry just beyond the foyer with his pass key. As he climbed the stairs he sniffed, almost expecting his nose to register something unpleasant, but it didn't happen. Maybe Santos had really gotten it aired out after all.

He had gotten a key to Mr. Ellis's apartment from the management office. Laurie, who handled matters pertaining to their property, informed him that Mr. Ellis's son was driving in from Ohio and would be arriving sometime the following day, and he had promised to contact her with a date when he would have his father's apartment emptied, adding that he didn't expect it to take very long.

The apartment was sparsely furnished, with just two contemporary style—by fifties standards—chairs flanking an end table in the living room and an old table and chairs in the dining area. The floors were bare. All the apartments had attractive parquet floors, but some tenants opted to put area rugs in strategic locations, which served the dual purpose of preventing them from stepping on cold floors in the wintertime and reducing the amount of work required to maintain the parquet. Mr. Ellis' floors were dull and had numerous long, black marks, the kind that come from dragging furniture from one spot to another. The only window coverings were shades that had once been white but were now yellowed. There was webbing in the upper corners that hadn't been dusted in ages.

The bedroom was no better. The sheets had turned a dingy brown from lack of washing. At least there wasn't much furniture to dispose of, and most of it would have to be literally disposed of. The heavy old-fashioned bedroom suite could probably be salvaged, but no one would want the filthy upholstered chairs and cheap wood tables in the living room. Maybe someone could use the kitchen table, but the two vinyl upholstered chairs, which Zack was sure were older than he was, had multiple rips in them. A thorough cleaning and a paint job and the apartment would be ready for a new tenant. It wasn't too bad at all.

He went down to Santos's apartment and knocked on the door. It was answered by Santos's wife, who had an obviously worried look on her face.

"Teresita, what's wrong?"

"It's Fernando. He's not feeling good. I think he's getting worse. I asked him all day if he wanted to see the doctor."

"Well, I'm a doctor. I'll be happy to look at him, if you'd like."

"Yes, please. Come in." Teresita stepped back, and he followed her inside.

Santos lay on the couch in the living room, the coffee table in front of him littered with comfort items: a carelessly folded newspaper, an empty plate and drinking glass, ashtray, cigarette pack and lighter. Teresita quickly removed the dirty dishes and disappeared into the kitchen.

"I understand you're feeling under the weather," Zack said. "Where does it hurt?"

"My belly. I ain't never had pain like this before. It's been bothering me all day, and now it's getting worse."

"Point to exactly where it hurts, will you?"

Santos pointed to the right lower quadrant of his abdomen.

"I'll bet it's a sharp pain that never lets up."

"How did you know?"

Zack called for Teresita, who rushed in, wiping her hands on a dishtowel. "What is it?"

"I want you to bring him to the emergency room right away." He turned to Santos and asked, "Have you ever had your appendix removed?"

"No."

"Well, I think you might have to have it taken out now."

"It's just a bellyache. I don't wanna go under no knife," Santos protested.

"It's either that or let it burst, which will kill you." Santos's face lost color, and Zack almost regretted being so blunt, but he knew that sometimes it took shock value to get people to understand the seriousness of the situation, especially when the person didn't like hospitals or doctors. "Of course, I can't tell from simply asking you a few questions if you actually have appendicitis, but I do believe it's worth looking into."

"Thank you, Zack," Teresita said. "We'll leave right after I get Fernando a shirt."

"I'll check with you tomorrow. I'll let myself out."

Vivian felt like she'd just been on a five-mile hike. Dealing with Bernard's mother was exhausting. The Williamses were already at the hospital when she arrived. Mr. Williams was charming, but his wife seemed surprised to see her.

"I didn't expect to see you here, uh . . ."

"Vivian."

"Yes, that's right. I just can't keep up with all Bernard's girls."

Vivian doubted Bernard's mother knew how much—or how little—her son dated, and she cheerfully let that remark pass. Mrs. Williams was like those annoying commercials featuring Cleo, the so-called psychic with the questionably authentic Caribbean accent, that played every five minutes on local syndicates and cable networks. The woman simply was not going to miss an opportunity to make her feel ill at ease any more than Cleo would miss a chance to invite viewers to "Call me now for your free readin'."

The doors to the intensive care unit were being

opened. "Why don't you two go in first. I'm sure they only allow two visitors at a time."

"Actually, you're supposed to be a family member," Mrs. Williams pointed out.

Vivian looked her in the eye unflinchingly. "I lied."

It was nearly seven twenty-five when the Williamses emerged, Mr. Williams holding his wife's upper arm like he was trying to get her to move a little faster. Vivian had a feeling he had wanted to leave a little sooner to allow her to spend some time with Bernard, but that Mrs. Williams postponed departure until the last minute.

"Your mother doesn't like me," she said to Bernard after ascertaining that he was feeling better and that hospital personnel anticipated transferring him to the medical floor.

"I hope she's not giving you too hard a time. I don't understand her. One minute she's saying how much she wants grandchildren and the next she says I've still got plenty of time to settle down."

Plenty of time? You're almost forty, for crying out loud. Vivian kept her thoughts to herself, not wanting him to feel she was trying to rush him into a commitment she was far from sure she actually wanted.

"I'm her only child, and I guess she's torn between my getting married versus still being her baby."

She stared at him, not liking the satisfied expression on his face.

"Attention, please. The time is now seven-thirty, and visiting hours are officially over . . ."

"I guess I'd better get out of here before I turn into a pumpkin," she said.

"I appreciate your coming, Vivian. I'm sorry we didn't have more time to spend together. But tomorrow I should be in a regular room . . . if you decide to come and see me."

Vivian decided to take the out he offered. "I've got a lot of things to catch up on, but I'll probably see you on Wednesday, if you're still here."

It seemed like everybody on the block was at home; Vivian didn't find a space until she was nearly at the next corner. She was glad she went to visit Bernard, but she felt strangely hollow, and in her heart she knew that whatever good feelings she had about a future with him in it had dissolved like Jell-O mix in hot water. His mother had been difficult, but something in the way he smiled while acknowledging her behavior told Vivian he rather enjoyed it, and that meant there was trouble ahead if she pursued the relationship.

Her body felt unwieldy and heavy as she slowly made her way down the street to her building. Lisa Mahoney had told her today that while Lisa was attending the big meeting in New Jersey the week after next, the one in which the future of many of the employees would be discussed, Vivian would have a chance to show she could run the department herself, just in time for her latest performance review.

In the lobby she paused to get her mail. She'd been in such a hurry to have a quick dinner and get changed that she hadn't bothered to pick it up. The latest issue of *Biography* magazine awaited her, the perfect remedy after such a long day. She was going to pour herself a glass of wine, fix some baloney and cheese on Ritz crackers, stretch out on the couch with her feet up, and enjoy her magazine.

* * *

"You come back and see us soon, now, Zack."

"You know I will. Good night, Mrs. Hughes, Mr. Hughes."

Zack checked his watch. It had been a pretty good day. He had done a coworker a favor and covered part of his shift this afternoon, and although he'd gotten out of there about an hour later than he planned, it still was only eight o'clock. If it were later in the week he would call a female friend—he knew a fair amount who lived in Southern Westchester—and issue an invitation for a drink at Smitty's and go on from there, but since this was the beginning of the work week he doubted he would meet with much success. He'd just go home . . . and try not to think about Vivian St. James.

"Hey, what's up?"

Vivian looked up from her work.

"Hi, Glenda."

"You all right? You seem kind of glum."

"Oh, I'm all right, I guess. I saw Bernard last night."

"Did you see his mother, too?"

"Yes. She left me something like five minutes to see him. They only allow a half-hour in intensive care, you know."

"Well, what did she do?"

"She was herself. That was enough. What bothers me is that Bernard seems to enjoy it. I have a feeling that whoever he marries will have to fight his mother—not literally, of course—for his loyalty for the rest of his mother's life . . . or until his wife runs for her own life, whichever comes first."

"I gather you've decided to pass on becoming the lucky bride."

"You got it. Here it is, March, and I have no prospects."

"Well, I don't, either, so you're not alone." Glenda glanced toward the door of the office and smiled in that sweet way she reserved for men. "Hi, Pete."

"Hi. Anybody here?"

"Sure. I think Harriet is getting coffee, but Vivian's in here."

Pete Arnold appeared, and Glenda flashed him another killer grin. "I was just leaving," she said before sashaying out.

Vivian leaned forward expectantly, her elbows resting on her desk. "Good morning, Pete. What can I do for you?"

"I've decided to roll over some additional funds into my 401(k). Would I be able to do that at any time, or will I have to wait until the next open enrollment?"

"Are you already in the 401(k)? I didn't think you were here that long."

"I just made it before the deadline to join in January. I talked to you about it, remember? I was a little late with my paperwork."

"Oh, yes, now I remember. I take it Glenda was able to get your deductions started for you."

"Yes, she did."

"Good. In answer to your question, you can roll over additional funds at any time."

"Good. The fund I'm invested in isn't doing all that great, and I think it's going to get worse. I'd like to get out now."

"You can bring the check to me, and I'll submit it for you."

"Hey, that's great. Thanks a lot." He turned to leave and promptly walked into the wall. "Oops. Sorry about that."

"Are you all right?" she asked with a smile.

"Uh . . . yeah. I thought the wall was farther over."

When he had gone, she used her palm to stifle her laughter.

Chapter 7:
Falling

"Wait a second, Zack. *You're* going to paint the apartment?"

"Why not? It'll save us a lot of money."

"I know, but *you?* Painting?"

"You make it sound like I'm going to paint the entire building. It's a one-bedroom apartment, Oz. Santos is just out of the hospital after an appendectomy. It'll be weeks before he can do anything physical."

"Well, hey, I think that's great. I'm just surprised Mr. Ellis's son got the place cleared out that quickly."

"The man didn't want to spend any more time here than he had to. He had the Salvation Army pick up what was salvageable, dumped the rest, had his father cremated, and went back home with a small cardboard box, which I have a feeling will be the old guy's permanent resting place. The whole thing took about three days. I think it's sad, but I suppose there's a reason why they weren't close."

"Don't worry, Zack. I know when you have kids

you'll be a great dad. So when are you going to paint?"

"This weekend, maybe Sunday. Teresita will clean it before that, and after I'm done she'll come back to do the floors, and it'll be ready for showing. I'll have Laurie put an ad in next week's paper."

"We're way ahead of schedule."

"Yeah, if we're lucky we can get somebody in by the middle of next month at the latest."

"Good work. And take it easy. You know you aren't used to that manual labor."

Friday afternoon Vivian had a meeting with Lisa Mahoney.

"Do you have any idea what will happen?" Vivian asked. The entire building was gossiping about who was likely to be laid off, and many of the employees were anxious about what the future held.

"Well, as I said before, all of us should be safe."

"Yes, I know, but what about the other departments? A lot of people are worried, Lisa. I have people stopping in here a dozen times a day asking if their jobs are going to be eliminated."

"I can't blame them. It's Glenda you're worried about especially, isn't it?"

Vivian shrugged. "Not really. I don't want to sound unfeeling, but Glenda herself isn't particularly concerned. She's already got a backup plan in place in case she needs one."

"Good for her. Just between you and me, Vivian, most of the eliminations will be at the upper level. If there's one thing the combined company won't need, it's two sets of corporate officers and other executives drawing six-figure salaries. The other problem involves consolidating the other departments. Unfortunately, there can only be one person in charge, and since there are two, that might present a problem. People won't be happy going from supervisor to assistant supervisor. But we're going to offer incentives for early retirement and see how many people want to take advantage of that, for starters. Now, remember, mum's the word."

"All right."

"You should be fine. I'll be checking in every day, and Connie can help you out, even though I did say it was okay if she took a few days off."

Vivian spent Saturday morning spring-cleaning her apartment, dusting the blinds, washing the windows with a mixture of ammonia and water, going through her closet and deciding which clothing and shoes she would not be wearing again and packing them up to donate to charity. By lunchtime the apartment sparkled and smelled like a spring breeze. She had some lunch, showered, and headed for the mall, planning to just browse while she got in some walking, but she purchased an attractive draped white blouse that was on sale. It would go with anything, and, as her mother always said, a girl could never have too many white blouses.

Sunday morning she got up early, drove to the spa she belonged to, and worked out. Since joining she was pleased with the progress her waistline was making; putting on slacks and skirts wasn't painful anymore. She wanted to maintain her figure. Soon it would be bikini weather . . . not that she was going to put on a bikini. She was a little old to be showing that much skin, although she would wear a two-piece with a more modest cut. She wanted to make sure she was firmed up.

Afterward, as she turned on her car's ignition, she had a sudden urge to see her parents. Within minutes, she was on Interstate 95 headed for Connecticut.

It took just under two and a half hours to reach New London. There was no car in the driveway, but Vivian wasn't concerned. Church was letting out just about now, and her parents should be home shortly. Besides, she had a key. Her parents insisted she hold on to it after she took her first apartment, and she'd kept it ever since.

She was in the kitchen making a sandwich from a leftover chicken when she heard them calling out her name. "Here I am!" She carefully laid the knife across the top of the open mayonnaise jar and went to greet her parents, embracing them warmly.

Her father was clearly thrilled to see her. She was his firstborn, and only daughter. "I was wondering when you were going to get up here and see the old folks," he teased.

"I know. It's much too long between visits. I promise to come more often." She carried her plate and drinking glass over to the square table in the corner.

"Don't forget your cake," Caroline said. She picked up the plate that held the large piece of chocolate-iced yellow cake and joined Vivian at the table. "We know it's a long drive for you," she added, "and that you're busy, but maybe you can take some time out from your social schedule and come for a weekend. You can always bring a friend."

Vivian smiled at her mother's none-too-subtle

hint. "Oh, I think most of my friends wouldn't be able to appreciate New London, but thanks, anyway."

"Well, then, when you come you can catch up with some of your old friends. I saw Grace DaSilva the other week at the supermarket. She's got two adorable little girls, three and six."

"I know. She put a picture of them in her Christmas card."

"Have you heard from Lauren Walters?"

"Yes. We talk every so often and try to get together at least every other month. We're going to meet in Stamford next week and shop for our safari."

"Oh, that's right. That trip. You know, it's an awful lot of money to spend to go somewhere where you won't meet anyone."

"The important thing is that we'll never forget it."

"I'm sure you won't."

"Nice girl, that Lauren," her father said. "I understand her mother's been ill."

"Oh, Eddie. That was months ago," her mother corrected. "She had pneumonia, but she's all recovered now. Haven't you seen her? She's always out in the yard working on her garden. How could you miss her?"

He shrugged. "Guess she hasn't been there when I've gone out."

The Walters family lived three houses down from the St. Jameses, and their daughter Lauren was one of Vivian's oldest friends.

"Tell you what," Eddie said. "I'm going to turn on the game in the other room. You girls can sit here and gossip. Caroline, will you make me a sandwich?"

"I'll bring it out to you," she replied, springing into action. She took Vivian's place at the counter. "I hope that potato salad is still good. I made it on Wednesday."

"It tastes fine to me. No one can make potato salad like you, Mom."

"Well, thank you."

Caroline quickly prepared Eddie's meal, which she served with the last of the potato salad. When she returned from delivering it, she filled a Dutch oven with water and put it atop the lit burner. "I'm making macaroni and cheese to go with my ham. I hope you're going to stay for dinner."

"I don't think I'll be here long enough. I've got a big week coming up at work, and I want to get home early."

"You mean you're only here for a few hours? It takes that long to get up here!"

"I know. It was a spur-of-the-moment thing, Mom. Aren't you glad I came?"

"Of course. Daddy and I feel a little abandoned, what with you in New York and Mark in Providence."

"You know you guys love having the house to yourselves."

Her mother joined her at the table. "I didn't say we missed having you *living* here with us; I said I missed you not living in the same city, or at least nearby. So, how's your friend Bernard feeling? Is he still in the hospital?"

"He was discharged Thursday. He's staying at his parents' while he recovers.

"Have you visited him there?"

"Not yet. I think he needs to rest for a few days. He said something about having me over for dinner, but of course that's his mother's call." She decided not to mention her decision to end the relationship; she didn't want her mother to start in on how much she wanted grandchildren while she was still young enough to enjoy them, which was her usual destination topic once she began to observe that both her children had left the New London area. She felt it wasn't fair that most of her mother's hopes were pinned on her. Mark didn't have to deal with all this interest in *his* love life, and he was only three years younger.

"Well, if you go, I want to hear all about it. Do you think it will become serious between the two of you?"

She took a deep breath. There was no end to her mother's curiosity. If someone were to tell Caroline St. James they were receiving obscene telephone calls, she would probably respond by asking what the caller had said. "No, Mom," she finally said, deciding honesty was the best policy. "I'm going to break it off as soon as I can."

"Break it off? But why, for heaven's sake?"

Because his mother doesn't want grandchildren as much as you do. "He's a nice guy, but he's an only child, and his parents—no, make that his *mother*—is too protective."

"You've met his parents?"

"Yes, at the hospital. I find his mother's attitude stifling. I also have a feeling that he rather enjoys it. I wouldn't be surprised if he never gets married, at least while she's alive." She knew that would silence any more protests, and she was right.

"I don't know why some women insist on turning their sons into mama's boys. He'd better watch out, or his mom won't let him leave her house to go back to his place."

"If it wasn't for his father keeping her under

control, he probably never would have gotten away to go to college."

"That's too bad, but at least you didn't waste much time on him. Is there anyone else on the horizon?"

The handsome face of Zachary Warner immediately came to Vivian's mind. She had been thinking about him a lot lately, ever since she decided it was over with Bernard, but it would probably be a long time before she saw him again. Last month's NBP activity had been a late-season ski trip to Vermont, which she and Glenda skipped. This month they were sponsoring a bowling night, but she was so busy with Bernard that she missed the deadline to register. Next month they would taking a train excursion to a casino in New England, but she wasn't much for gambling. She didn't remember what the June function was, but didn't see the point, since it was two months away. It was hard to get excited about anything with that long of a wait.

"Vivian? Can you hear me?"

"Yes, Mom. No, there's no one else." She pushed back in her chair. "I'm going to watch the game with Daddy. Why don't you come out?"

"I'll be there in a few minutes, after I get dinner in the oven."

At a little after three, Vivian announced she was going to drive home, which brought the expected protests from her parents, but it was still early. She refused to allow herself to be cajoled into staying "just a little bit longer," saying she had to leave immediately. Her mother insisted she bring home a plate to have for dinner and stacked it high with ham, macaroni and cheese, collard greens, and corn bread. "I know you had that sandwich and potato salad for lunch, but by the time you get home you'll be ready to eat again. I wrapped another piece of cake for you, too."

"There goes my workout."

On the long drive home, Vivian thought about how she should handle breaking off with Bernard. She had visited him in the hospital Wednesday night. By then, he was in a private room and was expecting to be discharged the next day. She was relieved to learn his parents had been in earlier. "I'm going to spend the first week out of here at their house," he told her. "Would you like to come to dinner next week, maybe get to know my mother a little better?"

She had been speechless. Get to know his mother? She preferred to forget she'd ever met the woman. Under the circumstances, she could only accept and hope Mrs. Williams would decide she didn't feel like doing any entertaining, and since Vivian was involved, the woman probably wouldn't.

Bernard reached for her hand and squeezed it. "I don't think I ever thanked you for getting me to the hospital promptly. I probably would have died if you hadn't been there to hear me fall."

She tried to make light of it. The last thing she wanted was for him to get sentimental because he felt she'd saved his life. Eternal gratitude would mean she'd never be able to get rid of him. "You would have done the same for me, I'm sure." Then she pointedly looked at her watch. "I guess I'd better be heading out."

"Already? You just got here. This isn't the ICU anymore, Viv. You can stay until nine o'clock."

Good Lord. It was only seven-thirty. No way
would she last another hour and a half. "It's not
the ICU, but it's still the hospital. You're not able
to entertain; you're here because you're sick and
you need to rest. Besides, Terry will probably be
coming by."

"He was here already. He stopped in right after
work."

Her mind raced to find another excuse. "I'm
sorry I can't stay longer, Bernard, but I've got an
early meeting tomorrow, and I want to make sure
I'm prepared. With this merger coming up, I'm
hoping to get a promotion. You know how it is."

Once more he squeezed her hand. "All right.
Give me a kiss good-bye, and then I'll let you go."

She tensed, not wanting to do anything to lead
him on and make him believe she was interested,
but knowing it wasn't fair to tell him she wasn't,
not while he was recovering. If there was anything
she hated more than seeing a working television
stacked on top of a nonworking television, it was
trying to give someone the brush. She bent and
kissed his cheek, then quickly moved out of his
reach. "Nothing hot and heavy for you. You're in
the hospital, remember?" She had practically run
to her car.

When she got home, she called her parents and
let them know she had arrived safely. Once she
hung up, she checked her caller ID. There had
been three calls from a telephone registered to
Levi Williams; at noon, two-thirty, and five, respectively. No messages were left, and she wondered if
it had occurred to Bernard that she could track
his calls.

Just as her mother had predicted, she was hungry again. She removed the foil wrapping from the sturdy paper plate, covered it with a paper towel and put it in the microwave. She was certain Bernard would be calling again, but she wasn't going to worry about it.

Zack was pleased with his progress. He had just one more wall to go. It was quite a workout, but he was in shape, thanks to his skiing and those sessions at the Y. Still, his shoulder muscles weren't used to the repetitive up-and-down motions involved. He would have to take a hot shower afterward and see if he could talk somebody into giving him a massage.

He chuckled. Normally a massage was a prelude to sex, but the only thing he was interested in now was getting his shoulders rubbed. He was too tired for anything else. Austin was right when he cautioned him against overdoing it. Still, it would be silly to take two days to paint an apartment this small. He had stopped to rest plenty of times, watching the NBA game on the portable set he brought with him. Fortunately, the reception was coming in clear. He didn't think those old-fashioned rabbit ears people used to put on top of their televisions were made anymore; and the apartment had no cable hookup.

He moved to the top of the four-foot ladder in order to paint the upper part of the eight-foot wall. Once he got the top done, he would have a full fourth of the wall completed. He'd be out of here in no time.

* * *

Vivian thoroughly enjoyed her meal. Her mother was a fabulous cook, but that wasn't the only reason for her satisfaction. It had been a surprisingly nice weekend. This was the first weekend she could remember where she wasn't either going out on a date or to an event with the hopes of meeting a future date. She knew that next weekend Glenda would want to make up for it, but it had been relaxing, that was for sure.

The phone rang as she was washing out her glass and utensils. A glimpse at the caller ID revealed it was Bernard calling from his parents' home. "Hi, Vivian."

"Hi, there. How are you feeling?"

"A lot better. I figured I would the minute I was out of that hospital, but I miss you. I thought I'd see you this weekend."

"I figured you'd need your rest, so I went to Connecticut to visit my parents."

"Are they well?"

"Yes, thanks. They miss me, though. It's hard for them. My brother doesn't live near them, either. I'm going to have to spend more time with them. I might go back next weekend." She hoped he got the hint.

"I know how you feel. My mother felt just awful when I went to Pennsylvania to school; and she was disappointed when I moved out after I worked for a couple of years. She already told me a dozen times how glad she is to have me back. I have to keep reminding her I'll only be here until the weekend. Oh, by the way, can you come to dinner on Tuesday?"

She could not think of a way out. "Oh, yes; I suppose so." She hadn't expected an invitation to materialize at all, and she certainly did not expect it to be for a weeknight. Now that she thought about it, it did make sense. The Williamses were retired, so a Tuesday was just as good as any other night for them. It would actually work out well for her. She could make an early escape, citing an early morning at the office. "What time?"

"Around seven, I guess. I'll let you know."

"All right." A crashing noise from above made her jump.

Apparently Bernard heard it, too. "What *was* that?"

"I don't know. It came from upstairs. That apartment is supposed to be vacant, but I think the super's wife might be working up there. Her husband just had surgery and can't do much yet. I'd better see if she needs help. Can I call you back?"

"Sure."

It all happened so fast. One minute he was attempting to step down, and the next he was on the floor. Doggone it, he must have missed the damn step. Zack was stunned. He was smarting, too. The floor was *hard*.

He managed to move into a sitting position, rubbing his right elbow, which he'd banged. Then again, just because he could sit didn't mean he could stand. He tried to get up. When he put his weight on his right foot he grimaced and fell back. "Hello?" called a female voice, simultaneously opening the door, which, fortunately, he'd left unlocked.

The two syllables were not enough for him to recognize the voice, but as she came closer with hesitant steps, he soon recognized her. For a split second he wondered if his injuries had been more severe than he thought. Was he unconscious and dreaming, or was it even worse than that?

"Zack? Is that you? What are *you* doing here?" No longer moving tentatively, she rushed to where he sat. "You're hurt! What happened?"

"I fell off the ladder. I hurt my ankle. My elbow, too." He looked at her with equal confusion. "What are *you* doing here?"

"I live downstairs. I heard a crash, and since I know no one lived here I came up to see what was going on. I thought maybe Teresita was working up here and had an accident."

"*You* live downstairs?" He was astounded by this information. How could it be possible that all the time he'd thought of Vivian, wanted to see her again, she was living right here in the building he owned, directly below where he'd been working all day?

"All right, now you know why I'm here, but why are *you* here?"

"I own this building. Well, I own it with my buddy Austin . . . and the bank. You probably know Austin's parents, Mr. and Mrs. Hughes. Santos, the super, won't be able to lift anything heavier than a phone book for about six weeks, and since a gallon of paint weighs more than that I figured I'd take care of it. In hindsight, it probably wasn't such a great idea."

Vivian nodded, not knowing what to say. Of course she had known he was one of the building's owners, but it had come as a big surprise to see him painting. Now it made sense. She looked at his elbow, which he continued to support with his other hand. "Do you think it's broken?"

"I hope it's just a bad sprain."

"Maybe you can lean on me and I can help you get out of here. I'd be happy to bring you to the hospital." She frowned. It seemed like she was always bringing her male acquaintances to the emergency room. Now she would be bringing Zack. She didn't like the pattern and wished it would stop.

"I don't know if that's going to work, not with two flights of stairs to get down. Why don't you knock on the Hughes's door? They're in 1-A. Mr. Hughes can probably help me get down the stairs. I'd rather lean on him; he's bigger than you are."

She took a deep breath. It was time to come clean. "I know the Hugheses. I know Austin, too, and his fiancée."

"Desirée?"

"Yes. I took her to get her hair done when she was staying with them. She caught malaria in Africa." She sensed the dawn of realization going on in his mind and decided not to be around when it bloomed. "I'll be right back. Don't go away, now."

Zack was too dazed to respond. First he learned that Vivian was his tenant, and then he was told she was a friend of Desirée's, which, given that Desirée only knew a handful of people in New York, meant Vivian was probably the one she had wanted to introduce him to. He could have met her something like a year and a half ago, before all this craziness started. Instead of being his angel of accidents—his this time, he noted wryly—she could have been the angel of his heart. *Damn.*

* * *

Vivian slowly walked down the two flights of stairs. Her advantage was over. The playing field had evened out. Of course, Zack might not even remember the efforts Desirée had used to fix him up. It had been, after all, over a year ago, but that look in his eyes said otherwise. It was the look of an inventor who just thought of the final action that would make his creation work properly. He knew, all right. He was probably thinking about how small a world it was. She wished he would think something else, like he wished he'd been able to meet her then. A simple introduction would have changed so much between them. Zack was probably telling himself the reason he'd fallen was because of bad vibes she was sending from the floor below.

When she got to the first floor landing she frowned. She was about to ask the wrong person for help. She turned around and climbed the two flights again.

"Yoo hoo, Zack! The rescue squad is here," Vivian said cheerfully.

Zack expected to see Mr. Hughes with her, but instead she was accompanied by a beefy fortyish male he didn't recognize. Damn, did she have a boyfriend right here in the building? He wouldn't want to be socially involved with any woman who lived on the same *block*, but of course that was him.

"This is Michael Harris, Zack. He lives next door. I thought it might be more appropriate for him to help you; it might be too strenuous for Mr. Hughes." She turned to her neighbor. "Michael, this is Zack Warner, your landlord." Michael bent to shake Zack's outstretched hand. "Don't bother to get up, man," he joked.

"Yeah, that seems to be my problem now. My ankle's messed up. The entire right side of my body is hurting, actually. That parquet is as hard as . . . I don't know what."

Michael went into action, squatting at Zack's right side and swinging his arm around his neck. "Okay, I've got you. Try to get up on three, okay? One . . . two . . . three."

Zack noticed that Vivian appeared to be holding her breath as Zack stood on his left foot. She went to his left side and guided his arm around her shoulder. Using the two of them as human crutches, he managed to hobble to the stairs. "I feel like I'm at the top of Mount Everest looking down over Tibet. Maybe we should tie a rope around me and hoist me down the side of the building like a piano."

"Aw, you can do it," Michael urged.

Zack turned to Vivian. "Why don't you lock up the apartment for me? The key is on the kitchen counter. Give it to Teresita. I can manage with Michael." He was embarrassed by his weakness.

"All right. I'll stop and get my keys and purse and meet you downstairs."

She had put the small television on the floor and was locking the apartment when the door to 3-C opened and Miles Harris—or maybe it was Mason—poked his head out. "Miss Vivian, where's my daddy?"

"He's helping the landlord. He'll be up in a minute."

She clumsily walked down one flight with the

television, which she deposited on her table, then
retrieved her purse. By the time she emerged, Zack
and Michael were almost to the first floor landing.
She could tell that Zack was becoming more adept
at moving with only one leg. She waited quietly
while Zack maneuvered the remainder of the stairs
with help from Michael, then called out, "Here I
come."

"How far away are you parked?" Michael asked.

"I'm right out front. I guess we'll go to Mount
Vernon Hospital, huh, Zack?"

"If that's the closest. All they have to do is an X
ray. They shouldn't botch *that* up."

Skepticism dripped from his comment like liquid
from cooked collard greens, and Vivian said with
a smile, "I suppose the only hospital you really
trust is Hudson."

"I feel more comfortable there, yeah."

She shook her head. "I feel sorry for whoever
treats you."

Chapter 8:
Role Reversal

"Thanks a lot, Michael," Vivian said, echoing Zack's sentiments.

"No sweat. Free rent next month, right, Zack?" he joked before growing serious. "You take care of yourself."

"I will." Zack closed his eyes. His ankle was throbbing now, and it felt like it weighed fifty pounds.

"We'll be at the hospital in a few minutes. It's Sunday, so I don't think they'll be too busy. We probably won't have to wait long."

"You got a date?"

"No, silly. I've just got to go to work tomorrow."

"Is Michael a friend of yours?"

She didn't know whether to smile or pout. On one hand, it was cute that he seemed to be a tad jealous of an imagined flirtation between her and her neighbor. On the other hand, he knew she had gone out with Gary, Gordon, and Bernard; and she certainly didn't want him to think she had been around the block more times than the mailman.

"Michael lives next door to Mr. Ellis, or *lived* next door, with his wife and sons."

"Oh. Well, it was good you thought to get him. You're right, it might have been a bit much for Mr. Hughes to go down two flights with me leaning on him."

As Vivian predicted, the emergency room at Mount Vernon Hospital wasn't very crowded, and Zack was seen right away. X-rays determined that there was no fracture in either his ankle or his elbow, but both were sprained badly. He also had bruises on his chest which would give him some discomfort in that area.

"I don't want you to bear any weight on that foot for four days," Dr. Christine Kalafus instructed after she had bandaged Zack's right ankle and applied a sling to his right arm. "On Friday morning you can try it, and I want you to follow up that day. By then you should be all right. We're getting crutches for you, but is there someone at home who can perhaps help you minimize your movements, help with your ADLs?"

Vivian wrinkled her forehead. "What's ADLs?"

"Activities of daily living." Zack and Dr. Kalafus spoke simultaneously, then laughed.

Zack proceeded to answer the doctor's question. "I live alone, Doctor, and there's a flight of outside stairs to the entrance of my house, plus another flight inside to my bedroom. And my couch is terribly uncomfortable to sleep on."

"That's far from ideal. Any family members you can stay with?"

"My parents are retired, but they're at my brother's in Virginia. They just left yesterday. My cousin used to be my tenant, but she took a job transfer to Detroit. My only contact with the guy who lives there now is collecting his rent check."

Dr. Kalafus glanced at Vivian before returning her attentions to Zack. "Any friends?"

Zack shrugged. "Well, I don't like to brag, but—"

"It's a slow night here, Dr. Warner, but not *that* slow. Do you think you can tell me the situation in ten words or less?"

"Actually, most of my friends are of the female persuasion. They think highly of me, but I don't know how they'd feel about me dropping in on them for such a long period. Might give some of them ideas. I might not be able to get out without making a lifetime commitment. You know how it is."

Anyone else saying those words would come off sounding like they had an ego the size of the Pentagon, but Zack looked so boyish and bashful as he spoke, like a wide-eyed, innocent child, that it only added to his charisma.

Dr. Kalafus smiled. "All right. What about you, Ms. St. James?"

Vivian lowered her chin to her chest in her best Say Whaaaat? look. "Who, me?"

"You look like a sensible girl. Do you think you can take care of your friend for a few days without wanting to make it permanent?"

"Wishing for permanency isn't a problem." *If anything, it'll probably make me want to kill him and bury his body in the basement.* "But I work all day. I can't take off to play Florence Nightingale." She thought of Mrs. Hughes, but then quickly remembered that the older woman spent her days in nearby Eastchester, caring for her young grandchild while her daughter was at work.

"Taking off from work wouldn't be necessary, as long as you have food for him. The fridge or the microwave is as far as he should go for his lunch."

"Well, I do have a sofabed that's pretty comfortable, but . . . I don't know. How long will this be for?"

"Vivling, I'm wounded by your reluctance." Zack's hand was on his heart.

She rolled her eyes. He was giving a performance worthy of Bernard Williams's mother. She hoped Dr. Kalafus would help her out, but the woman was clearly enjoying Act One, Scene One. Shame on her. Hadn't her mother taught her it wasn't nice to take delight in the discomfort of others? "All right," she said finally. "I guess it's the least I can do, after you've taken such good care of my fr—of some people I know."

"Well, it looks like that's all settled. I love happy endings," the doctor said, sounding so cheerful that Vivian wanted to smack her . . . or pelt her with popcorn. This was her life for the next week, not some MGM movie.

"Thanks, Vivling. I promise, you'll miss me when I'm gone."

"I'm already looking forward to it."

Dr. Kalafus chuckled. "I'm sure it won't be too difficult for you, Ms. St. James. All the doctor has to do is keep his foot elevated. Just remember, Dr. Warner, you shouldn't try to bathe or do anything that might require assistance while you're alone."

Vivian's head jerked. "Are you saying I'll have to bathe him? That's out of the question, Doctor." She cast a murderous look Zack's way. "One word out of you and I'll twist your bad arm."

"Ouch."

"No, you won't have to bathe him, Ms. St. James.

I just think it's best for someone to be at home when he does in case he should lose his balance or need help for any other reason. Something simple, like getting in the tub and finding out the soap is by the sink, can be a terrible inconvenience when only one leg is working."

"I'll make sure I leave a bar in both places." *And so help me, if he gives me a hard time I'll leave one on the floor as well.*

"Excuse me. I want to see what's holding up those crutches." Dr. Kalafus left the room.

Zack had been sitting up, but now he laid back and rested his left hand on his abdomen. "Well, roomie, I just have one question. What's for breakfast?"

"If you're about to tell me how you like your eggs, don't bother. I usually eat cereal."

"I hope you like Cocoa Puffs."

"I don't touch that sugary stuff. That's for kids."

"I said Cocoa Puffs, not Frosted Flakes."

"I eat Total."

He made a face.

"It's part of a balanced diet, but I know, you'd rather eat Cocoa Puffs. How did you manage to graduate from med school without passing nutrition?" He was unbelievable. *This* was unbelievable. She was his tenant, and now he was going to be her houseguest. What a crazy setup.

"Aw, don't give me that righteous jazz. I'll bet you're the first one in line when the doughnut cart comes around."

She glared at him. The truth was she had realized the probable connection between her sweet tooth and her weight gain and had given up on pastries, but she wasn't about to share that fact with him.

"Here we are," Dr. Kalafus said, returning with a set of long crutches. "Someone will be in shortly to train you on how to use these, but let's just check the fit." She continued speaking as Zack stood and positioned the crutches under his armpits. "I'd like you to follow up on Friday, either here or with your regular doctor." She handed Zack a white sheet. "These are your written instructions, which we've already talked about. Please look them over so I can clarify anything if necessary. And remember that you can always call in case you're unsure of anything."

After satisfying the staff that he could maneuver with his crutches, including making repeated trips up and down the practice stairs, Zack was discharged from the emergency room. They insisted he utilize a wheelchair for his exit, and he held his crutches across his lap while Vivian pushed the chair.

"I like this. It reminds me of that movie, *Rear Window* with Jimmy Stewart. He had the beautiful Grace Kelly catering to his every whim, and I've got the beautiful Vivian St. James . . . not catering to my every whim, of course, but nearby."

"My personal favorite is *Kiss of Death,* when Richard Widmark ties that lady in her wheelchair and pushes her down a flight of stairs." She thought she saw his shoulders shudder at the creepy picture she painted, but he couldn't see her smiling. How nice to know he thought she was beautiful.

"My sofa is comfortable," Vivian said. "My first apartment was a studio, so I bought a Castro Convertible. It was expensive, but it was worth it. I slept on it every night for four years. An ordinary sofa bed mattress never would have held up."

"Why don't I just sit down for now? It's too early to go to bed for the night." He sank down and sighed loudly. "If the mattress feels as good as these cushions, I may never wake up. I might just sit here all night."

She watched as he moved sideways and rested his bandaged foot on the cushion. "You don't have anything to sleep in, do you?"

"I don't even have anything that's clean. I'm afraid I don't have any other alternative but to ask if you would mind terribly going down to my house and picking up a few things for me? Maybe Glenda can go with you. I wouldn't want you to go alone; it's dark out."

Vivian was reluctant. Her restful evening at home was becoming an endless round of errands; she'd be lucky if she got to bed before midnight. Still, Zack was in a spot. He had no clothes except for his paint-spattered sweatshirt and jeans. Besides, he looked awful, his handsome face pale and drawn. The stress of his accident, combined with the pain medication he received at the hospital, and the energy required to climb a tall flight of stairs on crutches, had worn him out.

"I'll go call Glenda," she said as brightly as she could.

Before she could leave, he put a hand on her forearm and stroked it, creating a warm friction she could feel through her long-sleeved cotton blouse. "You know I hate to ask you this, Vivling."

Oh, my. Between his large hand covering her arm and the low tone he used, which managed to be both seductive and sincere, if he'd asked her to go to Jupiter to retrieve his personal belongings she'd do it. "It's all right. You've got to have clothes, and once you have them you'll be all set."

"Are you kidding. Get a chance to see his place without him being there? Hell, yeah, I'll go. I hope you're leaving right now."

"I can always count on you to want to help me out, Glenda. Your motives are so . . . unselfish."

"Never mind me and my selfless motives and get over here. I want to hear all about what happened . . . and I can't wait to see where he lives."

"I'm leaving now."

"I'll be in the lobby."

True to her word, Glenda was standing in the lobby of her apartment building when Vivian reached Riverdale. "Okay, where does he live?" she asked.

"Don't you think you should get in the car before you start asking questions?"

Glenda pulled the door closed and fastened her seat belt. "Okay, I'm in. Give me the scoop!" She rubbed her palms together for emphasis.

"He lives on 117th Street in Harlem. He has a brownstone."

"A brownstone! I should have known. The man's a doctor."

"He's a doctor, but I don't think he makes the money you're thinking about. Remember, he specializes in emergency medicine. It's the other specialties, like the plastics or cardiovascular guys, who are making the real ducats."

"All right, but I'm sure he's not going hungry."

"Of course not."

During the rest of the drive they exchanged details of their respective weekends, with Vivian telling her friend about coming home from Connecticut and finding Zack on the floor near an overturned ladder in the apartment upstairs.

"Oh, that is *soooo* romantic."

"What, finding him moaning in pain or bringing him to the ER?" Neither situation was anything she had dreamed about.

"The whole thing. I'll bet he's feeling real grateful, and to think he'll be staying with you the whole week. This is a great opportunity to get to know him."

"Speaking of getting to know someone, how is Terry?"

"Oh, he's fine. Trying to get me in the sack. I like him, Viv, but I think as more of a friend. If I was going to fall in love it probably would have happened by now. It doesn't take long, you know."

"Well, maybe you should stop seeing him. You wouldn't want to lead him on."

"I'm not leading him on. He's not saying anything about being in love with me, either. He just wants my body."

Vivian was too busy counting the passing streets to reply. Finally she turned onto 117th.

"Nice block," Glenda said. "All the houses have been refurbished . . . or at least most of them," she amended when they passed one with its windows and doorway boarded up.

Vivian had to agree that she was impressed herself. There were few structures more handsome than the old brownstones and townhouses of Manhattan. It was obvious that the residents of this block loved their homes. A few of the buildings were lined with attractive black wrought-iron fences, and some enterprising homeowners had planted flowers on the sides of their homes, giving an odd look of suburbia to the middle of one of the most urban sections of New York.

"This is it," Vivian said, pointing. "Let's park."

"Four floors. Does he live here alone?"

"Yes, that's what he told the doctor."

They got out of the car, and Glenda walked a little beyond the steps leading to the main entrance. "There's the apartment," she said in a stage whisper, pointing to a door a few steps below street level. There's a light over the door. Someone lives there. It doesn't look like they're home, but there's a light on upstairs. You're sure no one else lives with him?"

"He said he leaves a timer on, because his shifts rotate. If he's at work all night he doesn't want anyone who might be watching his house to figure out he's not there. He has an alarm system, too. I'll have to disable it."

"What?"

"Relax. All I have to do is push a button. But the door has to be closed, so as soon as I get it unlocked, get in quickly so we can close it behind us. I've only got thirty seconds to turn off the alarm."

The tall, oak door was heavy, and a loud beeping noise began as soon as she opened it a fraction of an inch. They rushed inside and closed the door, and then Vivian pressed the "off" button on Zack's keychain. The beeping continued, and she tried it again.

Glenda looked on anxiously, holding clenched fists at waist level and shaking them up and down. "Hurry up, Viv. If that thing goes off we're likely to be arrested."

She depressed the button and counted to five before letting go. The beeping sounded twice more in quick succession and then stopped. She and Glenda simultaneously let out the breath they had been holding. "That was close. Good thing I asked Zack to answer my phone."

"You did? What if Bernard calls?"

Vivian smiled. "I'm sure he will. He'll get the wrong idea about the man who's answering my phone, but this is one case where the wrong idea can be a good thing."

"Well, there's nothing on the third floor but a bathroom in the corner of a huge room," Glenda announced. "My cousins in North Carolina have what they call bonus rooms over the garage, where they put pool tables, computers, big screen TVs, but imagine having one right here in New York."

"You ought to be ashamed of yourself, traipsing all around Zack's house."

"I'm nosy, all right? I'm going to check the rest of this floor out."

Vivian was pleased with what she saw. Zack was a neat man. Other than a few dishes in the kitchen sink and some linty patches on the area rugs that could use a vacuuming, the narrow house was orderly. His taste in furniture wasn't bad, either. She especially liked his walnut bedroom suite consisting of a highboy, night tables, and a king-size four-poster bed. As she transferred clean underwear from the top drawer of the highboy into a nylon duffel bag, she couldn't help wondering how many occupants the four-poster had known.

"So, is it boxers or briefs?"

Vivian looked up to see Glenda standing in the doorway. "Briefs."

"That figures. He doesn't look like the boxer type."

Vivian knelt to get a few pairs of shorts from the bottom drawer. "What else did you see?"

"Two more bedrooms, both empty except for window blinds."

"Is there another bathroom?"

"No. The bath that connects from this room also has a door to the hall, so I guess there's just one bath per floor, if you count the half bath downstairs. I remember I was watching this old show where a couple had relocated to New York because the woman accepted a job offer. In one scene the husband was complaining about how expensive it was to live here and mentioned their rent alone was three thousand dollars. Then in the next scene they're coming back from bike riding, and the wife asks the husband if he wants to shower first. I said to myself, 'Their rent is three thousand a month and they only have one bathroom?' "

"Maybe they had a full bath and a powder room. That would explain why there was only one shower."

"Hmph. All I can say is if I was handing over that much for rent every month, I'd want *five* baths."

Vivian packed several shirts, T-shirts, and pairs of socks for Zack, as well as a pair of slide-in sandals from his closet, which was on the sparse side but was fairly orderly, except for the sweaters falling over each other on the shelf. No one could call Zack Warner a clothes horse. She fingered the textured material of the red blazer she recognized from the Valentine's dance, closed her eyes and allowed herself to remember how nice it had been

3 QUICK STEPS
TO RECEIVE YOUR "THANK YOU" GIFT
FROM THE EDITOR

Send this card back and you'll receive 4 FREE Arabesque novels! The introductory shipment of 4 Arabesque novels – a $23.96 value – is yours absolutely FREE!

There's no catch. You're under no obligation to buy anything. You'll receive your introductory shipment of 4 Arabesque novels absolutely FREE (plus $1.50 to offset the costs of shipping & handling). And you don't have to make any minimum number of purchases—not even one!

We hope that after receiving your books you'll want to remain an Arabesque subscriber. But the choice is yours to continue or cancel, anytime at all! So why not take us up on our invitation to receive 4 Arabesque Romance Novels, with no risk of any kind. You'll be glad you did!

Call us
TOLL-FREE
at 1-888-345-BOOK

THE EDITOR'S "THANK YOU" GIFT INCLUDES:

- 4 books absolutely FREE (plus $1.50 for shipping and handling)
- A FREE newsletter, *Arabesque Romance News*, filled with author interviews, book previews, special offers, and more!
- No risks or obligations. You're free to cancel whenever you wish... with no questions asked.

BOOK CERTIFICATE

Yes! Please send me 4 FREE Arabesque novels (plus $1.50 for shipping & handling). I understand I am under no obligation to purchase any books, as explained on the back of this card.

Name _____

Address _____ Apt. _____

City _____ State _____ Zip _____

Telephone ( ) _____

Signature _____

Offer limited to one per household and not valid to current subscribers. All orders subject to approval. Terms, offer, & price subject to change. Offer valid only in the U.S.

AN121A

Thank you!

Accepting the four introductory books for FREE (plus $1.50 to offset the cost of shipping & handling) places you under no obligation to buy anything. You may kee the books and return the shipping statement marked "cancelled". If you do not cancel, about a month later we will send 4 additional Arabesque novels, and you will be billed the preferred subscriber's price of just $4.00 per title. That's $16.00 for all 4 books for a savings of 33% off the cover price (Plus $1.50 for shipping and handling). You may cancel at any time, but if you choose to continue, every month we'll send you 4 more books, which you may either purchase at the preferred discount price. . . or return to us and cancel your subscription.

ARABESQUE ROMANCE BOOK CLUB
P.O. Box 5214
Clifton NJ 07015-5214

PLACE
STAMP
HERE

to be held in his arms while they danced that night. Maybe Glenda was right; this would be a good opportunity to get to know him better. As much as he got on her nerves, she already knew he wasn't completely exasperating from the compassion he had shown for that patient of his—the little girl with the facial injuries. "All right. I just need to get some of his things from the bathroom and then we're outta here."

"All I can say is that I could be *real* comfy cozy livin' here," Glenda said as they descended the elegant staircase with its polished banister. Vivian had packed Zack's toiletries in a plastic supermarket bag to separate them from his clothing.

"It's nice, but there's a lot of unused potential."

"I know. I haven't seen a man yet who's good at decorating. That's why they need us. The right woman would have those empty rooms furnished in no time."

Zack laughed into the receiver. "Yeah, well at least I'll be back on my feet by the time I go on my trip. That might not have been the case if I had broken my ankle. I've been planning this trip for over a year."

"I know," Desirée replied from the other end of the line. "Ozzie would be going along with you if he didn't have other plans."

"I hope you're not upset about that."

"Of course not. Maybe the two of us will go next year. It's something we'll have to do before we start a family. In the meantime, I don't think Ozzie will mind going to Taos for our honeymoon." She chuckled. "I've got to make a couple of other calls

to people who live out of town. I'll be talking to
Sydney. Anything I can tell her for you?"

Sydney Chambers was Zack's cousin, with whom
he'd grown up. She lived in Michigan now but had
been renting the first-floor apartment of his brownstone during the time Desirée was in town. "Tell
her 'hi' and give her Vivian's address, in case she
wants to send me a fruit basket for being on the
disabled list."

"I'm just tickled that you two have managed to
meet. Wait till I tell Ozzie about all the accidents
that keep bringing you together. I think it's price-
less. Now, you be sure to let Vivian know I called
about the wedding date."

"I'll do that. She should be back any minute.
Take care, Desirée, and give Oz my best."

He hung up, and just a few minutes later he
heard Vivian's key in the lock.

"Hi. You all right?"

"Yeah, just a little groggy. Did you find everything okay?"

"No trouble. That alarm scared me a little,
though. I had to try three or four times to turn it
off. Glenda and I thought it was going to go off
and the cops were going to come and haul us away
in handcuffs. Here it is." She placed the duffel bag
on the floor within Zack's reach. "You have a beautiful home, by the way."

"Thanks. I bought it at auction from the city."
He gestured at the narrow closed armoire on the
opposite wall. "Is that a computer in there?"

"Yes."

"Is it okay if I use it?"

"Yes. Were there any calls?"

"Yes. Guess who I just finished talking to."

She decided right away it wasn't Bernard; that

would certainly be no reason for Zack to get excited. "Who?"

"Desirée. She called to tell you they have a firm date for the wedding." Zack named a date in mid-July.

"Wow, that soon? I was afraid she might run into difficulty."

"She did, but she got it all settled. The ceremony will be at the chapel of her alma mater, and the reception is going to be at Phil Wallace's house in Golden. Apparently all the nice places were booked up." Phil Wallace was Austin's business partner in the consulting service that bore their surnames.

"Wonderful. Does she want me to call her back?"

"She just asked me to tell you the date. I think she's calling everyone who'll be coming from out of town so they can reserve the time and make travel arrangements."

"I guess she'll be busy on the phone, then. But I'll bet she got the shock of her life when you answered my phone."

"She actually thought she dialed the wrong number. And she reminded me that she wanted me to meet a friend of hers when she was here. I'd forgotten about that. She cracked up when I told her we keep running into each other because someone is sick or has had an accident."

"Well, now that you say that, I do remember Desirée wanting to introduce me to a friend of Austin's. It was so long ago I had forgotten." The whole thing about pretending she didn't know who Zack was all this time made her feel uncomfortable, and she didn't want to linger on it. "I didn't get to spend as much time as I would have liked with Desirée before she went back to Colorado, but I like her very much, and I'm happy she invited me to her wedding."

"Maybe you and I can fly out together."

"I think I'd like that. Uh, were there any other calls?"

"No."

That figures. Of all times for Bernard to be considerate. "Is there anything else I can get for you?"

"No, I'm fine. I was going to tie up your bathroom for a few minutes, if that's all right. I'm in desperate need of a shower." Clean clothes already in hand, he reached for his crutches.

"Go right ahead. I'm going to look at the paper and then get ready for work tomorrow, so I'll take my shower in the morning. I've got some microwaveable hot wings in the freezer. Why don't I make you some? I'm sure you're ready to eat something."

"As long as I know they're in the freezer, I'll go ahead and make them myself when I'm cleaned up. You've done a lot for me today, Vivian. Don't think I'm not aware of it, or that I don't appreciate it." He stood facing her now, and with his left hand he touched her cheek. "Get some rest. I'll be all right." Then he removed his hand and in an instant she felt his lips on her cheek. "Thank you," he whispered.

She turned and watched him make his way toward the hall. Was it her imagination or had his voice just broken, like he was overcome with emotion?

It wasn't until she heard the bathroom door close that she realized she was standing with her fingertips caressing her still-warm cheek.

Chapter 9:
Bad

Vivian sprang into action when the alarm buzzed the next morning. She threw on a bathrobe and checked on Zack before beginning her daily routine in the bathroom. He was fast asleep on the opened sofa bed, his bandaged foot elevated on the two sofa pillows.

She waited until she was fully dressed to wake him. His chest was rising and falling in even movements, but he didn't snore. She was glad. That would ruin the picture, like talking on the phone with a male job applicant with a sexy voice and having him show up weighing 300 pounds. "Zack."

"Uhhhh."

"Zack," she repeated, this time a little louder.

He muttered something that sounded like, "Go away," and rolled over.

Vivian leaned over and shook his shoulders. "Zack, I'm getting ready to leave. I just need to talk to you for a minute, then you can go back to sleep."

He opened his eyes and looked at her through narrowed eyes, his forehead wrinkled in annoyance. Vivian found his obvious displeasure startling, but then his expression suddenly softened and he reached out, taking her hand in his. "Come to bed," he said just before his eyes fluttered shut.

Come to bed? Was the man car-razy? She had to bring him back to earth, and quickly. "Zack, if you don't wake up this minute I'm going to sit on your ankle."

That did it. He opened his eyes, and this time she could tell he saw her clearly. Once again his forehead wrinkled, but this time he appeared confused. "Vivling. Why are you threatening to hurt me?"

He looked so earnest, so innocent, that she regretted her harshness, but couldn't he remember what he had said just a moment ago? "I'm sorry, Zack, but I've got to leave for work. I'm leaving you my number at the office. I'll put it by the phone and the remote control for the TV. Now, last night I stopped at the store and picked up some of that cereal you like. There's some cold cuts in the fridge, and the bread is on the counter. I put a couple of jars of soup on the counter, so you won't need to open a can. And help yourself to anything in the freezer. I always keep microwaveable foods in there."

"I really appreciate this, Vivian. You know I'll reimburse you for all this, your gas, the extra food, and for your time."

"Don't worry about it, Zack."

His eyes roamed down her body and then up again. "You look good."

That was just what she needed to hear, and she didn't bother to hide her delight. "Thank you. I've got to go now. Go back to sleep now. Call if you need anything."

"How about a kiss?"

Vivian felt so good about his compliment that she leaned down and pressed her lips against his stubbly cheek just for an instant. When she stood up she saw the outline of her lips, a deep berry color courtesy of her lipstick, on his skin. "Good-bye."

"I'll have some sweet dreams, that's for sure."

She didn't look back, but she was smiling.

At her office, Vivian checked her schedule. There was one new-hire starting today, a systems analyst, and Harriet told her he was waiting in the lobby. She also said Connie had called to say she was taking a day off. "Personally, I think she's job hunting."

"I wouldn't be surprised. She's been unhappy ever since that episode with the memo being photocopied. I can't say I'd want to work with people who would do that, either. But it'll be all right. Lisa gave me a key to her office, so in case I have to get in there it won't be a problem. Would you bring"—she glanced at her calendar—"Dennis in, please?"

"Sure. Be right back."

Dennis Chin was twenty-four years old and two years out of college, a studious-looking young man with a slight build and glasses. This would be his second job. She knew his type well—they changed jobs every two or three years, always for a better position and a larger paycheck. She predicted he would be the head of an MIS department by the time he was thirty. His soft-spoken manner and somewhat geeky appearance reminded her a little of Bill Gates of Microsoft.

When Harriet returned with Dennis, Vivian welcomed him to the company, went over the benefits package they offered, and finally inspected the paperwork he had filled out and determined it was complete. She then turned him back over to Harriet, who took him upstairs to his department.

When Vivian went to get coffee, the buzz on the cafeteria line was about the meeting the executives were having this week, and several people asked her if she knew what was going to happen. She had expected this and had a stock answer ready. "I don't know any more than you do. I'm sure their plans will be announced soon."

Zack called at nine-thirty. "Good morning."

"Good morning. I'm surprised you're up. You were practically in a coma just a few hours ago when I left. I'll bet you don't even remember talking to me."

"I remember how good you looked. And your telling me to help myself to what was in your cupboards and fridge. I don't remember anything else. I've always been a deep sleeper. Hope I wasn't too obnoxious."

"No more than usual," she said with a smile. "What's up?"

"Do you have any hot sauce?"

"Hot sauce? On cereal?"

"I decided to have two of those frozen sausage biscuits you've got."

"Hot sauce? On a biscuit?"

"You're starting to sound repetitious, Vivling. I like hot sauce. It's in my roots."

"Where are you from?"

"Actually, I'm from 158th Street, but my mother is from Trinidad."

"There should be some hot sauce in the pantry.

Look behind the ketchup and steak sauce. I try to keep all that stuff together. Are you okay otherwise?"

"Yeah. How's it going with you?"

"Oh, just another Monday morning. I'll see you tonight."

"I'll be here. I might even have a surprise for you."

" 'Might have' isn't fair."

"Maybe not, but unfortunately, it's the best I can do. See you later."

Vivian hung up the phone. She had lived alone for ten years, and it was odd to call her own number and have a man answer. It would probably feel even more so to go home and find Zack there. Not bad peculiar, just peculiar.

The day went without incident until four o'clock, when clerical worker Annemarie Giacomo stopped by the department. "Vivian, can I speak with you privately for a minute?"

"Sure. Come in and close the door."

Annemarie, an attractive brunette in her late forties, took a seat facing Vivian's desk. "This is so embarrassing. I don't know how to say it."

"I hope you're not unhappy working for George Anderson." Annemarie had recently transferred from sales to the purchasing department.

"I'd be a lot happier if he used some deodorant."

"What?" It was an involuntary response; Vivian had heard her perfectly. It was just that she expected Annemarie to say something along the lines of George was a tyrant, or that he had her running his personal errands.

"The man has BO, Vivian. I can't stand it."

She didn't know what to say. She hadn't had

much contact with George, who had been hired a few months before when the previous manager retired.

"Of course, I don't want to be the one to say anything to him. The man is my boss. He'll be the one to make out my next performance appraisal and recommend a salary increase. I don't even want my name mentioned when you talk to him."

She raised an eyebrow. *When* I *talk to him?* But in Lisa's absence, it was her responsibility. Of course, she'd be only too glad to let Lisa deal with this delicate situation, but being a manager meant managing, and this was part of it. She had to cope with both the sour and the sweet, or in this case, the fragrant and the foul.

"This type of situation can be rather difficult to handle, for obvious reasons," she said slowly.

"My sense of smell is probably more keen than most people's, but at this point I'm ready to respond to another job posting."

"I don't think anything is open for you right now," Vivian said quickly. She knew she had to take action and reassure Annemarie, even if she hadn't the faintest idea of what she was going to do. "As I was saying, it's a delicate matter, but I will take care of it for you."

"Thanks so much, Vivian. But please remember . . ."

"Don't worry. No one else will know you were the one to complain about it."

Vivian thought about the situation during the drive home. It would be so much easier if the offender was merely one of the purchasing agents, but George Anderson was a department head.

There was no way she could call him down and tell him there had been complaints about his personal hygiene. On the other hand, putting out a memo reminding everyone about something they should already know was silly. Past memos Lisa had written regarding sensitive topics like sexual harassment and excessive use of perfume had resulted in groups gathering around the various bulletin boards exchanging whispers about who they believed the respective guilty parties were.

Zack was at the computer when she let herself in with the day's mail in hand. He was sitting in one of the matching Queen Anne chairs flanking the armoire. "I hope you don't mind," he said. "I logged into my account so I could check my E-mail and send a few messages to let people know I'm not at home. I'm not giving out your phone number or anything—I didn't even tell my job—but there are some folks who need to know I'm all right. My parents might try to call me from Virginia."

"That's very considerate of you. No, I don't mind." While she felt he truly was concerned about his parents, she also believed he wanted to contact all his female friends who would be looking for him at home and at the hospital, but of course it was none of her business. Part of her wanted to tell him that she wouldn't be offended if he wanted to E-mail women from her machine, but she realized she wouldn't be able to without sounding petty and jealous. He was signed in under his own screen name; it wasn't like return mail addressed to him would clog her mailbox. Still, it bothered her that he had felt it necessary to mention his parents specifically. Just saying he wanted to contact the people he knew would have been sufficient.

She sniffed. "I smell Italian food, but it can't be coming from here, can it?"

"I made spaghetti sauce. I was bored out of my mind, sitting around with my foot up, so I figured I'd make myself useful. After all, how much TV can I watch?"

"But how could you manage with one whole side being out of commission?"

"Well, it's not really one whole side. My arm might be in a sling, but I can use it, as long as I'm not lifting anything heavy. I managed to pull out the stool you keep next to your refrigerator so I could sit on it. I used that chopped onion and green pepper you have in the freezer, and some of the minced garlic from that jar in the fridge. All I had to do after I sauteed it was open the jar of sauce and throw it in, plus some oregano. I'm sorry I couldn't make the actual spaghetti, but getting a big pot with a gallon of water on the stove is too much for my bad arm."

"I'm glad you didn't attempt it. That was sweet of you to make the sauce. I'll get the water going for the spaghetti." She deposited the day's mail on the table and went into the kitchen, where she filled a Dutch oven with water and put it on high heat.

By the time she added the pasta to the boiling water she had changed into a T-shirt and jeans. She frowned when she saw Zack was still on the computer. *How many people does he have to write to, anyway?* Then again, he probably was sending mail individually, not as a group. That way none of the women would be able to identify her rivals. Unless they were really dumb, they had to know there were rivals; the fact that he wasn't giving them a phone number should give them a broad hint about who he was staying with. Not that she was a *rival*, but theirs was an unusual situation, one that no one would really understand. She wasn't sure she understood it herself.

When she put the food on the table and called him she noticed he was no longer on-line, but was playing one of the strategy games in her software collection. She felt a sense of satisfaction, which she quickly shrugged off. Zack's social life was none of her business. She just wished there were more good men to go around, or at least more good men she felt compatible with. She was having such a terrible time finding a special man to fall in love with, and she knew other women were, too. Why couldn't there be five men running after every desirable female instead of the other way around?

"I like this," Zack said, interrupting her thoughts. "It makes me think."

"I enjoy it, too. But do you think you can pull yourself away from it long enough to have some dinner?"

"No problem with that. I'm hungry. Something smells really good. Did you bake bread or something?"

"They're bread sticks that come from a refrigerated can. The salad came out of a bag. I'm afraid I'm not much of a cook. 'Add water and stir' are my favorite instructions."

He crossed the room on his crutches, carefully sitting down at the table. "I'm sure by the time you're cooking for a family you'll be fine."

That was a topic she preferred not to discuss. Fortunately, there was an easy way out. "Would you like to say grace?"

Zack blessed the table, and as they accented the flavor of the pasta, salad, and bread with grated

Parmesan cheese, salad dressing, and butter, respectively, he asked how her day at work had been. "I don't even know what you do."

She told him. "Actually, I could use some diplomatic advice about a problem that came up at the office today," she said. She recounted Annemarie's problem with her boss. "Any suggestions?"

"Yeah. Let your boss handle it."

"She's out of the office this week. Besides, I want to handle it myself. I'm ready to make a move into management. There might be an opportunity opening up for me to get a promotion. I figure they'll need to have two managers, one for each site. If I go running to my boss with every little thing that'll only convince her I can't handle it."

"Good point. What'd you tell the woman?"

"That I'd take care of it."

"All right. Forget it, then."

"You mean do nothing after I told her I would resolve it? I can't do that, Zack! That's unethical."

"I don't know what else you can do. If it was someone low on the totem pole it would be different, but the man is a manager, Vivian. What are you going to do, call him in and tell him he stinks?"

"I can't do that either."

"Well, then. Your only option is to do nothing, unless you want to send him an anonymous note."

She frowned. It seemed so unprofessional to not do anything, like wait staff who delivered food and disappeared until it was time to present the check, leaving you to fend for yourself when you wanted Heinz 57 rather than A.1. on your steak.

But she could think about that later. "Zack, did you ever find out what happened to your patient, that child with the facial injuries?" He shook his head. "I stitched her up as best I could and sent her home with her father. I used absorbable sutures, so they didn't have to have them removed. I do know the mother recovered, but I don't know if she demanded they see a plastic surgeon. My hunch is probably not. Private consultations are handled differently from emergency situations. With no insurance they probably wouldn't have gotten any further than the reception desk. We rarely get to find out what happens to the people that come to the ER for treatment. People pass in and out all the time."

"I'm sorry I can't help you with the dishes," Zack said after dinner. "After all, because I'm here you've got twice as many."

"That's all right. The last thing I want you to do is do more damage to your elbow." As Vivian carried the dishes to the kitchen sink she noted that there was just a small amount of sauce left. How nice not to be overwhelmed with leftovers for once. She could get used to this . . . and having dinner with Zack every night, exchanging feelings and ideas as they enjoyed their meal, preferably a meal they had both played a part in preparing. What would happen now that dinner was over?

The telephone began to ring. She glanced at the caller ID panel on her kitchen extension. It was Bernard.

"You haven't forgotten dinner tomorrow?" he asked.

"No, of course not, but I'm doing my dishes right now. Can I get the directions from you tomorrow?"

"Sure. I'll call you at the office. How did it go today?"

"Pretty good. You feeling all right?"

"Better. I'll be glad to go home this weekend. I'm really looking forward to seeing you, Vivian. I haven't called because I know you're busy this week, but I've missed you."

She chose her words carefully. "It'll be good to see you, Bernard."

Tension underscored her mood as she washed the dishes, sprayed disinfectant on her counters and then put the dishes away. Her heart was thumping loudly, and her airway felt like it had shrunken. She couldn't wait until this dinner tomorrow was over. It wasn't like she could put down her napkin after dessert and tell him she wasn't going to see him anymore, but surely she could count on his mother to help pave the way.

"Hey Vivling, I'll bet I can beat you at this game," Zack yelled from the living room. "You wanna try?"

She wrung out the sponge and joined Zack, the unpleasantness of the forthcoming breakup with Bernard going down the drain along with the excess water. She moved the other Queen Anne chair in front of the armoire, next to where he sat.

She was the victor, although not by much. Before she knew it, it was nine-fifteen, and she had planned to be in bed by nine. "Time for me to turn in. I'll open up the sofa for you. I'm surprised you were able to get it closed."

"It wasn't hard. I leaned on it with my good arm and hopped a few times."

"Well, if you don't feel up to it tomorrow don't worry about it."

"You're so good to me, Vivling."

She looked at him sharply. Was he trying to be sarcastic? But he was gazing at her intently. Before she knew what was happening, he was leaning toward her, and she found herself doing the same.

They kissed once, softly, like a whisper; and then his hand cupped her jaw and began again. His firm mouth and searching tongue demanded a response, and she kissed him back with an eagerness that surprised her.

"I hope you didn't mind," he said when it was over. "Something about us playing this game, sitting here side by side like Ma and Pa Kettle . . . I guess I'm getting a taste of what I've been missing."

"Don't feel bad. I think I've gotten the same." She rose and pulled the chair back into place on the side of the armoire. Silently she removed the sofa cushions and pulled out the bed, spreading the blanket he had neatly folded, and placing the pillow in place at the head. She knew it would be a lot harder for him to pull the bed out than it had been for him to push it back. "Good night, Zack."

Zack watched her movements uncertainly. Her mouth had tasted so fresh and sweet, her skin felt so soft. He was glad he'd kissed her; he'd wanted to do it almost from the very beginning. He liked being at her apartment, working in her tiny kitchen like he lived there, too. He'd actually looked forward to the moment when she would unlock the door and enter at the end of her workday, dissolving his loneliness. The whole thing was rather absurd, like he was a househusband or something. After he kissed her she didn't seem angry—she'd admitted something was missing from her life, too—but she clearly wasn't comfortable with it, either. That was plain from the swift way she arranged the sofa bed, like it was timed to blow up in three minutes, and then disappeared into her bedroom like she was being chased. Maybe kissing her hadn't been such a good idea after all, but surely she knew she had nothing to fear from him. Perhaps it was unsettling to have a man whom she really didn't know all that well sleeping on her couch, but because of his injuries he certainly didn't pose much of a threat. She'd said it herself—all she had to do was connect to his bad arm, or his bad leg.

Vivian was trembling as she closed her bedroom door. Here she felt safe. She felt a little uneasy, having shared a passionate kiss with Zack and knowing he would be spending the night just a few feet away from where she slept. There had been such power in the way he held her jaw, yet such gentleness when he stroked her skin. It had been a long time since she'd been kissed with such ardor, where she felt its effects to the tips of her toes. Kissing a man as he left her apartment was one thing, but Zack wasn't leaving, and that was why she felt so flustered.

She was still cold when she got into bed, pulling the covers up to her neck and curling into an S position. The Quiet Storm love songs she usually fell asleep to bothered her tonight, so she changed the radio to the easy listening station. She quickly fell asleep.

* * *

She left for work on Tuesday without waking Zack. He already had everything he needed, knew where everything was, and how to reach her. If he needed anything he could call.

She pulled her 626 into the company parking lot behind a newer model by Mazda, a Millenia in dramatic midnight blue. She hadn't noticed it before in the always-crowded parking lot and wondered whose it was.

The vehicles parked side-by-side, and she alighted at the same time as the other driver. She recognized the tall brown-skinned man as the senior auditor from the big accounting firm the company utilized to inspect their financial records each year. "Good morning," she said, wishing she could remember his name.

"Hello. Vivian, isn't it?"

"Yes. I was admiring your car. I have a Mazda, myself, but I'll probably have to get a newer one next year. Are you happy with yours?"

"Very. I got it at a great price. These Millenias are nice cars, but they haven't been big sellers, so a couple of years back Mazda offered a purchase plan with a fat rebate and an interest rate next to nothing. I jumped on it, and I've never been sorry. I come in from Stamford, a fair drive, so naturally I want to be comfortable. This car fits the bill."

"Thank you. I'll remember that."

"Glad I could help."

"How's the audit going?"

"We're actually winding up."

That didn't surprise her. The auditors showed up in January and were there for all the snow and ice storms. By the time heavy overcoats gave way to suit jackets in the spring they were on their way out.

"Since I'll be leaving soon, I was wondering if you'd like to have lunch with me, say Friday?"

She was taken aback by the unexpected invitation—he wore no wedding ring, and at a good fifteen years her senior he certainly was no youngster—but she quickly recovered. It was only lunch. "I'd like that. Except, well, this is embarrassing, but I can't remember your name."

He laughed, a rich baritone sound that appealed to her ears. "It's Timothy Golden."

"All right, Timothy. I'm on the phone list under Vivian St. James."

He held the front door open for her to enter, and after quick smiles they parted ways, she down the hall to her office and he upstairs to his desk in the accounting department.

"You look happy," Harriet said when Vivian walked in.

She shrugged. "It looks like it's going to be a good day." *After yesterday I could use one.*

Chapter 10: Worse

"Is Connie coming in today?" Vivian asked Harriet on Tuesday morning.

"No. She just called. She's leaving to spend a few days in Pennsylvania with her mother. She says she'll be back to work on Monday."

"I wonder what Lisa will have to say about that."

"Connie said she knows she was going to take some time off."

"A day or two, yes; but not the whole week."

Vivian was listing the employees who would be added or deleted from the various health insurance plans the company offered when Lisa called from New Jersey.

"I tried to get Connie, but I didn't get an answer. Is she in today?"

"She's taking the week off. I think she told Harriet you knew about it."

There was a tense silence before Lisa spoke again. "I approved two days without pay. She didn't say anything about being gone the whole week. I never would have okayed that; I'm going to need her."

"Is there anything Harriet or I might be able to help with?"

"Yes, but I'll have to get back to you on that. Right now I've got something a little more pressing to handle. I need you to read me something from a memo I left on my desk."

"Sure. I'll put you on hold and pick up the line in your office." Vivian took the key to Lisa's office from her desk drawer, then ran down the hall. She had to unlock both the door to the outer office where Connie sat as well as the one to Lisa's private office. She picked up the receiver and pressed the blinking button. "Okay, I'm here." She listened as Lisa instructed her where to find the paper she was looking for. It was a memo to her from the company president. "Did you want me to fax this to you?"

"No, I just need you to read me part of it. There's a paragraph on the bottom of the first page that begins with . . ."

Vivian read the section Lisa requested, then waited while Lisa put her on hold to confer with someone. She was still waiting when the other line began to ring. When Harriet didn't answer by the third ring she hit the hold button and picked it up. "Human Resources, Vivian speaking."

Harriet was the one calling. "There you are. Pete Arnold is waiting to see you. He says he has something important to give you." She lowered her voice. "I'm going to ask him to wait in the hall so I can close the office door. I was on my way to the restroom."

"Go ahead. I'll be right in." She switched over to the other line. "Lisa?" Silence. She waited, but had to return the call to hold when one of the

other lines began to ring, then the other. Right
now she really missed Connie being here.

The caller on line three had a quick question,
and that call ended promptly, but the person on
two was still waiting. "I'll be right with you," she
said quickly, then returned the call to hold. She
had to see if Lisa was back.

She was. "Sorry about that, Lisa. Harriet had to
step out for a minute, and all the lines started ringing. You'd think we had an ad in the paper or
something. Would you mind if I go back to the
person still waiting? It might be something I can
answer quickly."

Lisa consented, and Vivian retrieved the line on
hold. It was the director of research and development. Alan Konishima was one of the lucky people
who knew his job was safe. It had been stated in
the initial announcement that the companies' respective laboratories would be consolidated to one
location under the direction of their present lead-
ers. He was a good-natured man who told her he
would continue to wait.

Not surprisingly, Lisa decided to get the memo
faxed to her after all. "Sure. I'll get it to you in
the next five minutes."

She quickly picked up line two and offered Dr.
Konishima an apology for the delay, then listened
to his reason for calling. "Yes, I have that information in my office. I'm in Lisa's office right now,
but if you can hold just one more moment I'll get
it for you. I promise it will only take me about
fifteen seconds. All right. Thanks." She put the
phone on the desk and, memo in hand, made a
dash for her office, stopping only to turn off the
light and latch the door before shutting it.

Pete Arnold was standing in the hall outside the

office. She had forgotten all about him. He probably had his rollover check, but she saw no reason why he couldn't just leave it with Harriet.

"Pete, just one minute. I've got to answer a question for someone."

She found the information quickly and told Dr. Konishima what he needed to know. "Okay, Pete," she said loudly as she hung up. "Come on in."

"I'm back," Harriet called.

"Good. It was crazy while you were gone. Now that you're back maybe it'll slow down."

"You're very busy this morning," Pete observed.

"Oh, yeah." She spoke pleasantly, not giving any clues to her distaste for obvious trivialities, like "It sure is coming down, isn't it?" when anyone with two functional eyes could see it was pouring.

"I wanted to give you that check for my rollover, and the completed form as well."

She took the envelope he offered. "That's fine. I'll see that this goes out today."

"Thanks. Have a nice day." He left.

She made a face. If there was anything that made her want to scream more than motorists who didn't use their turn signals, it was hearing that expression. It was so insincere sounding, no matter how heartfelt the intention. "You do the same," she returned, not wanting to be rude.

She scribbled a cover page to Lisa and asked Harriet to fax it, then resumed work on the insurance updates.

"Vivian, are you on two?" Harriet asked about fifteen minutes later.

"No." She heard Harriet saying "Hello? Hello?"

Harriet appeared in the doorway. "That's funny. There's nobody here, but the light doesn't go out when I hang up."

"I haven't been on two since I took a call while I was in Lisa's off—" Vivian broke off abruptly, remembering how she had put the phone down without hanging it up in her haste to get back to her office to answer Dr. Konishima's question. "Oh, I know what I did. I'll be right back."

She was halfway between the two offices when she drew in her breath, realizing that she had left the keys on Lisa's desk and locked the door behind her, taking only the document to be faxed when she left. Her pulse began to pound in panic. Not only was she unable to get back into Lisa's office if she should need to, she couldn't break the connection, meaning one of their lines was out of service.

She turned and went back to her own office.

"The light's still on," Harriet said.

"Yes, I know. I left the phone off the hook in Lisa's. I just realized I locked my keys in there."

"I have my key to the outer office. Maybe Connie keeps her key to Lisa's office in her desk drawer. I'll go see."

"Thanks, Harriet."

Together they went to the offices next door. Once in the outer office they rushed to Connie's desk, and Harriet tugged at the top drawer.

Nothing happened.

"Oh, no. It's locked." Vivian slammed her palm on the surface of the desk.

"And Connie's on the road by now. I'm so sorry, Vivian."

"It's my own fault."

"I just wish I had a key to Lisa's office."

"I know. It's all right."

"I'll go look up a locksmith for you." Harriet left the room.

Vivian didn't reply. Lisa would have to sign off on a locksmith bill. Some great impression she was making. Her hopes of a promotion were fading like a noncolorfast garment after a washing.

She slowly walked the few yards to her office. She didn't go back to the insurance; instead she leaned back in her chair, her clasped hands supporting her head, and stared at the ceiling. What she needed was a key, and if not that, a miracle. Of all weeks for Connie to take off.

She sat up. Wait a second. All those squares that made up the ceiling were removable, not just the plastic that covered the tubular fluorescent light bulbs. They concealed all the telephone and electrical wires. "Harriet, hold off on the locksmith. I'm going to call maintenance. I think they might be able to help me. Just cross your fingers that Lisa doesn't call again and want me to get something else from her office."

It was nearly noon by the time a maintenance man arrived with a ladder. He promptly disappeared into the ceiling, and if all went well he would be able to crawl next door, come down in Lisa's office and unlock the door. Vivian completed the insurance updates and placed calls to those who had not yet selected a plan.

The envelope from Pete Arnold was on top of her In Box. It was sealed, and she opened it with a silver letter opener. Her eyes widened when she saw the amount of the check. No wonder he wanted to hand it to her personally. Eighty-three thousand dollars was a nice piece of change, and it still had many years to grow before Pete would be ready to retire. The people at his old fund must have hated to part with such a sum, even though they must have millions. It was a personal check, so it hadn't been a direct rollover. He would probably have to pay some tax on that, not that it was any of her concern.

She checked the corresponding form and made sure it was complete, then addressed an envelope to the investment firm that handled the employees' 401(k) accounts. She picked up the check, preparing to put it inside the folded form. Eighty-three thousand dollars, made out to . . . Vivian St. James.

What! Payable to *her!* What was Peter Arnold thinking of? He should have made it payable to the investment firm.

Someone entered her office. "There you are. I've been calling you, but your line's been busy." It was Glenda. "What's up with that? You and Zack didn't talk enough last night?"

"It's got nothing to do with Zack. I'm having a miserable morning." Vivian told her friend about the telephone problem. "And if that's not enough, look what your boy has done now." She handed over Pete's check and enjoyed Glenda's bewildered expression.

"What's he giving you eighty-three thousand dollars for?" she hissed.

"Relax, I haven't been keeping secrets from you. It's for a 401(k) rollover. He made it out to me by mistake. Can you imagine?"

"Good thing you're honest."

Vivian was relieved when five o'clock came. Maintenance had been successful in getting into Lisa's office from the ceiling, and the line was now free.

She realized on the way home that Zack hadn't called. She supposed no news was good news. He was probably answering replies to all those E-mails he'd sent out yesterday.

She smelled the meat cooking as soon as she opened the apartment door. "What are you cooking now? It smells fabulous."

"I marinated a couple of steaks."

He was at the computer, but he was playing the strategy game, not writing E-mail. Once again she was glad, and once again she forced thoughts of his female admirers out of her mind. "You're a handy man to have around the house, Zack. But—"

"I confess I had ulterior motives. I'm dying to get out of this house. Not that there's anything wrong with it; it's just that I've been in for two days, and I'm not used to being housebound."

"I understand, but—"

"Maybe you and I can go out for drinks and dessert or something."

Vivian chewed on her lip nervously. "I'm sorry, Zack. I should have told you. I have plans for tonight. I won't even be able to have dinner." She felt terrible. It hadn't crossed her mind that he might make dinner again tonight. She figured he would have one of those microwave meals she had in the freezer. They were actually quite good. But that look on his face—he looked so lonely and unhappy. She had to say something encouraging.

"I'm sure I won't be too late. A friend invited me over for dinner, but since it's a Tuesday I don't think it'll run very late. If you feel up to climbing the stairs we can go somewhere later." It would make a late night for her, but she'd be all right. Surely tomorrow she would have a calm day. She was certainly overdue for some tranquility.

* * *

After she left, Zack fixed his plate. The steak tasted flat to him, the potato dry and the salad was like eating tree leaves. There was nothing wrong with the way the food had been prepared, but disappointment had dulled his taste buds. The draped white blouse and plaid slacks Vivian had changed into, casual but feminine, told him she wasn't dining with a female. She was going on a date. The only reason the guy wasn't picking her up was because she wouldn't be able to explain his being here.

He picked at the T-bone, in the end only eating half his meal. He left it on the table. Maybe his appetite would return when it was closer to the time for her to return.

The last thing he expected was to hear her say she had plans for tonight. He was afraid he had acted like a chump, wearing his disappointment as openly as he wore his clothing. It had been years since he'd been caught with his emotions showing. He hoped Vivian would see it only as a result of his being isolated for two consecutive days, even if he knew that wasn't it. He wanted company, but not just anybody. Last night had been wonderful, having dinner and then sitting together in front of the computer. All day he had looked forward to doing it again, not only spending time with her, but perhaps a repeat of that wonderful kiss they shared, this time assuring her there was no reason for her to be nervous. If he wanted to get out for a few hours, all it would take was one phone call to any of the women he knew who lived in the area and he would be picked up right away. But he didn't want to be with any of those women, he wanted to be with Vivian. She had made an indelible impression on him that first night in the ER

at Hudson Hospital, and he believed it was fate that
kept throwing them together again and again.

Vivian found the Williams home with no difficulty. It was one of those *Leave It to Beaver* stone-
and-shingle homes that began to dot American
suburbia in the prosperous post-World War II years,
well before any African-Americans lived in the village of Pelham. She forced herself to look pleasant
as she moved down the front walk. It was only a
quarter to seven, but she felt she should arrive a
few minutes early. It seemed tacky to arrive just in
time to sit down to dinner. At least this way she
could participate in a little predinner chitchat.

The dog began barking the moment she rang
the doorbell. Good Lord, it sounded vicious, like
a Doberman or a rottweiler. Or maybe there were
two. Vivian didn't like strange dogs, and they usually didn't like her, either. Now she knew how mail
carriers felt.

Bernard answered the door. It was good to see
him after nearly a week, and he looked much
healthier than he had last week in the hospital. He
held out his hand, and when she was inside he
discreetly kissed her on the lips.

She jumped on hearing the low moan of a dog.
A large Irish setter bounded into the foyer. How
could such a gentle-looking animal sound so threatening?

"Oh, that's just Cocoa coming to check you out.
He does that to everybody he doesn't know.
Don'cha, boy?" Bernard rubbed the top of the
dog's head. Cocoa ignored him, instead concentrat-
ing on sniffing at her, trying to put his snout between her legs while he panted like a plus-size man

making love. Why did dogs always do that? Maybe it would make sense if she had been stuck on a desert island or somewhere without facilities, but this was ridiculous. She was fresh out of the shower. It would be less embarrassing to be bitten.

Bernard's voice was sharp as he reprimanded the dog. "Hey! Cut that out." Cocoa obediently stopped his sniffing . . . or maybe he had had enough. He ambled off out of sight. "Sorry about that," Bernard said. He took her arm. "Come in. I want you to meet my uncle."

She frowned. His uncle! What was this, a family reunion? She walked with him into the living room. Mr. Williams was seated in a chair opposite the television, his feet propped up on a matching ottoman with Cocoa resting nearby. When he saw them he swung his legs to the floor.

"Oh, please don't get up, Mr. Williams," she said, walking over to him and extending her hand. "It's good to see you again."

"Hello, Vivian. Glad you could join us." He shook her hand.

Bernard led her toward another man seated on the sofa. "And this is my uncle, Oliver Williams."

"Hello, Mr. Williams." Vivian shook his hand. He strongly resembled his brother. "Are you and Bernard's father twins?"

Oliver laughed heartily. When he spoke she had difficulty understanding his words; he spoke in a barking manner with poor enunciation. As best as she could tell, he was saying, "Oh, people ask me that all the time. We look a lot alike, but we're not twins."

She turned to Bernard. "Where's your mother? I'd like to say hello."

"In the kitchen. She'll be out soon."

Vivian pictured Mrs. Williams patting flour on her face to make it appear that she had been slaving over a hot stove, when in reality she had probably thrown the uncooked meal in one of those oven bags and was in there reading a magazine.

She took a seat in the middle of the couch next to Oliver, with Bernard sitting on her other side. "Would you like a drink?" he offered.

"Some wine would be lovely."

Bernard disappeared, and she was startled when Oliver patted her lower thigh and said something unintelligible. "I'm sorry. I didn't quite understand you."

He repeated the statement, and this time she understood a little better. Still, she wanted to be sure. "How long have I been seeing Bernard?" she asked. When he nodded, she said, "We've gone out a few times. I was with him the afternoon his ulcer acted up."

Oliver made a reply, but it sounded like mush.

His brother came to the rescue. "Now, Ollie, kids today have different options than we did. I agree that there wasn't any stress delivering the mail. But we didn't get paid like Bernie does, either."

Vivian raised an eyebrow. *Bernie?*

Bernard returned with two glasses and handed her one. "Mom says she's ready."

"Good," Mr. Williams said, getting to his feet, quickly followed by Vivian, who nearly spilled her wine in her anxiousness to get up. Oliver had not removed his hand from her knee, and it was getting uncomfortable. It wasn't like she could give him a withering look or, to make certain he got the point, lift his hand and put it back in his lap. She hadn't bargained for the evening to include a lecherous uncle. She just hoped she wasn't seated next to him at dinner.

In the dining room Mrs. Williams greeted her with uncharacteristic friendliness. "We're so happy you could join us tonight, Vivian."

"Thank you. I'm glad I could be here. Can I help you with anything?"

"No, I've got everything on the table. Let's all sit down. Bernard, you're next to Vivian. Ollie, on this side."

Vivian wished Mrs. Williams had put a little more thought into her menu planning. Dinner was a colorless affair, with chicken with white gravy, rice, and turnips, which she detested. Only the burnt orange stoneware kept them from drowning in a bland sea of white food.

During the meal she learned that Oliver lived with the Williamses. Fortunately, Oliver didn't say much. The conversation was dominated by Mrs. Williams asking one loaded question after another. She was from Connecticut? Had her family lived there very long? What did her father do? Oh, her *mother* worked, too, as a librarian? How nice! Did she have any siblings? And what did her brother do? Did he like living in Rhode Island? Vivian was glad when Mr. Williams laughed and said, "Ceola, you're asking so many questions the poor girl can't eat her food"; it gave her a reprieve.

She was swallowing a bite of chicken when Mrs. Williams started in again. "Vivian, I noticed your eyelids are kind of reddish. Do you have some kind of rash?"

She froze. She had always used bright makeup; after all, she was brown enough to be able to handle the contrast. But she was careful in applying it. She decided Bernard's mother was just trying to give her a hard time. "I don't think so," she said, recovering. "I don't feel any itching. I'll take a look at it later."

She had fiddled with her wine glass for what seemed like an eternity after it was empty, but by the time Mrs. Williams cleared the table for dessert she made a quiet but desperate grab for the wine bottle and poured herself a second glass. Her movement was not lost on the sharp-eyed older woman, who pointedly remarked, "Bernard, perhaps you should drive Vivian home tonight."

"I'd like to thank you for a charming evening." She was surprised she could get the words out without bursting into laughter. She had been properly cordial when thanking Mr. and Mrs. Williams, knowing she would never see them again; and in saying goodbye to Uncle Ollie, who marked the occasion with a kiss full on the lips. So help her, if he had tried to infuse his tongue in her mouth she would have bitten it, uncle or no uncle.

Now she and Bernard were alone by her car. She wished she could tell him right now that it could never work between them. He was a nice man, but he'd have a lot more appeal if he was an orphan . . . or at least motherless. Uncleless, too.

Bernard laughed. "You know you didn't mean that."

It was pointless to object. "All right, I didn't mean it."

"I guess it wasn't fair to spring Uncle Ollie on you. He's a trip. He's lived with my parents ever since his wife threw him out."

"For cheating on her, I'll bet."

"How did you know?"

"Just a hunch. What's with him, anyway? I could barely understand a word he was saying."

"That's just the way he talks. I've been around him all my life, and I couldn't understand him either until I was about fifteen." He put an arm around her. "I'm going home Saturday. How about some seafood Saturday night? Just the two of us."

"I'm going to Connecticut Saturday."

"But you were just there Sunday."

"I'm not going to New London. I have a friend who lives up near Hartford. She's the one I'm going on the safari with. We try to get together once a month." That much was true, but she and Lauren Walters usually met in Stamford, the halfway point between their locations.

"All right. I guess I'll talk to you when you get back." Was she imagining it or did a knowing look cross his face?

"I'm awfully tired, Bernard. I'm going to go home now." She unlocked her car door.

There was something in his kiss that told her he knew what was coming. His lips touched hers for just for a second and managed to reflect power and defeat at the same time.

She waved to him as she drove off. The evening she'd dreaded for days was over. It hadn't been too bad, if you didn't count a lustful uncle, a horny dog, and a mother who thought she was a lush.

She glanced at the clock on the dashboard display. It was early, only eight forty-five. Good. All she could think about was going home to Zack. She hated to admit it, but she was going to miss him when he was gone.

Chapter 11:
Brutal

Zack looked at Vivian carefully. "You're sure you're up to it?"

"Absolutely. Whenever you're ready."

He hadn't expected her to want to go back out; he thought she was only trying to humor him when she made the suggestion. But he also hadn't expected her to return this early, either. He reached for his crutches.

"Hey, you've really gotten good on those things."

"Thanks. I've had practice." He eased down the stairs. It was a slow process, but when he got to the bottom he felt fine, not exhausted and weak the way he had after leaving the ER. This was actually the second time he'd ventured downstairs this evening; he'd paid a visit to Austin's parents while Vivian was gone.

She held the door open for him, and he breathed in a great gulp of night air. "Oh, that smells good. I've had the windows open during the day, but there's nothing like letting fresh air surround you."

"Where are we going?" she asked when they

were in his Ford, which he insisted they take; it had been sitting idle for two days and was due to be moved anyway; the street sweepers would be coming through overnight.

"A little place called Smitty's. It's not far from here."

"I've never heard of it."

"It's a nice place. The bartender sings."

"He sings?"

"He's good at it, too. You'll see."

Minutes later they arrived at the small establishment that had been a favorite of his ever since he had dated a young woman who lived nearby. They had broken up years ago, and the last he heard she was married and living in Maryland, but he still stopped in at the bar whenever he was in the area.

Lemuel Smith, the owner, was tending bar. "Hey, it's the Zack attack!" he greeted, smiling broadly. His gaze took in Zack's crutches and arm sling. "What happened, you get run over by a bus?"

Zack laughed. "I fell off a ladder."

"Broke your ankle, huh?"

"No, just a sprain. I should be back on both feet Friday." Zack turned to Vivian. "Vivian, this is Lemuel Smith. Lem, Vivian St. James."

"Are you the gentleman who sings?" she asked as she shook his hand.

"That's me. I'll serenade you while you're having your drinks. What'll you have?"

Zack ordered beer and Vivian requested wine. They brought their glasses to one of the booths lining the opposite wall, and he asked the question that had been on his mind ever since she returned. "How was dinner?"

She rolled her eyes. "To sum it up nicely, it was

awful. But I know I'll sleep good tonight—this is
my third glass of wine."

"And your last. You're driving." It probably
wasn't nice of him, but he was relieved to learn
the evening hadn't been pleasant for her. Perhaps
that meant she was ready to write off her date. Had
it been Bernard Williams, or someone else she'd
met?

He watched Vivian turn sharply when Lemuel began to sing along with the slow jam on the jukebox,
his rich baritone amplified by the microphone he
kept behind the bar. He was an excellent singer,
reminding him of Will Downing.

"Wow. He's really good." Her admiration was evi-
dent in her dreamy facial expression.

"I wish you'd look at me like that."

"Like what?"

"Like you're willing the person you're looking at
to sweep you up and carry you off."

"Can you sing to me like that?"

"I couldn't carry a tune if it came in a briefcase
with a million dollars."

They only stayed long enough to have one drink.
"You'd better get some sleep," Zack told her. "I'd
hate for the future manager of human resources to
be found slumped over her desk, snoring." He was
yawning himself by the time they got back to Vivian's
apartment. Today was the most active day he'd had
since he'd injured himself, and he'd been on red
alert during the brief ride home, making certain she
had no problems driving. "Sweet dreams," he called
out as she headed for her bedroom, her gait just a
tad slow after three glasses of wine in relatively quick
succession. He would have liked to kiss her again,

even if it was for just a moment, but he passed. If she'd been with a date earlier, no matter how bad it was, she had probably already been kissed. He preferred to be the only one.

Vivian fell asleep wondering why he hadn't kissed her.

When she woke up she wondered why he hadn't kissed her.

During the drive to work she wondered why he hadn't kissed her. She was beginning to see Zack Warner in a different light, and she would have welcomed his embrace.

When she arrived at work she had to put him out of her mind; she had too much to do.

Zack himself had given her an idea of how to handle her biggest problem. Writing an anonymous note to the purchasing manager seemed cowardly, but under the circumstances it would save embarrassment, both hers and his. The trouble was, she had been drafting official-sounding correspondence for so long everything she wrote had that human resources air about it. She needed to sound ordinary, not administrative; none of that "it has been brought to my attention" stuff.

She was pretty satisfied with what she had drafted when she took a call from the lab that processed their new employees' chemical tests. "Hi, Sharon! What's up?"

"We've got a positive, Vivian."

"Oh, no! Who is it?"

"Dennis Chin."

"Dennis Chin!" she exclaimed. "You're kidding."

"I was kind of surprised, too. He's so bookish,

reminds me of Clark Kent. But he's got marijuana and cocaine in his system."

"Are you sure you got the right results?"

"Positive."

Vivian sighed. "I guess I'll have to be the bearer of bad news." She wasn't looking forward to it, but company policy mandated that anyone who failed the drug test would be let go immediately. She wasn't expecting to have to handle anything like this. Why was all this stuff happening while Lisa was out of town?

She put in a call to the MIS director, Mel Norris. Maybe he would volunteer to give Dennis the ax. But even as she pecked out the four-digit extension, she didn't feel particularly optimistic. Mel was an affable chap in his sixties whose previously silver hair was now brown (courtesy of one of those dye products whose slogan to a public they obviously thought was stupid was that no one would notice). He was an excellent manager; but his style included leaving personnel matters to human resources.

She took a deep breath when he answered. "Hello, Mel. It's Vivian St. James."

"Hullo, Vivian."

She winced. Mel was brilliant, but he had a slow, deliberate way of speaking that suggested an IQ of fifty. "The lab just called, Mel. They said Dennis Chin tested positive for marijuana and cocaine."

"Dennis? Are they certain?"

"I had the same reaction. I asked if there was any possibility of an error, but they said it was correct."

"That's too bad. I'm certainly surprised. I guess you'll want to see him."

A euphemism for terminating him, she knew. So much for hoping he would handle it. But of course it wasn't his responsibility, it was hers. Dennis had fooled them all. "I was going to call him down now, but I wanted to notify you first."

"Thank you. I'll try to talk to him when he comes up to get his things."

Sheer nerves made her wait a half-hour before asking Dennis to come to her office. It was going to be unpleasant, and the procrastinator in her wanted to put it off as long as possible.

But she knew she couldn't hold off forever, so she called Mel's secretary to get Dennis' extension, then placed the call. "Hi, Dennis. It's Vivian St. James in human resources. Fine, thanks. I need to see you about something important. Can you come down to my office?"

"Sure. Be right there."

Dennis didn't appear suspicious of her motives when he announced his arrival by knocking on her open office door. "What'd I do, forget to sign something?"

"Come in, Dennis, and sit down."

In the few seconds it took for him to be seated, his demeanor went from joviality to anxiousness. She saw him grip the arms of the chair and knew the first gnawings that something was wrong were taking effect.

She got up and closed the door, then returned to her seat. "Dennis, I'm afraid I have bad news." She reminded herself that he certainly knew his own habits. Maybe he had misjudged the time it would take for the substances to clear his system.

"What happened?"

"Our lab tells us that you tested positive."

If the distress on his face was any indicator, Dennis was a fabulous actor. His forehead wrinkled as he shook his head, looking as disbelieving as anyone would if she'd just announced that Martians had landed in the parking lot. "It's a mistake," he said. "I don't use drugs. I've *never* used drugs."

"They said they were certain, Dennis. I'm sorry."

"You're *firing* me? For something I didn't do?"

"We don't allow anyone who tests positive to remain in our employ. That's the rule, and there can't be any exceptions. I'm sure you understand."

"But they're *wrong!*"

Oh, my. His voice had broken, and were those tears in his eyes? This was so difficult. She didn't understand how people could deliberately be cruel, like a landlord who chose the day when a snowstorm hit to evict a family with small children. "I'm so sorry, Dennis, but those are the rules. I have to abide by them."

"The lab made a mistake. Let them retest me. They won't find any drugs in my system."

"I'm afraid we can't do that. Giving second chances isn't practical. The drugs in your system could have cleared out in the interim."

"Drugs? *Plural?*"

"They found traces of both marijuana and cocaine."

He opened his mouth, but no words came out. He looked almost comical, sitting there wild-eyed with his mouth wide open. And then, as he closed his mouth, the tears poured out in earnest. His upper body trembled, and he removed his glasses to wipe his eyes with his palms.

She leaned forward and handed him her box of tissues, trying to think of something comforting to say. She had little sympathy for people who used drugs or indulged in any behavior they knew had

serious consequences, then expressed remorse
when they were caught, but something about Dennis inspired compassion in her. "I wish there was
something I could do," was the best she could
come up with.

He stopped crying and wiped his eyes. "I swear
to you, Vivian, it's not possible for them to have
found drugs in me." He waved a hand when he
saw her mouth open in protest. "It's not fair. They
make a mistake and I pay for it. I have no job, no
way of paying my bills, my reputation is ruined . . .
I went for that test on Friday afternoon. Someone
was thinking about their plans for the weekend and
mis-labeled my results."

"I'm sorry, Dennis," she repeated.

"I am, too." He got up and left. She was glad
to see he had recovered his dignity enough to leave
with his head held high, but she found the entire
experience unnerving.

"I tell you, Glenda, the man was *sobbing*. It was
so embarrassing." Vivian was sitting in a hard plastic chair facing her friend's desk in the payroll office.

"I'll bet. All I can say is he doesn't look like a
party animal to me."

"What a *week* I'm having!" she exclaimed.

"It's not all that bad. You don't have to worry
about Bernard anymore." A curious Glenda had
called her at home last night, but she was too
groggy to talk. Vivian wasn't surprised when Glenda
came to the human resources office first thing in
the morning, armed with a cup of steaming coffee
and a cinnamon bun, to get the scoop about dinner at the Williams's. "And at five o'clock you can

go home and relax with Zack. What's he making you for dinner tonight?"

"Probably nothing. I have to go food shopping. My freezer's empty except for maybe a pound of ground beef." She paused, not sure if she was ready to confide a feeling so startlingly new to her. "Glenda, I like Zack. I mean, I *really* like him."

"Uh-oh. Are you saying what I *think* you're saying?"

"I don't know what you're thinking. All I know is that I like him. He's witty, he's charming, he's handsome . . ."

"He's a doctor."

She shrugged. "You've got to admit that doesn't hurt."

"Well, you've got an ideal opportunity here. He'll be your prisoner for two more days yet."

"It's a little more complicated than that, Glenda. He's so popular with the ladies. You should have heard him at the hospital. He makes no secret of the fact that there are women who'd jump at the chance to marry him. It's hard to compete with that, and I'm not sure I want to."

"Come on, Viv. Do you really want to have a man nobody else wants? At least let him know you're interested. It doesn't mean you have to give up any other invitations you might receive. Especially if you know *he* isn't."

"Speaking of which, you'll never believe who asked me to lunch. Timothy Golden. The auditor."

"That old guy? His first job was probably keeping records for Noah, making sure only two of each species got on board the ark."

"Come on, Glenda. He's not that ancient."

"He's fifty if he's a day."

"Maybe. Do you know anything about him?"

"Not really. I've never worked with him. He does the important stuff, corporate balance sheets, accounts payable, things like that. Payroll is easy to audit, so they assign me the newbies, the kids right out of college with the dumb nicknames. This year I had Whitey."

"Whitey!"

"Yeah. He's one of those people who are so fair they're almost colorless. He told me that when he was a kid his hair was so blond it was almost white. I'm sure he'll learn soon enough that he'll have to drop that name in favor of the one he was given, or else the only star he'll be is on the firm's softball team."

Vivian thought about Glenda's advice after returning to her office. Technically, Zack *was* a captive in her apartment. She decided the best thing she could do was spend as much time as possible with him while he was staying with her. It was clear from the way he kissed her the night before last that he found her attractive, but she also knew he was cut off from his usual social connections. He had probably never gone so long without female companionship, and she had to consider a possible connection between that and her suddenly looking good to him. Still, it warmed her heart when he said he had gotten a taste of what he was missing. She was going to do her best to drive that point home, show him what he could have if he was willing to settle down.

At a quarter to five she had her hand on the receiver when someone called out her name. She removed her hand and forced herself to sound jovial. "Hi, Jim. What can I do for you?"

"I wanted to talk to you about getting my son a summer job. He's a junior in high school and has expressed an interest in chemistry, and I think it might be a good experience for him to work in the lab."

"I'm sorry, but we don't allow any kids to work in the lab since the explosion that Mr. Arndt's son caused two years ago." The man appeared a bit taken aback; she wasn't certain if it was because of the news itself or the way in which she delivered it. She probably should have forced a solemn note into her voice instead of sounding so cheerful, but at least he made a hasty retreat. *Good,* she thought. He should be able to figure out that if one of the VP's kids had done major damage, his own son didn't stand a chance of being hired. She grabbed the phone and began dialing, anxious to hear Zack's voice. "It's me. Everything okay?"

"Fine. You won't be late, will you?"

Was she imagining it or did he sound like he was eager to see her? "No."

"I forgot to tell you. I went down to visit with the Hugheses for a little while last night while you were out. Mrs. Hughes insisted we have dinner with them tomorrow night. Can you make it?"

"Yes. That was sweet of her. I'll bet they were surprised to see you all banged up."

"And even more to learn I'm staying with you. But don't worry, I explained we're not having a torrid affair."

She laughed, in spite of the sudden flush of heat in her face. "I'm calling to ask if you want to go to the supermarket with me. I know it's not very exciting, but at least it'll get you out of the apartment. If not, I'll stop on my way home."

"I'll go. After being in the house all day it'll be

fun to hang out in the produce department and sample the grapes and the cherries."

She laughed. "It sounds like I'll have to pretend I don't know you."

"Even if somebody notices me they won't say anything. People treat you different when they think you've been hit by a speeding bus."

She was still smiling as she straightened her desk in preparation for tomorrow's work, but she frowned when her line rang at five minutes to five. If there was anything that made her clench her teeth more than people who didn't tear coupons out of the sale circular until their totals had been tallied at the register, it was people who called just before she was getting ready to leave for the day. She grabbed the phone and tried to keep the irritation out of her voice as she greeted, "Human Resources. Vivian St. James."

The female voice on the other end was breathless. "Oh, Vivian, I'm so glad I caught you."

She frowned. "Who's this?"

"I'm sorry. It's Sharon from the lab."

"What's up?"

"I don't know how to tell you this . . ."

She no longer tried to conceal her frustration. All she wanted to do was go home. "Tell me what?" she asked impatiently.

"The technician made an error. Dennis Chin is clean."

"What!"

"I'm so sorry, Vivian. Has he been let go?"

"You're damn right he has! The man was crying in my office. He kept repeating it was a mistake, and now you're telling me it was, even though this morning you were sure it wasn't. How could this happen, Sharon?"

"It was an error in labeling."

"Has this ever happened before?"

The answer came fast. "No, never."

"You realize he could sue you for this."

"He seemed like a nice young man. I'm hoping he'll be content to just get his job back. You *will* offer it to him, won't you?"

"I don't know. It's his boss's call. And if word's gotten out that he was terminated for testing positive for illegal substances he might not want to come back." But she doubted this was the case; Mel Norris wasn't the type to feel he owed explanations to his subordinates. "I need to reach him right away. I'll let you know what's happening tomorrow."

After an acknowledgment from Sharon, Vivian clicked over to an available line and poked out Mel's extension with her index finger. "Mel, Vivian St. James. You're not going to believe this. The lab just called me. They made an error labeling Dennis's specimen. He's clean."

He voiced his displeasure with a grunt.

"I'm sorry, Mel. It's not like it was my fault. I feel like a fool, having fired him. I need to know if you want me to offer him his job back."

"By all means. There should be no problem. I don't think anyone except my secretary even knew he was gone."

She sighed. At least Dennis wouldn't have to contend with endless jokes from his coworkers about the mishap. "I'll call him right now."

There was no answer at Dennis's home phone. She declined to leave a recorded message. This simply wasn't the type of message one left on someone's answering machine. She wrote the number down and put it in her purse. She'd try him later, from home.

When she got home Zack was in the kitchen, sitting in front of the stove on a step stool. "Hi. Ready to go to the store? I want to go now so I can make something for din—" she broke off, noticing the four small beef mounds in a shallow baking dish atop the stove at the same time a hint of barbecue sauce drifted toward her nostrils. What's this?"

"Dinner. It's meat loaf, my specialty. All I have to do now is add the dry potato mix to water and milk and mash them. I didn't want to do that until you were ready to eat. We can go to the store after."

"You are amazing, you know that?"

"I must confess, I'm a man of many talents. How was work?"

"You don't want to know. I fired someone this morning because he failed his drug test, and then the lab called back this afternoon and said they goofed."

"You're pulling my leg, right?"

"I wish. I'm trying to reach him to let him know they made a mistake and we'd love to have him come back."

Zack shook his head. "And I thought my job was stressful. Those people you work with are downright nutty."

"Not really. It's just that everything seems to be going wrong this week." She put down her purse and pulled out silverware and glasses for the table. "You're spoiling me, having dinner ready as soon as I walk in the door."

* * *

She tried without success to reach Dennis after dinner. Maybe he was somewhere venting, even though he'd had all day to do that.

Zack turned on the television to the news as she hung up, and suddenly she panicked. What if Dennis had done something crazy, like gone to the lab armed and taken hostages?

She took a seat next to him on the sofa. "Any big stories today?"

"Nothing that would make you want to pack up and leave the area."

Her shoulder muscles slackened. "Good." She always watched this station. Skye Audsley was her favorite reporter, and tonight he was anchoring. He was handsome in a movie-star way, and he wore no wedding band.

"I see Skye's got the anchor desk," Zack remarked. "I know he's happy about that, even if it's only because the regular guy's on vacation."

"You know him?"

"We got kind of tight after we showed up at some of the same functions. About a year ago he was engaged to Austin's old girlfriend." He chuckled. "Lucky for him he came to his senses and called it off."

"What happened?"

"He just realized how superficial his intended could be. She would have made him miserable. She would have made Austin miserable, too, or any man. She's just that type of woman."

"What happened to her?"

"I think she moved to Atlanta. She's big on image, and hers was ruined when Skye dumped her."

"Too bad, but from what you say she had it coming to her."

"She did."

When the sports segment came on she went to clean the kitchen. "Are you ready to go?" she asked when she was done.

They went to the gourmet supermarket, at Zack's insistence. As soon as they arrived he got behind the wheel of an electronic scooter with a built-in wire basket in front, zooming off with a jaunty wave in her direction. Vivian tried to catch up, but he moved too quickly. She walked past each aisle, looking for him and occasionally calling, "Zack?"

She found him by the butcher block, ordering steaks. "There you are. I was looking all over the store for you."

"Sorry about that. This thing really moves. They ought to reduce the speed. A lot of older people use this, and in the wrong hands it can really be dangerous."

"Are you all right, sir?"

Zack nodded to the teenager who wore a polo shirt with the store's name and logo sewn over the left breast.

"Please be careful. We wouldn't want you to get hurt."

She looked at Zack, not understanding. "What was that all about?"

"Oh, nothing. I had a little mishap. No big deal."

She watched the employee walk past several aisles, eventually joining a few of his coworkers who were picking up rolls of paper towels from the floor, restacking them in a pyramid-style arrangement at the end of the aisle. "Was your little mishap running into that display?"

"No harm done."

"Hmph. I'm glad you didn't knock over those glass bottles of apple juice next to it."

He turned his attention to the butcher, who handed him a paper-wrapped package. "Give me two of those lobster tails, too, please. I want the biggest ones you've got."

"Lobster!"

"You've been such a good sport about all this, the least I can do is make you a fabulous dinner on Friday. Uh . . . you didn't have any plans, did you?"

"No." The word was spoken softly; the thought of him leaving made her feel a little down.

"Good. I got some of those loaded twice-baked potatoes, too. And while we're here, I want to replenish your food supply."

"You don't have to do that, Zack."

"I insist." He tossed the wrapped lobster tails in the basket of the scooter with his other selections, then backed up.

"Doesn't it hurt your foot to press down on the pedal?"

"It just tingles a bit. Pressing down isn't quite the same as bearing weight. Okay, I'm off like dirty underwear." With that he depressed the pedal and took off once more.

She found him in the produce department, gently squeezing tomatoes. She watched as each inspection brought a frown to his face. "What's the matter, are they too soft?"

"Just picking them up leaves indentations." He reached higher on the diagonal pile, and before they realized what was happening the tomatoes began to spill to the floor in an avalanche of red balls, some of them making *splats* as they hit the floor.

Zack's expletive was lost in his rush to back away from the falling fruit. Vivian called frantically for help. Where was the produce clerk? Surely they didn't all go home at six o'clock.

"Damn. It didn't look like it was *that* many tomatoes," Zack said.

An apron-wearing man in his thirties appeared. "Oh, no," he said upon seeing the mess of red on the floor. "What happened?"

"It was an accident," Vivian and Zack said simultaneously, then looked at each other in amusement that quickly turned to guilt when they noticed the displeased look on the employee's face. She recognized him as one of the people who were restoring the paper towel display Zack had run into.

"I was trying to get a tomato from the top, and then they all came tumbling down like the walls of Jericho. I've got a leg injury and I'm not supposed to walk on it, and I can't reach too high being in this chair," Zack explained.

She knew he was trying for sympathy, but the clerk wasn't buying it. To him Zack was just an overgrown kid who wanted to see how the electronic scooter worked and was wreaking havoc in the store. He frowned at them, then went to the wall phone in the corner by the less popular vegetables like rutabagas. "Clean-up needed in produce," he said into the speaker.

"Let's get out of here," she hissed to Zack.

"Wait a sec. I haven't had any grapes, yet."

"Forget the free samples and just throw some in a bag to eat at home. You don't live in this area, but *I* might want to come back here one day."

They got in line behind a couple in their fifties. Both husband and wife were quite heavy, and Vivian was glad to see they had included several desserts with their purchases. She would hate for their marriage to go on the rocks because one party repeatedly consumed all the Cherry Garcia.

The woman smiled at her warmly. "Did you ever find your son?"

"Yes, but now I think maybe I should have let him stay lost." She laughed, amused by the woman's misconception, then met the gaze of an obviously sheepish Zack.

Back at home, she made another attempt to reach Dennis. This time he answered.

"Dennis, I'm so glad I reached you. It's Vivian St. James from—" she started to say, "from work," but quickly amended it and named the company.

"Did those people tell you they made a mistake?"

"Well, yes, they did. But how did you know?"

"Because, like I told you, I don't do drugs."

"I'm sorry, Dennis. I'm only trying to do my job here. I did speak to Mel, and he would love it if you would come back to work tomorrow morning."

"I'll be there. Thank you, Vivian. This confusion has caused me a lot of grief, but I know it's not your fault."

"I'm glad. I'll see you tomorrow."

"How'd it go?" Zack asked when she hung up.

"If you ask me, he's getting ready for his testimony. He said something about being all stressed out over this. I half expected him to say he had an appointment tomorrow morning but would be in later."

"He probably saw a lawyer today."

"Oh. I hadn't thought of that."

"Don't sweat it." He turned on the computer and monitor. "Come on, let's see if you can still beat me at this game."

Chapter 12:
Enough Already

Vivian watched Zack descend the stairs on his crutches. She'd been so surprised to come home from work and see him inspecting his unwrapped ankle and taking a few awkward steps without the aid of his crutches. She could tell from his grimace that it still hurt, and he rewrapped it. She carried the wine and the dessert down the one flight . . . just in case.

They were greeted by both Mr. and Mrs. Hughes, as well as the appealing aroma of roasted pork.

Mr. Hughes patted Zack on the back affectionately. "I hope you'll be back on your feet again soon, my boy."

"It'll good to be back, even though I won't be doing any running for a while yet. I'm going to take off the bandage tomorrow and work it out so I can walk."

"You'll be running in no time."

"He has a follow-up tomorrow," Vivian said.

But Zack waved a hand in dismissal. "I'm not going to worry about going back. I know enough about orthopedics to know whether or not my ankle needs further attention."

"Your trip is coming up soon, isn't it?" Mrs. Hughes asked.

"In June. I've got time. I'll be running and doing push-ups by then."

"I'm glad." Mrs. Hughes noticed Vivian's quizzical expression. "It's so exciting. Zack is going on an African safari."

"You are?"

"In just about two-and-a-half months I'll be watching all those animals running free."

"This is incredible. So will I!"

It was his turn to be incredulous. "You are?"

"Yes. I'm going with a girl I grew up with. It's something we always said we would do when we were grown."

"I've wanted to go for a long time, too."

"Austin's been wanting to go, too," Mr. Hughes said, "especially since he's already been to West Africa. He'd probably be going with you if he wasn't getting married."

"Are you two actually going on the same trip?" Mrs. Hughes asked.

They looked at each other.

"Kenya," she said.

"Tanzania," he said.

Everyone laughed.

"Still, that's a heck of a coincidence," Mrs. Hughes remarked. She rose. "Excuse me, I'm going to put the food on the table. We can all sit down in about five minutes."

"Just get back safely," Mr. Hughes said to Vivian and Zack. "The wedding's just a few weeks later, and I know both Austin and Desirée want you two to be there."

* * *

Friday was designated casual dress at their offices, which meant most of the women wore slacks and the men tossed aside the tailored look for khakis. Vivian wanted to look nice for her lunch date with Timothy, so she chose a denim skirt with a dropped yoke and a white blouse. Jeans and T-shirts were not allowed, but a skirt made of jean fabric was acceptable.

She hoped today would be as calm as yesterday had been. Dennis Chin was back at work, Peter Arnold had given her another check with the correct payee, and all was quiet. It had been nice to take care of her responsibilities and go home to Zack for what she'd known would be a pleasant evening with the Hugheses. Since he had already explained to them how he had come to be staying at her apartment, there was no shock to cope with. Mrs. Hughes did ask if there was any romance going on when the two of them were clearing the table, and she laughed it off—convincingly, too, she thought.

But she was actually beginning to feel a little frantic. When she and Zack returned to her apartment after dinner, they exchanged chaste good nights, and she retreated to her bedroom.

Even the night before, when they had played a computer game after returning from the supermarket, there hadn't been the slightest hint of desire on his part. She was running out of time. Tonight was the last night they would have together. Tomorrow his sprain would officially become a thing of the past, and he would probably want to leave right after dinner.

She smoothed her short hair close to her head

with the aid of gel and applied her makeup. It was ironic, primping for one man while her thoughts were with another.

Timothy called at nine-thirty. "Hi! I hope we're still on for lunch."

"Sure. I'm looking forward to it."

"What time would you like to leave?"

"Twelve-thirty is a good time for me. It's right in the middle of the day."

"That's fine. I'll see you then."

The morning went by swiftly, and Timothy appeared promptly at twelve twenty-eight. He was wearing a long-sleeved collarless shirt tucked into cuffed dark trousers and a beige waist-length zippered jacket.

He suggested a nearby seafood restaurant, and she agreed. She ordered coconut-fried shrimp, and he requested the shrimp scampi.

"Someone at the office must have told you about this place," she remarked after the waitress had taken their menus. "It's kind of hard to stumble across accidentally."

"Yes, one of the accountants recommended it to me. I usually get here once a week. Their scampi is the best I've tasted."

She was glad he was familiar with the bistro. Neptune's Catch had a capacity of less than one hundred and was nestled in a woodsy section of a Westchester village too small to be included on any map. It was the only restaurant she knew of that didn't accept credit cards, a set up which she knew had caused at least one person considerable embarrassment. She remembered Glenda telling her about one of the executives coming to her for a loan from the petty cash fund to reimburse his secretary. He had taken her to lunch for her birthday, and upon presenting an American Express card to pay the bill and being told it was cash only, his secretary had to ante up because he only had fifteen dollars on him.

Over lunch they participated in the obligatory exchange of background information, learning that they were both from Connecticut—Timothy hailed from Bridgeport—and had attended the same college. He was divorced, with two children, seventeen and twenty, and since he mentioned the year of his college graduation, she was able to put his age at forty-seven or forty-eight, a little younger than her initial belief. It made her feel better. Fifty frightened her; it was so distant. She wasn't even forty yet.

He called her office a little over an hour after they returned. "I just wanted to say I enjoyed having lunch with you, Vivian. I hope we can do it again."

His voice sounded softer than usual and a little strained. "Are you all right?"

"I've got a little stomachache, but I'm sure I'll live."

"Oh, I'm sorry."

She called him back at four-thirty. "Just thought I'd check how you were feeling."

"Actually, it's getting worse. You just caught me. I've been away from my desk for half of the afternoon, and now I'm getting ready go home."

"Can you take my home number? I'd really like to know how you're feeling a few hours from now, and I don't know how to reach you."

"Sure. I've got a pen here. Shoot."

Glenda showed up at her door a few minutes later, after Timothy had hung up with a promise to call her. "Now, I want to know everything that happens with you and Zack, and don't leave out anything."

"All right."

"Don't be blue, Viv. It'll be all right. You'll see him again."

"Actually, I wasn't thinking about Zack. I was thinking about Timothy."

"Timothy? Why are you thinking about him? I know you had a good time at lunch and all, but—"

"He hasn't been feeling well since lunch. I'm a little worried. Why is it every man I go out with either has an accident or gets sick?"

"Not every man, Viv. Remember, Bernard was complaining of pain even before you met him. It's true that Zack fell, but it's not like the two of you ever dated."

"Thanks for reminding me."

"It's just one of those weird coincidences. Have you talked to Timothy in the last hour or so? Maybe he's feeling better."

"I just talked to him. He went home."

"He did? Wow, he must really be feeling crummy. Those auditors might not show up until nine-thirty, but they're usually still here at seven. I got suckered into staying late one Friday night to help with some project Accounting was doing, and when I left at six-thirty they were still plugging away. I can't imagine putting in that many hours, unless I was working for myself. But try not to be too concerned. You don't want it to put a damper on your evening with Zack."

On the drive home Vivian's thoughts began to shift from Timothy to Zack. It was true that she

could do nothing about Timothy's condition, but
she did hope he would call and say the spell had
passed and he was back to normal. This business
with Gary's lacerated arm, Gordon's ankle sprain,
and Bernard's ulcer was too much. No wonder
Zack had dubbed her the angel of the accident
prone. At least this was one incident he had no
way of knowing about.

She found Zack in the kitchen, struggling to cut
through a lobster shell with a long knife . . . and
standing on his own two feet. "Hi! How's the
foot?"

"Feeling pretty good, now that I've had all day
to get it in shape. It felt really weird at first, but
it's definitely strong enough to support me. Do you
have any more knives? This one seems dull. I found
your sharpener, but it doesn't seem to have made
a whole lot of difference. Oh, wait, there it goes."
He guided the knife down the length of the shell.

"Sorry. I'm not much for carving. That one knife
usually serves my purposes."

"Well, next time we have dinner you're coming
to my place. I've got everything a cook can want."

She looked at him, startled. Next time?

"Can I help you do anything?" she offered when
he didn't elaborate on what he meant by *next time*.

"You can set the table, I guess. There really isn't
much to do. The steaks are broiling now. The salad
is in the fridge, and the potatoes just have to be
heated."

"I'm going to change, and then I'll set the table."

On the way to her bedroom she noticed his duffel bag on the floor by the coffee table, all zipped
up, next to his television. She stared at the items
for a few moments, then hurried in to change.

In her bedroom she removed her skirt and slip and pulled on a pair of jeans that felt tighter than usual around her waist and thighs. She'd eaten larger dinners than usual all week because of Zack's cooking, and then there was that fried shrimp and all that bread at lunch today. Tomorrow when she lunched with Lauren Walters she would order a simple soup and salad. Soon it would be summer, and there was no way to hide extra pounds while wearing a swimsuit.

Twenty minutes later they sat down to dinner. Zack held up his wine glass. "Here's to a caring lady who took me in when I had nowhere else to go."

His seriousness surprised her. "Are you trying to make me cry? You talk like a homeless person, not the owner of a four-story brownstone that probably has a dozen rooms."

"All right, I'll amend that. But you've taken good care of me, and I know it hasn't been easy to do that, plus go about dealing with your own life."

She decided to be honest. "It's not like there's so much going on in my life, Zack."

"Oh, I don't know about that. You seem to have a pretty full plate to me. You're busy at the office, you'll soon be going on the trip of a lifetime, and I happen to know that you date a lot. I'm sure not every man you've gone out with since New Year's has ended up as one of my patients."

She made a noncommittal murmur, not wanting to admit that the odds were a lot higher than he thought. Of course, if Timothy decided to see a doctor, it would be someone in the Stamford area.

"Sometimes we get so involved with the day-to-day stuff that we don't realize how full our lives are. Speaking of the day-to-day stuff, I'm due back at work tomorrow afternoon."

She kept her voice casual. "I'll bet you're anxious to get home."

"I've been very comfortable here, but you know what they say—there's no place like home."

She'd known all along that he would be leaving after dinner. He was moving about fine, and there was no need for him to stay longer. Still, there was a dull ache at the base of her throat that she knew was disappointment.

He insisted on helping her clean the kitchen. "I have to do this when I'm at home, you know."

"Yeah, but you've got a dishwasher." She instantly regretted having said the words. The kitchen was on the first floor in the rear. His bedroom, where he kept his clothes and where she was supposed to have been, was on the second floor. She'd just put her foot in it, telling him that she'd helped herself to a tour of his home.

Zack graciously did not comment on her blunder. "True, but that's only a small part of cleaning a kitchen. I think this past week may have spoiled both of us. You won't want to cook and I won't want to clean."

And then it was time for him to leave.

He picked up his duffel bag and portable television, but put them down when he reached the door and turned to her.

Her heartbeat raced. Surely he wouldn't leave without kissing her. . . .

He took her hands in his, then raised her right hand and kissed the back of it. His eyes never left her face. As he lowered her hand he continued to hold it. In a smooth motion he let go and slid his hands up the length of her arms. When he reached her shoulders he drew her close to him, saying just one word before he kissed her hungrily.

"Vivling. . . ."

She accepted his embrace like she'd known it all her life. When the kiss ended they just stared at each other, and then he put an arm around her, encouraging her to rest her head on his shoulder.

"This is a lot harder than I thought it would be," he said.

She didn't respond right away, too happy to be nestled in the space between the back of his ear and his shoulder, enjoying the warm tingling from being so close to him. "I can help you downstairs."

"No, I can manage. I'm all cured, remember?" He let go of her and bent to get his belongings, slipping the duffel bag onto his right shoulder and grasping the television with his stronger right arm. "Thank you," he said simply. Then he was gone.

She closed the door behind him. With him gone her cozy apartment seemed to have lost all its life. Her first thought was to grab her purse and drive somewhere, anywhere noisy and full of people. But she had to give Zack a chance to leave first; he would think she was chasing after him.

The ringing of the telephone was a welcome distraction. She grabbed the receiver and voiced a pleasant greeting.

"Vivian? It's Timothy. I wanted to see how you were feeling."

"I'm fine. The question is, how are *you?*"

"I just left the emergency room. They diagnosed me with gastroenteritis. It had to be the shrimp."

"Oh, how awful!"

"It's a mild case. Since you had shrimp also I just wanted to make sure you're all right."

"That was thoughtful of you. I'm fine, actually. I'm glad you'll be all right."

"Yes, they had me hooked up to an IV for a couple of hours for hydration and for medication. I'll be at work on Monday. Maybe we can do lunch again next week . . . somewhere different, of course."

When their conversation ended she felt even worse. Learning that her latest date had developed food poisoning, no matter how mild, did little for her ego.

She walked over to the armoire and opened it. Getting involved in the strategy involved in attempting to conquer the world was just what she needed to get over her low mood.

She turned on the computer and pulled one of the chairs around to face the screen. As she waited for the machine to boot up, she noticed a small white envelope to its left and picked it up. 'Vivling' was written across it in bold printed strokes. Maybe it was a note, something that would make her smile . . . and something that would make her forget that he hadn't even asked for her phone number when he left.

She used the letter opener she kept inside the drawer to open it. It wasn't a note, but three fifty-dollar bills.

She stared at the money for a long time. When her desktop came up on the screen, she shut it down and turned it off, leaving the envelope and its contents exactly where she had found it. Five minutes later she was on her way to the spa. They didn't have a punching bag, but any frenzied activity was in order.

Chapter 13:
What Goes Around
Comes Around

"Well, I don't know, Bev," Vivian said into the receiver. "You know how badly it went between Thomas and me, and I'd be sure to run into him at a party at your house."

"Oh, don't worry about him. He's in the hospital."

"In the hospital? What happened?"

"Gallstones. He'll be fine."

"Well, as much as I don't want to run into him, I'm sorry to hear he's in the hospital. I wouldn't wish that on anyone."

"It's about time he's had them taken out. They've been bothering him for months now. I think it goes back to around the time he met you."

Vivian sank back into the cushions, and part of her wished she could drown in them. "All right, Bev. I'll see you Saturday."

* * *

Vivian smoothed her dress. She felt a little uncomfortable going to a party alone, but Glenda was on a date with a man she had met at the NBP-sponsored bowling tournament, and none of the other few people she knew in the area could make it. Since Beverly and John lived on a residential street in the Westchester hamlet of Elmsford, and because it was clear night with none of the mist and dark shadows reminiscent of Jack the Ripper, she decided to go.

Because Beverly and John were married she figured most of the people they knew would be married as well. She had no expectations of meeting anyone here, but she needed to get out. The dismal note on which Zack's stay had ended, as well as the knowledge that Thomas Joseph also had not been spared misfortune after crossing her path made her very morose, and she could count the times she'd smiled in the last week on the fingers of one hand. Everyone had noticed her melancholy mood, and a concerned Glenda had offered to break her date in order to go to the party with her, but Vivian assured her she was fine with going alone.

She felt buoyed from the moment she first heard the music, which was loud but not eardrum damaging, and felt better still at the sight of attractive people mingling in small groups in the living and dining rooms. Beverly introduced her to a few people, and soon she was standing with a group of women who, judging from their hushed tones, were gossiping. She had joined them because they were female, but it had clearly been a mistake. "I'm sorry. I didn't mean to interrupt." She turned to find another group to join when the woman named Tina stopped her. "Oh, don't go. We didn't mean to shut you out. It's just that we're all feeling so bad for poor Gordon."

"Gordon?"

"One of the guys who's here. He had made special plans for tonight because it was the birthday of the girl he was seeing, and she canceled on him with some excuse, and then she shows up here on the arm of another fellow."

"Oh, how awful! Is Gordon still here, or did he leave?"

"He's still here. Right now he's dancing. He's putting on a good front, but what else can he do?"

"If he leaves he'll lose face," another woman agreed.

"It just goes to show, Westchester is a small place. You never know who knows who," the third woman added.

Vivian only half listened as the women exchanged remarks about it being a small world. She was rapidly losing interest in the saga of "poor Gordon" and wondered how all of them had even found out about his humiliating situation. Then again, that was the way of parties. All it took was one person to know the inside scoop, and the story spread faster than the flu.

From there the women went on to discuss how Gordon didn't stand a chance against the good-looking escort the two-timing woman had arrived with. "I don't know. If I was her and he called me, I might have done the same thing."

"He's *so* fine."

"Did you see those eyes? They practically glowed in the dark."

"Do you suppose they're real, or is he wearing contacts? He's kind of brown to have blue eyes."

"I remember my grandmother had blue eyes and

she was dark brown, but it had something to do with her cataracts."

"Anyone else would look like a freak of nature, but on him they look good. I'm sure they're real. Men don't get into colored contact lenses; it's just us women who like to experiment with eye color."

The mention of an exceedingly handsome man with blue eyes piqued Vivian's attention. She carefully scanned the room, which wasn't that large, but her eyes were still adjusting to the dim lighting. She didn't see anyone who looked like Zack, but who else could the women be talking about? Apparently not only was Westchester small when it came to single thirty-something African-American professionals, but so was the entire New York metropolitan area.

She gestured to Beverly as she was about to pass by, stepping away from the others and spoke as softly as possible while still being heard above the loud music. "Do you know if there's a man here named Zack Warner?"

"Zack? Yeah, I think so. Does he have blue eyes?"

"Yes."

"He's involved in Big Brothers with John. You know him?"

"Yes."

"I wish you'd invited him. He caused a hell of an uproar with that woman he showed up with."

"If this is about poor Gordon, I've already heard the story."

"I feel terrible, since I'm the one who invited him. He works with me and is a nice guy, nice-looking, too. I was so surprised to see him, since he'd told me he couldn't make it because he had a big night planned. He'd made dinner reservations and bought theater tickets. At least he was able to sell the tickets to somebody when she canceled on him." She shook her head. "Women who do things like that give all of us a bad name. But at least he's hiding his hurt well."

Vivian looked in the same direction as Beverly. "Wait a minute. It's Gordon *Wilson?*"

"Yes. You know him, too?"

"Yes. The son-of-a-gun stood me up a couple of months ago, and now I'll bet I know why. This girl must have told him she wanted to see him, and he unloaded me like the proverbial hot potato."

"That's too bad, but at least you were able to keep the incident to yourself. I think the story of what happened to him has gotten around to everybody here."

"I do feel sorry for him, but I can't help thinking that what goes around comes around. So where are Zack and the girl, Bev?"

"I think they're out on the patio. John asked everyone who wants to smoke to go out there. He's afraid someone might burn a hole in our brand new furniture. Besides, that hussy is probably too ashamed to show her face inside, as well she should be."

"Thanks." All she could do was wait for them to come back in. She wasn't about to go out there looking for him. She hadn't seen or heard from Zack since he'd left her apartment over a week ago, and she was still smarting from the way he'd left the money for her. It seemed so cold, so impersonal, not to mention too much. She hadn't done anything for him that warranted him giving her a hundred and fifty dollars. The money was still sitting in the envelope inside her armoire. If she'd known he was going to be at this party she would have brought it so she could return it to him.

She was asked to dance and promptly got caught up in the music. She'd forgotten how good it felt to dance. Next time she had the blues she would put on some music and dance up a storm in the privacy of her living room.

When the song ended she and her partner thanked each other, and, feeling a tap on her shoulder, turned and saw Zack. "Hi! Hey, are you following me?" The lightheartedness of her tone surprised her.

"I thought that was you. And I'm not following you, not that that's a bad idea." He looked around. "Are you with someone?"

"No, but I hear *you* are." She regretted the words as soon as they were out. Zack blinked, and his eye color appeared to darken, like he'd been wounded. It was her own hurt feelings that had made her lash out. *She* was the one he should have brought with him, not some other woman.

"I'm not staying. I just apologized to Gordon."

"The way I heard the story it wasn't really your fault."

"No, it wasn't. When I invited Sherry to this party she didn't mention she was going to cancel the plans she'd already made. I felt bad for him, and I wanted to tell him I was sorry. Sherry was someone he obviously thought highly of."

The sincerity in both his expression and his voice reminded her of that night in the ER when he was treating the little girl whose face had been cut. She'd learned from Beverly that he served as a Big Brother, another indication of his sensitivity. Still, his thoughtfulness stung her ego. He was being so considerate of everyone else's feelings but hers. Didn't he consider her worthy of dating? Did he really believe she would bring him bad luck? What about the kisses they shared at her apartment? Surely he had derived as much pleasure from them as she had. But instead he left her home without even asking her for her phone number, leaving money in an envelope, like theirs was a business relationship, and of an unsavory nature. She wished she could just come out and ask him just how he regarded her.

She forced her curiosity aside. "How did he react?"

"He was a gentleman, and he appreciated *my* being a gentleman. I think it's safe to say that Sherry no longer ranks as a possible date for either of us. But because he really cared about her, giving her up will be a lot harder for him than it will be for me."

"Well, I'm sure you won't have to make too much effort to find another date. There are plenty of possibilities right in this room." She met his gaze squarely in a silent dare for him to get the point.

He stared at her wordlessly, his gaze holding hers. He opened his mouth to say something, but in an instant what he had been about to express was lost.

"There you are. I thought you'd forgotten about me, Zack."

Vivian watched as a woman slipped her arm through his. She was petite, her shapely figure shown to its fullest advantage in a clingy shell with matching cardigan, and short, tight skirt. It had to be the notorious Sherry. A closer look revealed this was the same woman who had intercepted Zack as they left the dance floor at the NBP Valentine's dance. From the cozy way she was smiling at Zack,

Vivian guessed he hadn't told her she had lost her position on his hit parade.

"I think it's time for us to be leaving," Zack said without emotion.

Sherry gave Vivian one of those triumphant smiles that said *keep away, he's taken,* and moved on. Vivian pretended not to see. If there was anything she disliked more than people who took two parking spaces to protect vehicles that were already dented and scratched, it was a possessive female.

She almost laughed aloud when she saw Zack yank his hand away.

Zack couldn't get Sherry home to the Bronx quickly enough. He saw her to her apartment door, his tight-lipped demeanor leaving no doubts about his anger. Despite this, she had the gall to invite him in, her body pressed against his and arms around his neck extending an invitation she didn't need to put into words. But he couldn't stand conniving females. What would have been a pleasant evening was in ruins because of her dishonesty.

As he drove home to Harlem he thought of Vivian's comment about possible dates amongst the females at the party. He knew the unspoken message—that the best possible choice was standing before him. He had been about to take her up on her challenge when Sherry appeared.

The truth was that he'd thought about her ever since he left her apartment last Friday. The time spent with her there had forced him to think deeply about his attitudes. He had never lacked for feminine attention ever since he was a child. The same girls who teased him about his unusual coloring in the schoolyard managed to fall into step beside him when classes let out. The behavior became more aggressive in higher education, and in nearly twenty years of dating he learned quite a bit about the female species, what so many of them wanted in a man. He was attentive, charming, witty, and truly cared about what was important in their lives, but few had made a real impact on him or stayed on his mind when an evening ended, which, more often than not, was the next morning.

There had only been two involvements that had become serious. One had fallen apart during medical school, the other during residency. Preparation for careers in medicine, as well as the early years of work, didn't mix well with relationships. All the men he knew who had married while in med school were now divorced, and some were on the second, and hopefully last, go-round.

Then there was the dollar-sign factor, as he had dubbed the reaction he sometimes got from women who learned about his initials—the MD, not the ZW—and immediately became caught up in the idea of what that would mean for them. If real life was a cartoon, these material mongers would blink, during which time their irises and pupils would be replaced by dollar signs that went ka-*ching*, ka-*ching*, as they imagined the lives of luxury that awaited them if they could snare him. At first he'd found it amusing, but as time went on he saw it for the insult it was and avoided anyone whose eyes gave that telltale look.

He had been a carefree bachelor for a good number of years now, but he was in no hurry to settle down and get married. He missed Austin, of course, since his move out West, but he'd sensed his friend had been searching for his Ms. Right for a long time. Unlike himself, Austin had always

pretty much been a one-man woman, to the point
of dating one woman exclusively for over a year,
which had given her the mistaken impression that
they were moving toward something more permanent. He could still hear Austin's bewilderment before he'd broken it off with her. "I never told her
I loved her," he'd said. "How could she think we
were serious?"

Zack had explained to him that simply not pro-
fessing love wasn't enough to prevent a woman
from getting the wrong idea. As weeks turned into
months of steady companionship, a woman was going to think they were headed for the altar, no matter how slow the journey. "That's why I go out with
so many different women. I'd rather humble myself
by calling after two or three months and learning
they're seeing someone steadily than see them over
two consecutive weekends and let them think
they've hit pay dirt." On those occasions when he'd
been told that the object of his desire was now in
an exclusive relationship with someone else, he felt
no embarrassment, he just wished her sincere happiness and moved on to the next phone number.
There were no bad feelings, and actually he was
frequently a guest at the nuptials of former flames.

He had his routine down pat, but he didn't know
what to do with Vivian. She hadn't seemed particularly impressed with either his looks or his medical
degree when they first met, and he liked that. Of
course, he told himself it probably had something
to do with the unusual circumstances. He'd met
women in all kinds of situations and conditions—
one time a minor traffic accident had led to a
memorable, but brief, fling—but never one who
had come into the ER accompanying a date. Her
thoughts that day appeared to have been with that

dude she was with, Gary, if he remembered correctly. He still remembered the relief he felt when he learned they had just met, but when he couldn't think of a way to approach her he forced himself to forget about her, telling himself he'd never see her again.

He had considered meeting up with her again on the NBP ski trip a marvelous stroke of good luck, but he had blown it by suggesting she was a jinx when the guy she was skiing with hurt his ankle. The closest he'd gotten to asking her out was at the Valentine's dance. The only thing that stopped him was the attention she was getting from Bernard, but when he held her that night as they danced he experienced a unique blend of excitement and contentment that he had never had before and didn't have again until he spent five days at her apartment. The time they spent together, talking over dinner and as they competed at computer games, ranked with his more special memories.

He'd thought about taking her out for dinner that last night instead of cooking at home—there were plenty of casual-but-nice restaurants that wouldn't object to the jeans that were the only form of trousers he had with him—but he was afraid of breaking the magic they had inside her apartment. He believed in the old proverb, 'If it ain't broke, don't fix it,' and besides, he'd already made more mistakes than he should have with her, and he was determined not to make any more. He hadn't even taken her home phone number. He did have her work number, but he was afraid to use it. He knew he would see her again. When he returned from safari he would contact her about their plans to fly out to Colorado together. That

was a month and a half away, but if he felt like he
absolutely, positively had to see her, he did know
where she lived. . . .

Chapter 14:
Grazing in the Grass

Vivian was captivated by the family of elephants walking the plain just yards away from their vehicle, two small ones led by a huge one she assumed was their mother. She was awed by the size of the adult animal. Her ears alone were a good four feet wide. The guide was explaining that young elephants often stay with their mothers for as long as ten years. She'd never thought of animals as having families or staying together like humans, at least beyond infancy. She noted it was a single parent family. Had daddy elephant gone after a younger model? How would one elephant even know another elephant's age?

The elephants plodded on, and it soon became apparent that the family was headed toward a nearby stream. The driver stopped to allow the safari participants to watch the family go into the water and dip their trunks to drink.

"Look, Viv. Giraffes!"

At the sound of Lauren's voice she turned her attention to the windows on the right side of the minibus. Their party of eighteen plus guides rode in three vehicles, in which every passenger had a window seat. Two giraffes, their caramel-colored hides decorated by white mosaic designs, nearly blended into the bush. They were breathtakingly beautiful, managing to look almost graceful with their incredibly long necks.

She was five days into what was turning out to be the trip of her dreams, and this was the first day they were actually viewing game. It had taken the better part of twenty-four hours just to get to Nairobi—an overnight flight to London, followed by a connection to Kenya the following day. When their party arrived at the Jomo Kenyatta Airport in Nairobi that night they were brought to their resort hotel, where they spent a restful evening after the long trip, followed by a day of leisure and partaking in the activities their accommodations offered: Swimming, tennis, and squash. Vivian had allowed Lauren, a regular golfer, to get her on the course for nine holes. It had taken another day to reach the Samburu National Reserve, the site of their first tented camp, driving over abysmal roads. The distance the Americans in the group had traveled was staggering; they had gone nearly halfway around the world.

She and Lauren had opted to rough it on a tented safari rather than one where nights were spent at lodges. The sight of tents that had been erected by the safari staff, who had arrived well before the rest of the group to set up camp, came as somewhat of a shock to their systems after the luxury of the hotel that had hosted them their first two nights on the continent, but at least the tents were insectproof, with comfortable cots; and a separate tent with a shower and toilet was just steps away.

And the food was incredible. Their dinner last night, served in a long three-sided tent, had rivaled what she'd had in fine restaurants stateside. The meat was tender, the vegetables crisp, and the potatoes had melted in her mouth. She could hardly believe it all had been prepared outdoors in the heart of the bush. "These people would probably be miserable if they had to work in the confines of a kitchen," Lauren had whispered. The setting was as elegant as the food was delicious; tablecloths, china, candles on the table—Vivian suspected they were citronella, to deter insects—and the maître d' hovering nearby only added to the ambience.

They returned to the camp for a buffet-style lunch before taking another game drive in the afternoon. There were no real roads to speak of. They drove over the earth, and acceleration of the minibus made the dust fly. Each dual-occupancy tent had accompanying facilities, and everyone was anxious to clean up and perhaps rest a bit before dinner. They had been driving most of the day in search of big game, and no one really realized how tiring it was until it was over. Vivian also wanted to see the sunset, which had dazzled her the night before.

Freshly showered and changed, she stood staring at the rapidly darkening horizon, the sun a blazing orange ball so low she knew it would soon disappear completely, and the sky varying shades of purple. The silvery clouds were partially blocked by the tremendous lone flat-topped thorn tree in the foreground, its trunk gnarled and its wide branches proudly proclaiming it as master of all it surveyed. She snapped pictures, grateful that she could preserve the image of the awesome tableau.

"It's got the be the most beautiful sight on earth," Lauren said solemnly.

"This is wonderful, isn't it?"

"It's everything I dreamed it would be, and more. The guide was saying how lucky we were to have seen so many animals. There was no guarantee we'd see any, and we saw elephants, giraffes, a zebra, and a leopard. Or at least a leopard's tail hanging from a tree."

Vivian laughed. "And did you see how quick Ken and George got out of the pop top when they saw that tail?"

"I would have gotten out of there, too. It looked like it was sleeping, but you never know when it might wake up and jump down on them. But it was kind of funny, the way the two of them were knocking each other over to get back inside."

Vivian was delighted to see that there was another campfire set up after dinner. Last night all eighteen participants had sat in comfortable canvas director's chairs arranged in a circle around the yellow-orange fire, sipping coffee and drinks and enjoying the warmth the crackling flames provided in addition to the jackets or sweaters they all wore to ward off the cool weather that came with sundown.

Tonight they again gathered around the fire, and she learned this was a safari tradition. Low square tables covered with dark green tablecloths held drink glasses, coffee cups, and ashtrays. Most of the group came from the US, Britain, and Germany. There were three married couples, a father and son, a grandmother and teenage granddaughter, and eight singles: Vivian, Lauren, and six men. The group's ages ranged from fifteen to sixty-four. Vivian was the only brown face among them, but she wasn't surprised. She knew many African-Americans went to the culture-rich countries of West Africa, and if she hadn't always dreamed of going on safari she probably would have been one of them.

The following days were a happy mix of game-viewing days at two additional national parks and cool nights around a fire. Their last day in camp coincided with Vivian's thirty-fifth birthday, and the vanilla-frosted birthday cake she was presented with that night after dinner came as a pleasant surprise. "How did you know it was my birthday?" she asked the white-clad chef after she blew out the seven candles.

"Miss Lauren told us."

She smiled at her friend. "I should have known. But now I'm kind of glad she did."

Six of their group had purchased the Kenya Coast Option, which was three nights and two days in the beach town of Diani. Vivian marveled at the bright blue water of the Indian Ocean. At the edge of the beach, a concrete staircase led to the pool of their hotel. Large, square portions of the concrete had been dyed pastel colors, and the aqua water of the lagoon-shaped pool glistened in the ever-present sunlight, with shade available for those who preferred it, courtesy of a generous number of palm trees at the edge of the concrete.

Despite the prettiness of the pool area, it was the beach where she and Lauren spent most of their time. Swimming in a chlorinated pool was not a big deal, but the opportunity to frolic in the Indian

Ocean might not ever come again, so they spent an afternoon windsurfing and snorkeling before having dinner and exploring the lively local nightlife.

The next morning, which would be their last full day in Africa, they put on shorts and gym shoes and set out on foot to do some exploring. Diani consisted mostly of hotels, restaurants, and retailers, but the accommodations were of differing architectural types, ranging from mid-rise structures of glass and steel to individual thatched roofed villas. It was on the grounds of the latter type that they came across a huge boabab tree with a hole in its trunk at eye level large enough to climb into.

"I'll take a picture of you inside the tree," Lauren suggested.

Vivian hastily shook her head. "No, thanks. There might be snakes hiding in there."

"Nah. There aren't a lot of snakes here. I read that most of them are on snake farms."

"What about ants?"

"You just came off a safari and saw wild animals in their natural habitats, Vivian. You think you're going to be done in by ants at the beach? That's like climbing all the way to the top of Mount Kilimanjaro and then being afraid to look down."

"Okay, *you* get in and I'll take *your* picture."

Lauren called out to a young man wearing khakis and with a brass name pin on his red polo shirt, just above the hotel's logo. "Excuse me. Can you tell us if it's safe to climb inside this tree?"

"Yes, ma'am. It's very popular with all the guests. We keep a step stool inside. You might have to stoop a bit to have a picture taken, even on the bottom step; but we suggest you refrain from stepping on the ground because of the possibility of insects. Also, a lot of children like to climb in, and the stool gives them the height needed so they can look out." He glanced at Vivian. "Would you like me to take a photograph of both of you inside?"

"Sure!" Lauren said enthusiastically. "C'mon, Viv." She handed the employee her camera and grabbed hold of the trunk at the opening. "Shucks. It's too high to climb into."

"I'll get you a footstool," the employee offered. "Just a moment."

"What a great photo this will be," Lauren said when he was gone.

"We'll have to give him a tip for his trouble. I feel a little guilty. He probably thinks we're guests here, or else he wouldn't be so helpful."

"No problem. A tip's a tip, whether we're guests or not. Oh, here he comes. That building he came out of must be where they keep the lawn mower and stuff."

The young man was coming out of a small structure a few yards away, carrying a flashlight and a folding step stool, which he promptly set up in front of the tree. He inspected the inside of the trunk with the light and then motioned for Lauren to go ahead. Within seconds Lauren was inside and was beckoning to Vivian.

She was still reluctant. "I don't know. Are you sure there's enough room in there for two of us?"

"Are you kidding? This tree is humongous. I think only a giant redwood is bigger."

She reluctantly climbed the stool and put one leg inside, balancing herself on the thick bark, her upper body outside the trunk. "Where's the stool?" she asked, frantically waving her leg in the darkness in search of terra firma.

"Right here."

She was startled when Lauren grabbed her leg and held it over the stool, but then gingerly slid down, her left leg automatically raising until her right foot reached the step, when she could comfortably bend it to get it inside. "Ooh, this is creepy. It's so dark!" Her voice sounded as hollow as the tree bark.

"I thought it would be better once you were in here, but I guess not." Lauren waved to the employee. "Okay, you can snap now. Two with each camera ought to do it, in case one doesn't come out right."

He moved the stool to the other side of the massive trunk, where it would not be visible, then stepped back to get as much of the tree in the shot as possible. As Lauren had requested, he took two pictures with each of their cameras.

The moment he began walking back toward them they began scrambling to be the first to get out. The more agile Lauren won, getting one leg out on her first attempt. She climbed up and slid out, and although she stood right outside the tree, Vivian felt more uneasy than ever. She carefully took a step up—the last thing she wanted was to lose her balance and fall in the darkness—and held on to the bark as she lifted her leg, balanced herself and slipped her upper body out.

Lauren had again taken possession of their cameras and was reaching into her purse, presumably to compensate the employee for his assistance. Throughout their posing they had caught the attention of hotel guests along the path, who usually stopped and pointed with amusement, but she noticed something achingly familiar about one of the two men who had stopped to look. She froze, half-in and half-out of the tree. It *couldn't* be. . . .

But as he and his companion came closer there was no mistaking his identity, and she remained transfixed as Zack moved closer, until he stood directly in front of her.

"Dr. Livingstone, I presume?"

Chapter 15:
Sailing

"I still can't believe it, Zack, running into you halfway around the world like this."

"I was pretty shocked myself. I wondered if it was really you I was seeing or if I'd been out in the proverbial sun too long."

They were at an open air restaurant on the hotel grounds. Vivian had been stunned to see Zack, to the point where she had frozen in her precarious position and he wordlessly helped her out of the tree, his hands firmly ensconced in the area just below her armpits and just above her breasts, giving her no choice but to put her arms around his neck and hold on as he swung her out and to the ground. The close contact of the sink-or-swim position, her front brushed against his, made her forget herself and possibly had the same effect on him, for neither of them moved out of it once her feet were on the ground. They merely stared at each other with undisguised longing. Only Lauren's discreet throat-clearing, followed by a request for introductions, prompted them to break apart, flustered. Zack introduced his travel companion Bill Byrd, and she introduced Lauren.

Then Zack suggested lunch, casually reaching for her hand and holding it until he pulled out her chair at their table.

The waiter appeared and took their drink order. "I'd like a vodka with grapefruit juice, and I'd appreciate it if you could bring that right away, please," Vivian requested.

Her words came out in a monotone, like she was in a trance, prompting Zack to laugh. "You sound like you're in shock."

"Maybe I wouldn't be if you had mentioned you were coming to the coast of Kenya after you left Tanzania."

"I honestly didn't think of it, since we're only going to be here three days, two of which we lose about half a day because we're arriving and leaving, respectively. Today is our only full day here."

"Ours, too. I know you'll be flying out of Tanzania, but maybe we'll be on the same flight to London Wednesday."

Zack shook his head. "I wish we were, but our connection is through Amsterdam."

"How many were in your safari party?" Lauren asked.

"There were a dozen. Four of us went as a group, but the other two took the excursion to Victoria Falls," Zack answered.

"It was a hard choice to make," Bill added, "but I've always been a beach person, and I've seen the Atlantic and the Pacific Oceans but never the Indian. Maybe I'll get to the falls next time."

"We all work at the same hospital," Zack said. "Bill's an anesthesiologist."

Lauren asked which hospital that was, and Bill answering her directly was the beginning of their four-way conversation breaking up into two one-on-ones.

Vivian began to relax even before her drink was delivered. Perhaps all she really needed was to sit down. This was real. Zack was actually here in coastal Kenya. They would both be leaving in the morning, but that left the rest of the afternoon . . . and all of the night.

She noticed other diners smiling at them. They must have looked like a cozy foursome, since Bill Byrd, like Lauren, was Caucasian, and the two of them seemed to be carrying on an intense conversation.

"Did you guys see a lot of game?" she asked.

"Lions, tigers, and bears. Oh, my." He spoke in a childlike singsong fashion.

"Come on, Zack. I know there aren't any tigers in Africa. I don't think there are any bears here, either. It's too hot for them."

"Okay. We saw three elephants, a zebra, a lion, and a couple of different species of antelopes with funny names."

"You saw lions? I'm so jealous. We didn't see any. But we did catch a glimpse of a leopard napping in a tree."

"Now *I'm* jealous."

They continued to compare notes, and when Lauren and Bill rejoined the conversation they made plans to meet on the beach after lunch.

Vivian's hands shook as she brushed her hair. She tossed a small jar of gel into her bag. Yesterday a wire brush had been sufficient, but today she wanted to look perfect. She made sure the skirt of her azure two-piece swimsuit wasn't bunched up inside her cover-up, a white, strapless culotte that was no longer than a pair of shorts and barely extended past the skirt of her swimsuit. Sunglasses, white slip-ons and a white sailor hat completed the look.

"Imagine coming all this way and seeing someone you know," Lauren said on the way downstairs.

"I knew he was taking a safari in June, but he said he was going to Tanzania. He didn't mention the extension to the Kenyan coast."

"I wish we were spending more time here."

Vivian knew what her friend was thinking. "I have a feeling Bill isn't going to forget you, Lauren."

"And what about Zack? You two looked like you were about to spontaneously combust, and you've never even mentioned him to me."

She shrugged. "It's complicated," she said, knowing it sounded lame.

"Well, I think when you two get back to the States you should set about simplifying matters."

"We'll both be in Colorado next month."

"The wedding you're going to?"

"Yes. Desirée is a friend of his also. Actually, he's known her fiancé since they were kids. He's going to be the best man."

"I don't think Denver is as romantic a setting as Kenya, but I guess it'll have to do. Oh, I see them." Lauren waved.

When the parties met Zack took Vivian's arm and propelled her aside. "I've taken the liberty of renting a sailboat for the two of us."

"What about Lauren and Bill?"

"Bill said he can think of a lot of things worse than spending an afternoon alone with Lauren. Trust me; it's not a problem."

* * *

The boat swayed gently in the ocean water, safe from the waves that formed closer to shore. Neither Vivian nor Zack wore a life preserver, but the bulky orange vests were within easy reach.

"You know, we probably should wear these things. You never know what might happen," Zack said.

"Especially with me in the boat, huh?"

"That wasn't what I meant. The last time I kidded you about that you nearly bit my head off, remember?"

She shrugged. "I guess I've gotten over it." The truth was she was so happy to be sharing part of her African experience with him she didn't mind him joking about their history together.

"I think your confidence has been restored. Now that you've gotten through your safari without so much as a scratch, you're realizing all that other stuff was just flukes."

"It's not me I was worried about. It's the people *around* me who have things happen to them."

"No one can say that life with Vivling is dull."

"You're right, no one would say that. Because you're the only one who calls me Vivling."

"I don't know where I got that from, but it suits you. It's good to see you, Vivling. *All* of you." His eyes swept over her body in obvious appreciation.

"Thank you." She didn't feel in the least self-conscious of his appraisal of the skimpy cover-up she wore; instead she practically preened from his approval. She had lost five pounds and felt she looked pretty good. She felt equally favorable about his attire. If there was anything that turned her off more than people with dirt under their fingernails, it was men who wore those tight-fitting trunks that hugged their genitals. Zack's loose-fitting navy trunks were more discreet, as was the navy nylon sleeveless undershirt that covered most of his chest but allowed a full view of muscular arms and a hint of beefy pecs. She, too, had never seen so much of him; when he slept on the sofabed in her living room he had worn a crew neck T-shirt with sleeves. Zack was not a large man, but he was definitely well built.

"I was going to call you when I got home."

"That's a pretty neat trick, considering you don't have my number."

"No, but I know your work number."

"True. So what were you going to call me for?" *And whatever it is, why didn't you do it sooner?*

"I wanted to talk with you about flying out to Denver together. You haven't made your reservations yet, have you?"

"No, but it's at the top of the list of things to do when I get back. The wedding's on a Saturday, so I figured I'd go out Thursday and come home Sunday."

"That won't give you much time for sightseeing. Ozzie says it's beautiful out there. Or have you been there before?"

"No, this'll be my first time. I did want to save some of my vacation time. This trip took most of it."

"Why not go out on Wednesday? One day shouldn't make much difference. Remember, there won't be much free time on Saturday, and Friday will be cut short because of the rehearsal and dinner."

"Aren't you forgetting something, Zack? I'm not in the wedding party."

"No, but I thought it would be nice if you came with me to the dinner. I'm sure Desirée won't mind."

She didn't bother to conceal her happiness. Maybe now they would get somewhere. "Really?"

"Sure. And if you're coming to dinner you might as well come to the rehearsal. You can stand in for Desirée. You know how the bride never participates in the rehearsal drill; it's considered bad luck or something. Will you come?"

"Sure."

"Good. With you there I won't have to worry about Desirée's friends. Ozzie's warned me they're all man hungry."

Her good disposition promptly became a memory. "Is that the only reason why you want me to go with you, to protect you from famished females?" Her voice was like a scale, each word ascending as she approached the category where she would shatter glass.

"No, of course not. I'm sorry, Vivling. I don't know why I'm always saying such thoughtless things to you." He reached for her hand. "Maybe it's because I'm trying too hard to make you like me."

Her eyes widened; this was the last thing she expected to hear. She could feel the vitality flowing into the previously limp hand he held. "What makes you think I don't like you, Zack?"

"That probably wasn't the right choice of words. I want you to like me as much as I like you. I've been wanting to ask you out from the start, and especially after that week I spent at your place."

"And you thought I'd say no?"

"I didn't think I was your type. Remember, I've met a lot of your male friends, and I thought you went in for those corporate types. To be honest,

I'm not used to being turned down. I don't know if I could handle it."

"Maybe it wouldn't be an issue."

"Are you saying you'd go out with me?"

She laughed. "After all we've been through together, it would be a sin *not* to go out with you." It was incredible. The picturesque scenery of blue ocean water breaking into frothy waves crashing into the white sand had faded the moment he stated his reasons for wanting her to accompany him to the rehearsal and dinner, but his confession of wanting to spend time with her made everything brighten again. She had waited months to hear this and was beginning to think it would never happen, and now that it had, she couldn't remember the last time she had felt so happy.

Her joy was about to increase. Zack raised her chin with his index finger and was kissing her before she could blink. It was only when they felt the boat rock that they broke apart, laughing when each recognized the terror on the other's face.

"I guess we'd better keep an eye out for the ocean. What say we continue this after dinner?"

"Sounds like a plan."

They had dinner in the setting of an underground cave, then went dancing at the popular Bush Baby disco. Because their respective flights left early in the morning, all four of them agreed it wouldn't be a late night. Still, Lauren and Bill were still dancing like teenagers when Vivian and Zack returned to the women's hotel, a seven-story building that, unlike the more provincial setting where the fellows were staying, could have been anywhere in the world. They sat in the comfortable cushioned rattan chairs in the lobby and talked.

Vivian usually napped after water sports, but the day's hectic schedule hadn't allowed time for it. To her dismay she yawned while Zack was talking. "Oh, I'm so sorry!"

"It's all right. I'm kind of tired myself. It was being out on the water that did it, I think." He took her hand. "I'll tell you what. I'm going to take down your home phone number, and when we're back in New York I'll call you, invite you for dinner and a movie, and we'll have a good time. I can't keep relying on fate to bring us together, Vivling. You might move and change jobs, and then I'll never be able to find you. So what do you say?"

"I say, six-six-seven—" she recited the rest of her phone number.

Vivian was just dozing off when she heard Lauren come in. She cast a half-open eye on the alarm clock. "You're out awfully late."

"I know. I'm going to hate myself in the morning, but I can always sleep on the plane. You were right, Viv. Bill wants to see me again!"

"I'm not surprised."

"How did you make out with Zack?"

"I practically fell asleep on him in the lobby."

"Didn't you invite him in?"

"No. He brought me upstairs, and that was it."

"Not even a kiss? It's not like you two are exactly strangers to each other." While they were preparing for dinner Lauren had insisted on hearing all about their prior contacts.

"Just a little peck. That was all that was appropriate. We were in the hall, remember?"

Lauren pulled a cotton nightgown out of her bag. "I've got a feeling you guys are going to make up for lost time when you get back to the States."

Vivian was thinking the same thing. She stretched lazily, rolled over onto her stomach, and closed her eyes. "Sweet dreams."

She knew hers would be.

Chapter 16:
New York
State of Mind

Vivian and Lauren arrived back in New York on Thursday. Glenda met them at JFK Airport, and graciously drove to the New Rochelle train station so Lauren could get a train home on the New Haven line.

While Lauren was in the car the conversation centered around the trip. It wasn't until they were almost at the train station that Lauren mentioned "the fellas," prompting Glenda to ask, "What fellas?"

She was incredulous when Vivian told her they saw Zack in Kenya. "Can't you go across the street without running into that man?"

Vivian laughed. "You're right. It was so weird. When I caught sight of him I just froze, which was a little awkward, since I was in the process of climbing out of a hollow tree trunk. Lauren and I had just had pictures taken posing inside it."

"You owe a lot to that tree," Lauren pointed out.

"If we hadn't stopped to take a picture, you never would have known Zack was in the country. And *I* never would have met Bill."

"Who's Bill?" Glenda asked.

"One of Zack's friends from the hospital. There were four of them on the trip, but the other two took a different excursion after the safari." Vivian saw her friend's expression, her forehead wrinkled somewhere between confusion and indignation, and she simultaneously shook her head and waved her hand in a dismissive motion, silently conveying to Glenda that the mysterious Bill was not African-American and Glenda hadn't missed the chance to meet an eligible doctor herself.

"Thanks so much, Glenda," Lauren said when they arrived at the station. She and Vivian embraced, and with a weary-sounding, "It'll be good to get home," she took her bags and disappeared inside.

Glenda's questions began right away. "What happened with you and Zack? Is everything all right?"

"If you mean did somebody end up in the ER, no. I have a feeling my luck is about to change." She paused for a few seconds. "Zack's going to call me in a few days. We're going to fly out to Desirée's wedding together. But before that we're going to go out on a date. Maybe even more than one if it works out."

The AC in Glenda's car was on and the windows were closed, trapping her shriek inside.

Vivian quickly covered her ears. "Are you trying to make me go deaf?"

"I'm sorry. I'm just so happy for you!"

"It's just a date, Glenda. Hold off on mailing those wedding invitations."

"I know. But he finally asked you out. By the

time you two go to Colorado you should be hot and heavy, you can catch the bouquet, and *then* we can mail the invites. But what I don't understand is what in heaven's name took him so long? From what you told me about when he stayed with you, you two seemed like an old married couple."

"Can you believe this—he thought I wouldn't want to go out with him because Gary and Gordon and Bernard were all suit-wearing types."

"And he thought you had something against a smock? I could see him feeling a little inadequate if he taught art to eight-year-olds or something, but the man's a *doctor,* for crying out loud."

"He's a lot different than I thought he was originally, Glenda. He used to radiate confidence to the point of being smug, like someone who had shared pillow talk with a female bigwig at Ernst & Young just before the Academy Awards. But when he told me how he didn't want me to turn him down, he seemed so vulnerable. Zack can be a lot of fun, but it's the sensitive side of him that I like the best."

That was the side of him she'd already fallen in love with.

Vivian begged off going with Glenda to the NBP dance to celebrate the summer solstice, held the night after she returned home. Even though she didn't go to work that day, her system was trying to adjust to the multiple time zones she had traveled through and settle back on eastern daylight time. Besides, Zack would probably call. A disappointed but sympathetic Glenda told other single African-American women at the office about the function, and a group arranged to meet there.

Glenda called early Saturday morning. "You'll never guess who I saw last night!"

Vivian drew in a breath. *Not Zack* . . . He hadn't called like she hoped he would, but she felt it was because he was probably as whipped as she was. Had he actually gone dancing while she sat at home waiting for the phone to ring?

"Pete Arnold!"

"What!"

"Yes. Arnella Walker told him about it."

"That figures." Arnella was a technical writer in R&D and worked close to Pete. "So did Mr. Clumsy have two left feet or what?"

"He's no Gregory Hines, but he'll do. And that's not all—we're going out tonight."

"You are! I'm so happy for you I could scream . . . but I won't."

"What about Zack? Are you going on your date tonight?"

"No. He . . . I haven't heard from him yet."

"Oh. He must be really tired. I'm sure you'll hear from him today."

The surprise of Glenda's first sentence and the optimism of the rest of her statement were so separate and distinctive that Vivian felt like she could reach out and touch both emotions, the same as she could put her fingertips on the lamp shade. She knew her friend was trying to cheer her, but her excuse-making for Zack's silence sounded forced, like she wasn't really sure she believed her own words; and if she wasn't careful, Glenda's unspoken doubts would seep into her brain. She wanted to remain upbeat, and the only way that would happen was if they talked about something else.

"How about a pedicure this afternoon? We can have lunch afterward."

"Not a bad idea. I can wear sandals tonight."

They met at noon. It was too late to schedule an appointment, but fortunately, most of the women waiting were there for manicures. All of those stations were occupied, but after only a few minutes they were seated at side-by-side pedicure chairs.

"I love getting my feet done. It's a lot quicker than a manicure, and there's something about it that makes me feel really special, almost like royalty," Vivian remarked when the pedicurists positioned themselves on the padding on the floor and began sloughing away dead skin.

"Maybe, but somehow I can't picture Queen Elizabeth sitting in front of someone on their knees who's scraping the soles of her feet with a pumice stone."

Vivian's first action upon returning home was to check the wall phone in her kitchen to see if any messages had been left. There weren't any, and the optimism she had forced herself to retain left her like air from a torn tire.

This was the third day they had been back at home. Where *was* he?

Zack was asleep in the lounge in the ER. He'd been on duty since eleven the previous night and was nearing the end of a double shift. He had been scheduled to come in this morning, but they had asked him to stay late—eight hours late. That was what he got for agreeing to cover when needed in exchange for the extra vacation time he was taking this year, but he didn't expect them to take him up on it so soon. Instead of spending time in Vivian's company like he'd planned, he hadn't even had a chance to call her.

The vinyl sofa was uncomfortable, and he knew he was done with sleeping until he was at home. He yawned, then checked his watch and was pleasantly surprised to see it was two-forty. Just another twenty minutes to go, and he would have eight whole hours before he was due back in. He could get some real sleep in his own bed . . . and he could call Vivian, explain what happened, and arrange to see her tomorrow afternoon if she was free.

One of the nurses burst in the lounge. "Dr. Warner, there you are. There's been a five-car smash-up on the GW. The paramedics estimate arrival in four minutes."

He stayed past the end of his shift to assist with the care of the accident victims, leaving just before four when it became apparent that the staff of the second shift had the tense situation under control. Anxious to leave before another emergency could occur, he decided to wait and call Vivian from home. She probably thought he'd fallen off the face of the earth.

At home he took the stairs two at a time and in his bedroom promptly stripped to his underwear, throwing his clothes on the floor. He was generally too neat to indulge in such careless behavior, but after seventeen hours on duty he was too tired to care. He'd pick them up later.

In bed, he dialed Vivian's number, silently willing her to pick up. She did, after the second ring.

"Hi. It's Zack."

"Hi. It's Vivian."

He laughed. She wasn't going to make it easy. But before he could say another word he yawned. "Excuse me. I worked last night, and they asked me to work another shift. I just got home."

"You went back to work already?"

"Didn't I tell you? I'm on nights this week."

"You didn't mention it. I just assumed you were off till Monday. I keep forgetting you're not part of the eight-thirty-to-five crowd."

He chuckled. "No, that would be the boys in private practice."

"You must be beat."

"I've got to be back at eleven o'clock. I wanted to let you know I've been dreaming about you."

"Oh. Anything exciting?"

Lost in his own daydream, he smiled and rubbed the palm of his left hand over the cold emptiness beside him. "I wish you were here with me now."

"Why, so you can go to sleep on me?"

"So I can squeeze you, nibble on your ear . . . Um um um."

She quickly broke into his fantasy, as he knew she would. "I'm glad you called, Zack. I admit I was beginning to think I'd dreamed our conversation in Kenya. But I think you should go ahead and get some sleep. It'll be eleven o'clock before you know it."

"I'll call you tomorrow."

"I look forward to it."

Zack, his eyes already closed, hung up the receiver by feel. He wasn't sure if it was actually back in its cradle, but it felt like it, and that was good enough for him. He grabbed the other pillow and held it close to him, his hand wrapped around its center. It didn't feel even remotely close to holding Vivian, but it was all he had.

He was asleep in minutes.

"That's the building we lived in," Zack said, pointing to a four-story structure of rust-colored brick.

"I can't imagine growing up in the city, with no grass, no trees. Where did you play?"

"In the street, just like these kids." The wide sidewalk was filled with adults just standing, enjoying the sunshine of the June day, as well as youngsters jumping rope and playing hopscotch or tag. "It was hot in the apartment. I was a teenager before we had an air conditioner, and then that was only in the living room."

"And where is this that we're going?"

"A restaurant called Wilson's. It's right on the corner. My parents used to bring us on special occasions. As long ago as that was, it's still one of my favorite places to eat. I love their coconut cake."

The street was crowded, and he took her hand, threading his fingers through hers. It was a perfectly natural gesture, but it made Vivian want to sing and shout out to everyone that this man was her date, the date she had been hoping would occur for six long months.

The restaurant was simple, with many multigenerational families dining together, the children wearing their Sunday best and trying to keep still as they sat in their chairs, napkins tucked into their collars to protect against oily spots. Baked goods filled a display case near the door, not the heavily decorated, flawless cakes and pies typical of most bakeries, but imperfect-looking everyday items like pound cakes, slightly unevenly iced chocolate and coconut cakes and lumpy-looking apple pies with nice brown crusts. Any of the items looked like they could have come from her own mother's oven . . . and they probably tasted just as good.

"I wish my schedule was more receptive," he said apologetically after asking what she wanted and giving both orders to their waitress.

"I think I can live with it. You do get an occasional weekend off, don't you?"

"Yes, but it won't be next weekend. Not only that, but I'll be on the worst shift of all, three to eleven."

"Three to eleven! That *is* bad news. Which days are you off?"

"I'm off this Wednesday, and then again on Sunday and Monday, so maybe we can see each other Sunday, in the late afternoon. Earlier in the day I'll need to spend a few hours with the kid I'm mentoring through the Big Brother program."

"I think that's a wonderful thing for you to do."

"Kareem's a great kid. Eleven years old and smart as a whip. He wants to be a vet. *So,*" he said briskly, changing the subject, "can I plan to see you then?"

"I'm sure we can work something out. Did you check into the reservations for Denver?"

"Yes. I got a good rate on the Internet, nonstop both ways, leaving from LaGuardia." He told her the dates and the fare, and she agreed it was perfect. "Ozzie recommended a bed-and-breakfast near downtown for us to stay in. I thought it might be easier if I made the reservations for both of us."

"All right. I hope you don't mind using your credit card to hold my room. I'll give them mine when I get there."

"No problem. But the car rental is on me."

"That's sweet of you to offer, but I see no reason why you should pick up that tab. I'll split it with you. Oh, that reminds me." She reached into her purse and handed him an envelope. "This is for you."

He frowned as he looked at the envelope. "Wait a minute. This is the envelope I left for you when I went back home. He peered inside. "I don't get it. The money is still in here."

"I know that."

He studied her impassive expression, which she knew gave no clues. "I gave this to you to show you that I appreciated your taking care of me that week. Why are you returning it?"

"I felt you showed adequate appreciation. You cooked dinner every night, plus you filled up my cupboards and refrigerator with all that stuff you bought at the supermarket. This was overkill." His eyes were all over her face; he was still trying to read her. Her shoulders stiffened.

"There's something more to this, isn't there?"

She hedged, then decided she should tell him exactly how she felt. Maybe then he'd stop studying her like an architect analyzing a blueprint. "All right. There's something that makes me uncomfortable about your leaving me an envelope with a couple of fifties in it. I thought we were friends, but you can't put a price tag on friendship, Zack. I felt like I was being dismissed, like a patient you'd released at the hospital." *And when you didn't contact me, I knew I'd been dismissed.*

He nodded thoughtfully. "I see. You thought I was trying to avoid feeling like I owed you anything, ease any guilt I might be feeling for accepting your hospitality and then disappearing."

"Can you blame me?"

"No, I guess I can't. I knew what I wanted, but you didn't know what I wanted; at least not then." He stuffed the envelope in his pants pocket. "Open envelope, insert foot. I guess I did it again, huh?"

"It's not an unpardonable sin, Zack."

"Maybe not, but it's important that you know there wasn't anything dismissive behind it. I was only thinking about your inconvenience."

"I understand that, but I can't accept your money. You were a guest in my home. I don't allow anyone to sleep on my couch if I don't want them to, and I certainly don't expect them to pay me for it, like I'm running a Marriott or something."

"Point taken. Now, just let me pay for the car rental in Denver. Not because I don't want to feel like I'm in your debt, but because I want to. I'd have to get a rental if you weren't coming, so why should I soak you for half the cost?"

She laughed at his phrasing. "All right, I guess that's not unreasonable."

"Good. And you were right, Vivling."

She rolled her eyes, not wanting to let on that she thought his name for her was kind of cute. "Right about what?"

"About us being friends. We are. But I don't want it to stop there." He reached for her hand across the table, raised it and pressed the back of it to his lips, his eyes not leaving hers the whole time. "So tell me, am I forgiven for my latest blunder?"

"Yes," she said without hesitation. He continued to hold her hand with one of his, and with the other he was tracing the length of her fingers, up one side and down the other, with the pad of his index finger. It was a simple movement that was off the sensuality scale, especially when he made contact with the sensitive webbing between her digits. It was comfortably warm in the busy restaurant, but she found herself struggling to keep from shivering from the erotic sensation.

The delivery of their food interrupted his erotic exploration of her fingers. It had been an unusual date—most of her dates were Friday or Saturday evenings, not Sunday afternoons—but one she thoroughly enjoyed. They'd walked through the Studio Museum of Harlem, enjoying the historic photographs of James Van Der Zee and the paintings of Jacob Lawrence, among others; and before parking near his former home Zack showed her where he had gone to school. She pictured him as a child, running along the street of his block. She felt pleased that he had wanted to show her his old stomping ground, and that he'd brought her for dinner to a place that had been the site of some of his happiest childhood memories.

"Are you sure you won't be too tired for work tonight, going out in the middle of the day like this?" she asked when they arrived back at her apartment building.

"I'll be fine. There's still plenty of time for me to sleep. I'm glad you consented to go out with me on a Sunday afternoon." Zack knew from experience that a lot of women wouldn't. He didn't understand how anyone could take an entire day, one that didn't involve going to work, to prepare for work the next day. That struck him as a tremendous waste of free time.

"Actually, I found it refreshing." She unlocked her door and stepped inside. "Aren't you coming in?"

"Just for a minute. There was something I wanted to give you."

"What's that?"

He draped a casual arm around her shoulder. "The last time we said good night we were in a hall. This time I wanted a little privacy."

A ripple of awareness traveled through her body as his strong hands rested on her shoulders and pulled her close. His lips came down coaxingly on hers, his tongue gently probed her mouth. The kiss was brief, and when it ended he gazed at her with the same foolishly happy grin she suspected was on her own face.

Chapter 17:
Rocky Mountain High

Denver was beautiful. As their plane landed she could see the majestic Rocky Mountain chain just to the west, snow-capped peaks that shone in the sun. Suddenly, she was glad that Zack had suggested coming out on Wednesday. This, their day of arrival, was already half over—it was already two in the afternoon—and if it was Thursday they would have less than one full day to see the area before they were due at the rehearsal and subsequent dinner.

It would also give them more time to spend together, something that had become as rare as an undercooked hamburger. When she'd returned to work on Monday she had been delighted to learn that she was being promoted from administrator to manager. Lisa had insisted that she attend a week-long seminar on human resources management, which would not be held in New York for another five months, so arrangements had been made for her to go to Boston. She had had to cancel her Sunday date with Zack; in order to be in Boston at nine A.M. Monday morning she had had to get a train out Sunday afternoon.

Zack's days off the week after that coincided with Independence Day. She had promised her parents she would spend it with them, since at the time she had no plans. She thought about asking Zack to join her, but decided it was too early to bring him home. Her mother would be so excited at her dating a doctor that she probably would have tried to arrange a private fireworks display in the backyard.

Last weekend she was busy with the hairdresser, the manicurist, and other preparations for Colorado, while Zack worked double shifts to make up for his upcoming time off. While they had talked regularly on the phone, neither of them expected that lone Sunday afternoon over two weeks before would be the last time they would see each other until it was time to leave for Denver.

She turned to him as he hung up the courtesy phone to the car rental agency. "I'm glad we came out a day early."

"Good." He took her arm and guided her toward the exit. "They said they've got a van on the way. In just a few minutes we'll be in the car and on our way."

They found their hotel easily, with Vivian reading the directions while Zack drove. The homey atmosphere of the antique-filled Victorian home came as a pleasant surprise. The century-old structure had been completely modernized, with whirlpool tubs and cable television. "I'll never stay in a cookie-cutter hotel again," she said as they climbed the curved staircase to their second-floor room.

"Better not let the happy couple hear you say that."

"I doubt that all the big hotels will go out of business just because I've decided I'd rather stay somewhere with more personality. Desirée and Austin will have plenty of clients in need of their consulting services. Besides, when they go to Taos for their honeymoon I'm sure they'll be staying someplace along these lines."

Zack unlocked the door to their accommodations and followed her inside. "Pretty nice, huh?"

"I'll say." Zack had gotten a special rate on a two-bedroom suite that gave them a connecting sitting room for a rate only slightly higher than paying for two single rooms. The fireplace in the sitting room looked so inviting she found herself wishing it was October instead of July so she could light it. The colorful small floral bouquet in a vase on the coffee table consisted of real flowers, not silk, and the large plant by the window was also authentic. Both bedrooms were furnished with four-poster beds. It was, Vivian thought wistfully as she eyed the mini-pillow door handle crocheted with the words DO NOT DISTURB, a setting made for romance.

It was too late in the day to do any sightseeing after they unpacked, so they relaxed for a bit and then drove downtown, where they parked and walked along the pedestrian mall on Sixteenth Street, window-shopping and keeping an eye out for a place to have dinner. They settled on a popular-looking bistro with a patio and enjoyed a leisurely meal, sipping wine while they people-watched in the warm summer night.

After dinner they drove out to Elitch Gardens, an amusement park that reminded Vivian of Coney

Island. She buried her face in Zack's shoulder when their car of the Ferris wheel stopped to load passengers with them at the top, a hundred feet up.

His arm immediately went around her shoulder in a protective action. "What's wrong, Vivling?"

She felt embarrassed to admit the truth. "I'm scared of heights."

"*Now* you tell me."

"Don't make jokes, Zack!"

He pulled her close. "It's all right. We're going down now. Just stay like you are and keep your eyes closed."

That certainly wasn't a tall order. It was rather nice where she was now, and even nicer now that he was holding her so tightly. Still, she would feel a lot better once they were at a lower height.

Once the ride was fully loaded and moving at a steady pace without stops, it wasn't too bad. Vivian kept her eyes open until the surrounding landscape came into view, when she promptly closed them and hid her face in Zack's chest until they were descending.

"If you don't mind my asking, why did you agree to get on a Ferris wheel if you're afraid of heights?" Zack asked.

"It didn't look so high up from the ground," she said softly.

"It never does. I guess you won't want to go on that ride where we free-fall two hundred feet at sixty miles an hour."

She leaned back slightly and narrowly opened one eye, staring at him skeptically. But even with her limited range of vision, she realized how high up they were, and her eyes opened in panic as she looked to the ground so far below. Zack quickly slapped a hand over her eyes.

She couldn't even look at the free-fall ride when he was on it, but she did agree to ride the roller coaster with him. The constant movement of this type of amusement park attraction didn't interfere with her height phobia. It was her favorite kind, a wooden coaster that creaked and rattled as it climbed to its pinnacle, and they both enjoyed it so much they rode it twice.

They were very tired after what had been a full day, and when they returned to their suite they retired to their respective bedrooms for a good night's sleep. After enjoying the hearty breakfast that was served to hotel guests the next morning, they embarked on a tour of the area, beginning with a trip to see Austin, who lived nestled in the mountains in the suburb of Evergreen. Vivian hoped to see Desirée, whom she knew spent most of her time there, but Austin informed her she had been staying at her mother's home in Denver because it was closer to the services she needed.

"So, how was the hotel?" Austin asked casually.

Vivian studied Zack, curious to see how he would respond. Instinct told her the two friends had discussed her recently. Perhaps Zack had mentioned the rooms he reserved connected to either side of a sitting room, which would have given away the platonic nature of their relationship. Was Austin hoping to help them move along to the next level?

"It's very nice. It's got character instead of being antiseptic, like so many of the hotels are."

"I like it, too," Vivian said. "But this is really nice, Austin." She waved a hand at the tastefully decorated room. "Tell me, did Desirée help you decorate?"

"She sure did. I wouldn't have had it any other way. I didn't even make an offer on the house until I knew she approved of it." He grinned sheepishly. "I had a feeling she was going to be living in it with me eventually."

"What was it like out here last winter?" Zack asked.

"Let's put it this way. We make it a point to never run out of food. On the bad days it might be two or three days before we venture out."

"Just a few days? I'd imagine it would take at least a week," Vivian said.

"It doesn't take long for the roads to become passable. A lot of it melts, actually, because it often warms up after a snowfall."

"That road is frightening enough when it's green. I can't imagine driving down it with snow and ice on the ground," Vivian said.

"I can't imagine you doing that, either," Zack said in a teasing tone, squeezing her upper arm. "You should have seen her on the way up here, Oz. Her hand was gripping the door handle, and her foot was pressed against the floor like there was an invisible brake pedal on the passenger-side."

"It was unnerving," Vivian said in her own defense. "We're in the middle of the Rockies, and with me in the passenger seat I was the one closest to the edge. Those yellow signs that tell you which way the road is about to curve don't help, either. The only thing worse than a steep mountain road is a steep mountain road that goes like this." She made a zigzag motion with her hand. "And I'm afraid of heights."

* * *

They managed to see as much of Denver's sights as possible, from the Red Rocks Amphitheater—Vivian got in her day's exercise when they walked to the bottom and then back up again, she huffing and puffing in the July heat, feeling inadequate as she watched Zack glide like he was on wheels—to the Molly Brown House, where Vivian insisted on going. "Didn't you see *Titanic?*" she prodded the disgruntled Zack. He went along, but declared that to reciprocate she had to accompany him to the renowned Denver Zoo. She protested, saying it was cruel to stare at animals who were obviously uncomfortable in the summer heat, "plus it smells bad," but she went along and found the experience to be surprisingly pleasant.

On Friday they spent hours in the Black American West Museum, then borrowed bicycles from the hotel and rode through City Park, pigging out on hot dogs and potato chips and stopping to rest and talk under the shade of sprawling oak trees while they observed other bikers ride by.

Desirée was radiant, and Austin seemed almost silly in his happiness. Vivian found herself feeling a little envious of them. She hadn't spent a whole lot of time with Zack, but as Glenda pointed out, it generally didn't take long. He was the man of her dreams, the one she wanted to grow old with.

Only the bridal party had attended the rehearsal, but a larger number of guests had been invited to dinner, which was held in the private room of a casual neighborhood bar and grill. Vivian was happy to see Austin and Desirée's familiar faces

again, as well as those of the senior Hugheses. At
the rehearsal Zack introduced her to the people
he knew, and she tried hard to remember all their
names. Charlene Harris was Austin's sister; she and
her husband Irwin were both members of the wedding. Phil and Sandy Wallace were easy to remember; they were the only nonblack people in
attendance. She also would not forget the dashing
Mickey Spivey, who, like Phil, would serve as an
usher for the ceremony. He was a large, handsome
fellow who seemed quite happy to be in the company of Desirée's attractive honor attendants. Two
of the four women were single.

There were more people to meet at the rehearsal
dinner. Zack's cousin Sydney Chambers was another easily identifiable face, since she looked
enough like Zack to be his sister. She had relocated
to the Detroit area after being transferred by her
employer, where, in a wonderful coincidence, she
had run into her former high school classmate,
Donald Nesmith. Donald now called that area
home as well, and had accompanied Sydney to
Denver. Most of the other names that went with
the faces left her as soon as she learned them.

Except for two. She was shocked when Zack presented her to his parents; he hadn't even mentioned they were coming.

She recovered quickly. "I'm so happy to meet
you, Mr. Warner . . . Mrs. Warner. What a nice surprise. Zack didn't tell me you would be here."

"Oh, we wouldn't miss it. Austin's like another
son to us. And it was a nice opportunity for us to
come west," Mrs. Warner said. She was a tall, fair-
skinned woman with blue eyes who appeared to be
biracial, and even at roughly sixty years old it was
still obvious that she had been a beauty when she

was young. "We've never been before. We just got
in a few hours ago."

"It's my first time as well."

"I'm not impressed," Mr. Warner said. He was
an older, heavier version of Zack. "It's scenic and
all that, but this altitude doesn't particularly agree
with me."

Zack reached out and rested his hand on his father's shoulder. "Are you feeling dizzy, Daddy?"

"I was earlier, but not right now. Now it's more
like a nauseated feeling."

"It's a common reaction, especially in smokers."

"Boy, what're you talkin' about? You know I haven't had a cigarette in fifteen years."

"It doesn't matter. Former smokers are just as
susceptible as current ones. I want you to stop at
the drugstore on the way back to your hotel." He
instructed his mother on what product to ask for.
"It should help you."

"My son, the medicine man," Mr. Warner said
with a shake of his head that failed to disguise his
pride. Then he turned his attention back to Vivian.
"So Zack didn't tell you we would be here, eh?
Well, he sure told us about you."

"He did?"

"Uh . . . I think they want us to take our seats
now," Zack said quickly, taking Vivian's arm and
steering her away, talking over his shoulder as they
went. "We'll see you guys later, huh? I need to sit
close to Ozzie, since I'm his best man."

"That was a quick getaway. Does that mean
you're not going to tell me what you said to your
parents about me?" Vivian asked when they were
seated at the long table near Austin and Desirée.

He spoke close to her ear in a low voice no one
else could hear. "If you must know, I told them

I've continually been running into a succulent young lady under the most unusual circumstances, and that she had agreed to fly out to Denver with me."

"Succulent? You make me sound like a chicken leg." The slightly glazed look in his eyes told her he liked her ideology. In spite of how good she felt, she elbowed him gently in the ribs, feeling this wasn't the place for innuendo. She noticed the unmarried bridesmaids, Desirée's friends Lorna and Eva, eyeing them with undisguised curiosity and more than a little envy of what surely appeared to be an intimate relationship. *If only they knew.*

Austin stood up and addressed the group, "Desi and I are so happy to see that the people nearest and dearest to us are all here to celebrate our marriage. We gave a lot of thought about where to hold our wedding, knowing that whichever choice we made meant many of you would have to travel a long way, and to see all of you here . . ." His voice cracked a little. ". . . It means a lot to us. I know I'm getting a bit emotional"—he joined in when someone laughed loudly—"but believe me when I say I'm sincere." He glanced over at a member of the kitchen staff who was gesturing to him. "I'm told we can begin serving ourselves now, so let's all eat, and remember, there's plenty of food."

The group applauded him and then formed a line at the buffet, where they proceeded to fill their plates with ham, turkey, and roast beef, plus macaroni and cheese, stuffing and gravy, potato salad, tossed green salad, greens, and cornbread.

"This is de*licious!*" Vivian exclaimed. "Who prepared all this?"

"They work with a caterer," Desirée replied. "They do a great business in private parties. My mother came to one and suggested we have the dinner here. It's larger than most rehearsal dinners; we wanted to say a special thank you to all the people who traveled."

"I haven't met your mom. Where is she?"

"She's with her boyfriend. They're sitting with Ozzie's parents. I'll introduce you after dinner."

Zack sniffed and frowned. "Vivian, do you smell something funny?"

"No. What does it smell like? Rotten food?" She had a flashback of Timothy Golden's food poisoning and felt her muscles tighten up.

"Nothing like that. It smells a little like . . . car exhaust. Nothing to worry about, I'm sure. I just have a sensitive nose."

She relaxed. It was actually rather sad that Timothy, quite a nice fellow, had been relegated to her memory for the incident of food poisoning, but she had been honest when, the day the audit was complete, he asked her if she imagined anything could ever happen between them. He had been utterly charming when she told him she couldn't see it, and she knew his Ms. Right was waiting for him somewhere. Even if her heart wasn't with Zack—and there was no doubt in her mind that it was—she didn't think she could cope with a newly divorced man who had children. It was a delicate situation she just didn't want to be in the middle of.

Jaws that had been chewing at twenty miles an hour began to stall as everyone's bellies reached capacity, and the conversation up and down the table was peppered with variations of, "I'm stuffed." Mickey Spivey tapped on his coffee cup with a spoon to silence them, then stood up. "I've known Austin for a long time, and I even met Desirée before he did, which means it could have been *me* getting married tomorrow . . ." he cleared his throat delicately to laughter, then continued.

"I knew they would be an item by the time they returned from that assignment in West Africa, and I was right. That's where it all began, and who knows where it will all end." He turned to the betrothed couple. "Pretty soon you'll have a ton of little rug rats who'll be begging you to take them to Casa Bonita for dinner."

"What's Casa Bonita?" Vivian asked Alisha, Desirée's matron of honor, who was sitting across from her.

"It's a Mexican theme restaurant all the kids love. It's got a lot going on to keep them occupied, kind of a cheaper version of Disney."

Mickey continued with his speech, but Vivian became aware of the buzzing of whispering voices.

She remembered thinking it was very rude of people to talk while Mickey was making a toast, but then everything became hazy. She thought she heard coughing and choking sounds, maybe coming from her own throat. Her hand caught on to something tubular-shaped, and she held on tightly. She wanted to ask what was happening, but her brain wouldn't cooperate.

Then she went limp and passed out. If Zack hadn't caught her she would have fallen to the floor.

Her body jerked at the strong odor that filled her nostrils, and she opened her eyes. She didn't recognize the strange man who stood over her. "Who are *you?*"

"Emergency Medical Services, ma'am. Apparently, there's some kind of fumes coming out of the air conditioning. A lot of the people inside were overcome. Some, like yourself, fainted."

It was then that Vivian realized she was lying on a stretcher outside. "Where's Zack?"

"I'm sorry. I wouldn't know who that is, but whoever he is, you'll see him at the hospital."

"Hospital?"

"Everybody has to be checked out. We're trying to bring everybody to the same place. Most of you will be looked at and let go."

"I can't go to the hospital! My friend's getting married at two-thirty tomorrow afternoon."

"I don't think there'll be a problem with that. From what I've seen no one looks bad off enough to be admitted. Once they call us we've got to bring you to the hospital. It's up to them to release you." Then Vivian felt herself being lifted and put in the back of an ambulance. Desirée's friend Alisha was already inside.

On her arrival she was rushed into an exam room. The EMS technician had started an IV, which made no sense to her whatsoever. She hadn't thrown up even once, and there was no way she could be dehydrated.

But she felt lousy. There was a sourness in her stomach, and it hurt to even breathe. And she was worried about Zack and the others. No wonder Mr. Warner said he felt nauseated before they sat down to dinner. Just as Zack had inherited his mother's blue eyes, he had his father's keen sense of smell.

"There you are!"

"Zack!" She tried to get up, but quickly fell back.

"Don't get up. And don't worry. I have it on a very good source that you're going to live to a ripe old age."

"How are your parents?"

"I think they're going to keep my dad overnight. He has a touch of COPD anyway. Chronic obstructive pulmonary disease. It's a respiratory ailment that comes from smoking."

"Oh, no!"

"Actually, I think it's for the best. He'll be monitored overnight and released in the morning. Phil and Sandy's place in Golden is at an even higher elevation than Denver, and I want to make sure he'll be all right."

"And your mother?"

"She's fine. As far as I know my dad's the only one they're keeping for observation. Even the matron of honor, who's four months pregnant, is expected to be released."

"Alisha. She and her husband were in the ambulance with me. I didn't know she was pregnant. I'm glad she's okay."

"Everyone is just a little shook up and maybe nauseated, but that should go away in a few hours."

"What about Austin and Desirée?"

"They're both fine. Has the doctor been in to see you yet?"

"Yes. He said he'll be back to check on me in a few minutes. I guess that means at least a half hour in MD time."

"Well, I brought you a little present." He handed her a small, plain white box.

She stared at it, instantly trying to figure out what it contained. A four-leaf clover or other good luck charm would be appropriate right about now. "I guess I could be coy and say, 'Oh, Zack, you shouldn't have,' but, hey, I'm a material girl." She opened the box eagerly, revealing a round gold compact. She raised an eyebrow. He'd gotten her some kind of makeup?

"Don't just stare at it, open it."

She complied. It was a mirror, but the shrill female scream that accompanied it made her shut it quickly. The screaming promptly stopped, and she began to laugh. *"This* is supposed to cheer me up? This thing suggests I'm so ugly I'm frightening." It was so like him, but she knew him well enough now to know it was a harmless joke.

"It made you laugh, didn't it?"

Vivian was released an hour later. She tried to comfort Zack's mother. "I'm sure Mr. Warner will be fine. Zack said he thinks it's the best thing for him."

"I can't remember the last time we spent a night apart. We've both been blessed with good health. I just can't remember."

"We're going to bring you back to your hotel, and you get a good night's sleep. Tomorrow morning Zack will bring you to pick up your husband. At least you know he's getting round-the-clock care."

"If I know my husband he won't sleep a wink. I have a feeling I'm going to have a hard time going to sleep myself."

"Are you sure you'll be all right, Vivling?"

"I'll be fine." She sniffed playfully. "Go ahead, leave me to go somewhere that has seminaked ladies—and I use that term *very loosely*—shaking their boobies in your face."

Zack gave an embarrassed shrug. "Something

like that. Mickey invited the fellows to his place. I think he and Phil have arranged for entertainment. But I won't be late."

"You don't have to say that, Zack. You're a big boy." *I'm not your wife.* "But I do hope you don't get too carried away. Boulder is a good drive from here, and you don't want to be hung over for the ceremony. You wouldn't want to embarrass yourself and trip over your feet."

"No hangover for me. I'm not much of a drinker anyway. Besides, I've got to pick up Dad from the hospital in the morning." He kissed her lightly. "Get a good night's sleep."

She closed and locked the door behind him, only reacting with a smile. She didn't expect to have any difficulty sleeping—she felt fine, but the experience of breathing the fumes and its aftermath had drained her—but she couldn't help thinking of Zack's mother, who would no doubt be tossing and turning all night.

"Hi, is this Vivian?"

She didn't recognize the female voice on the other end of the line. It wasn't Desirée. Maybe it was Zack's mother calling to inquire when he would be picking her up. He was actually on his way; he'd left right after they had breakfast, looking no worse for the wear after his night out. "Yes. Who's this?"

"This is Lorna Nairn, Desirée's friend. One of the bridesmaids. We've got a problem, and I'm thinking you might be able to help us out."

"What is it?"

"We had the final fittings for our dressings just

last week, but Alisha can't get into hers today. She's pregnant, you know."

"Yes, I know. Four months, right? It's that tight around her stomach already?"

"It's not her stomach that's the problem. It's her chest. It's made this rather sudden expansion in the last week."

"Oh, no!"

"I'm at her house now. We're afraid to say anything to Desirée. But we were thinking . . . you're about five-five and a size ten, aren't you?"

"Yes."

"So is Alisha. Would you be willing to fill in as matron—I mean, maid of honor?"

Vivian hedged. "I don't want to seem uncooperative, but wouldn't it be more appropriate if you or one of the other girls took that part? And then I can take your place. The maid of honor should be a very close friend of the bride, and I'm not even close enough to be a bridesmaid."

"I understand what you mean, and we thought of that, but Alisha's dress won't fit any of us. Actually, it would fit me, but it'll be too short because I'm four inches taller than she is. Eva's a size eight. I just met Austin's sister at rehearsal when I met you, and I can tell she's larger than a size ten. She was telling me she's still trying to lose the weight she put on when she was pregnant. Incidentally, what size shoe do you wear?"

"Eight." Vivian listened as Lorna relayed this information, and from Alisha's delighted squeal she knew it was a perfect fit.

Lorna delivered the dress and shoes in a half-hour. "I'll be holding my breath," she said when Vivian brought the ensemble into the bathroom to change.

The dress fit fine. Made of some sort of filmy fabric, the bodice was tightly fitted—no wonder Alisha couldn't wear it anymore—with a flare out at the waist. The crinoline-lined skirt was full and ended just above her ankles; and it was shirred at the shoulders. The only difference between this dress and the bridesmaids' was that her dress was cream-colored printed with roses in varying shades of pink, and theirs were solid dusky rose. Unlike most bridal attendants' dresses, this was a dress that really *could* be worn again, to a garden wedding as a guest, perhaps.

"Ta da!" She held her hands outstretched as she left the bathroom.

"Oh, it's perfect. We'll see you at Desireé's mother's house, then?"

"Yes. I'll ask Zack to drop me off on his way to the chapel."

"Good. It's easy to get there from here. Here are the directions. If you have any trouble just call. Alisha will break the news to Desirée. Right now she's trying to find something to wear. Thanks so much, Vivian."

"I'm glad I could help."

"You know, this is going to be work out very nicely. This means you'll be escorted by Zack, since he's the best man."

Vivian was still smiling after she left. Lorna had been right—Zack *was* the best man, as far as she was concerned.

Chapter 18:
I Take This Woman

All sets of eyes were on Desirée as she glided up the chapel aisle, her arm linked with that of her mother . . . that is, all sets except one.

Zack had known Vivian was going to be the maid of honor. When he returned from getting his parents settled after his father's uncomfortable night at the hospital and his mother's uneasy night at the hotel, he had been astonished when Vivian told him about Lorna Nairn's call and subsequent visit. Although she had shown him the dress she would be wearing, he hadn't actually seen her in it before now, for she had carried it over her arm when he brought her to Mrs. Mack's home, where the bridal attendants were dressing, and from where they would be driven in limousines to the site of the ceremony. It was amazing. She was a last-minute substitute, but it looked like it had been made for her. From the way she was smiling at the guests as she made her way up the aisle in time to the music—Desirée had chosen the emotionally powerful theme from the historic miniseries *Roots*—he felt sure she had done this more than once in the past.

He half expected her to raise her arm and wave, like a politician . . . or like a queen.

Even throughout the ceremony, he found his mind wandering, thinking about how delectable she looked. Austin and Desirée saying their vows was lost to him. Vivian gave him a little wink when, performing her duties as honor attendant, she gently pulled back Desirée's veil to free her face.

When it was time for the recessional—the music Austin had surprised Desirée with was *The Most Beautiful Girl in the World,* by that fellow who changes his name about as often as most folks trade in their vehicles—he linked his arm in Vivian's and escorted her toward the door. This time, she did wave to the guests, regardless of not knowing most of them; and he found himself doing the same.

He suddenly felt very happy, and he knew that his best buddy's wedding day was going to be an important date in his life as well, for in that instant he realized he was in love.

Vivian was puzzled. It only took a few moments to get out of the chapel, for unlike the carefully timed processional, this time they walked at a normal pace. After they were outside, Zack let go of her arm . . . but he took her hand. Maybe she was just imagining it, but it seemed like he was holding her hand very tightly. They posed for photographs on the chapel grounds, and he stood much closer to her than he needed to. Then he shocked her by asking the photographer to take a shot of just the two of them. What on earth had gotten into him?

* * *

On the way to the chapel, Vivian had ridden in the limousine with Desirée, Mrs. Mack, and Alisha Gibbs, who had taken the ride to offer moral support to her best friend in the moments before her marriage. It was fun; the four of them sang repeated choruses of the Dixie Cups classic, *Going to the Chapel*, but for the ride to the reception the lineup changed. The bridesmaids and ushers got into one limo, Mrs. Mack and Alisha rode in private vehicles, and she and Zack, the honor attendants, rode with the bride and groom. Austin and Desirée were holding hands and looking at each other lovingly. Every so often they would hold up their left hands to gaze at the new bands they wore. "All right, you two," Vivian teased. "I know you guys tried those rings on before you bought them."

"Of course we did," Desirée said, "but it's not the same as it is when you've actually taken your marriage vows."

"We don't mean to be sickening," Austin added.

"Well, Desirée, I must say you're handling the change in the lineup of your bridal attendants very well," Zack remarked.

"I almost had a cow when Alisha told me the boobie fairy visited her overnight, but when she said she had it all worked out and that Vivian fit into the dress . . ." she shrugged. "What could I say? She was as disappointed as I was, but because she didn't want me to worry she didn't even tell me about it before she had everything all taken care of. And I can't thank you enough, Vivian. You've been a real lifesaver, both in New York and out here." The two had become friendly when a distraught Desirée surveyed her hair, which had become a matted mess after weeks of being ill with malaria, and Vivian offered to bring her to a skilled hairdresser.

"I'm just so glad everything worked out."

"I'm glad the rehearsed part is over," Austin said. "I intend to enjoy every minute of our reception."

"Won't you two be leaving early?" Vivian asked.

"There's really no reason to," Desirée replied. "Our flight tomorrow isn't until three o'clock. We've got time to lounge around—we booked a suite at the Brown Palace—until checkout time, then grab our bags and head for the airport. It won't even be a long trip."

"Taos is just a hop, skip and jump by plane," Austin added.

"I'm going to forget all about what I have to do when I get back."

"What do you have to do, Desi? You're just about all moved in, except for your winter clothes."

"Thank you notes. I want to have them done within a month. If there's anything I can't stand it's brides and grooms whom I only hear from on the back of my checks." Desirée turned to Vivian. "You know what I mean, don't you?"

"I think all of us have had that experience at least once. It's one of my pet peeves, but I've got lots of those."

"I don't think it's really fair that it's the wife who has to do all the work, but I guess that's part of the job," Desirée said with a sigh.

Austin pantomimed the act of writing. "Dear Mr. and Mrs. Smith, Thank you so much for the silver serving dish . . ."

"Oh, you!" Desirée playfully punched his upper arm.

Austin nuzzled the neck of his new bride. "I have

a feeling I'm going to like this marriage thing," he said. "Zack, you'll have to try it one of these days."

He smiled at Vivian before answering. "I intend to."

The reception, held within the confines of a huge white tent, began as a dignified affair, with trio of musicians playing classical music as a background for the mingling of the guests while they awaited the arrival of the bridal party. The musicians disappeared just before the ushers and bridesmaids were presented to the guests, replaced by a band who played classics of a more popular nature. "I hope they remembered to tell them my name," Vivian said, her arm linked with Zack's as they awaited their turn.

The announcements were being handled by Desirée's mother's boyfriend, a circuit court judge whose booming voice barely needed amplification. "And as maid of honor and best man, I present to you Miss Vivian St. James and Dr. Zachary Warner of New York."

"There's your answer," he whispered as they moved forward to the center of the tent to thunderous applause. The smiles on the guests' faces told Vivian that she and Zack looked good together. She gave them a sunny smile, like she was in a Pepsodent commercial. This must be how if felt to be a bride, she thought.

It was party time. The large tent set up in the backyard of Phil and Sandy Wallace's home had full-service bars in three of its four corners. The

roof was filled with silver and white helium bal-
loons. Vivian became so full from sampling the
hors d'oeuvres, especially the crab cakes, that uni-
formed waiters were passing around at every turn,
that she feared she wouldn't be able to eat her
dinner. The music played continuously; whenever
the dance band took a break the classical musicians
returned. Even the six Port-O-Sans for the conve-
nience of the guests were roomy and complete with
sinks with running water. Helen Mack had spared
no expense at the wedding of her only child.

The dance band was exceptional, with a wide rep-
ertoire ranging from standards to the sixties heydey
of labels like Motown, Stax, and Philly Interna-
tional, right into contemporary sounds. Vivian
watched as the guests lost their inhibitions, led by
the older generation, who of course had been
around for the original Function at the Junction.
She got into the spirit herself, mastering the Shot-
gun danced to the classic of the same name as she
danced with Mr. Warner.

She and Zack weren't sitting next to each
other—he sat on Desirée's left and she on Austin's
right—but he offered his hand when the band
slowed down the tempo.

They had danced together when the lead singer
invited the guests to join in during Desirée and
Austin's first dance as husband and wife, but this
time it felt different. The floor was less crowded,
for one. Then again, maybe she was just getting
accustomed to dancing with him.

"I've got to tell you something, Vivling," he said.

"What's that?"

"I know it's soon, but I think I'm falling in love
with you."

She promptly took a misstep.

Zack tightened his hold around her waist. "You all right?"

"Yes." She quickly regained the beat. "I just didn't expect to hear you say that. I'm glad you feel that way . . . I've been thinking the same thing myself about you."

"So it doesn't frighten you?"

"Of course not. I think you're pretty special, Zack."

"Good. But I've got to tell you, it scares the hell out of *me.*"

Vivian, a little self-conscious of her unmarried status, sat out the tossing of the bridal bouquet, which was caught by Desirée's widowed mother. Judge Frank Mitchell, Mrs. Mack's boyfriend, caught the garter in a surprising display of agility for a man of his bulk, and the guests were delighted that the longtime couple would, if the legend persisted, be the next to marry.

The sun had set when the first guests began to leave. Vivian was enjoying a two-step with Zack when she suddenly remembered something. "Zack!" she exclaimed. "We both got here by limo. How are we going to get back to our hotel?"

"My dad turned in his rental this morning on the way home from the hospital. After I dropped you at Mrs. Mack's, I picked them up and brought them to the chapel. They drove the car out here. We'll all leave together, and we'll drop them at their hotel. Their flight home tomorrow is the same as ours, so we can stop and get them on our way to the airport. I hope you don't mind."

"No, of course not. I'm glad you were able to work it out so well."

* * *

When they all got into the rented Chrysler, Vivian noticed that Mr. Warner appeared to be breathing heavily. "Are you all right?" she asked him.

"Oh, I'm fine," he replied heartily. "That was some wedding. I tell you, it was worth the trip out here."

"It really was," Vivian agreed. "But from old photos of weddings I've seen from forty years ago, nice weddings don't seem to be anything new."

"I don't know about that," Mrs. Warner said in her soft manner. "I'd say they do things much better nowadays. I remember going to many weddings where they just served sandwiches."

Vivian and Zack looked at each other incredulously. "Sandwiches?" they repeated simultaneously, breaking into laughter.

"Those folks really must have been poor," Zack remarked.

"Well, they did remove the crust from the bread so they looked a little fancier, but they were still sandwiches," his mother said.

Zack reached for Vivian's hand, covering the back of it with his palm, handling the wheel adequately with his left hand. Vivian wondered if his parents had noticed the gesture in the darkness of the car, then told herself not to worry. Mrs. Warner was a completely different type of person from Mrs. Williams.

Traffic on this Saturday evening was relatively light, and they were back in Denver within thirty minutes. Zack and his father agreed on the time they would leave for the airport. Mr. Warner invited them to brunch, but Zack declined, citing the wonderful breakfast included in their stay.

There were a few other guests having drinks and playing the piano in the lobby of the inn, where it was a house tradition to gather. Everyone asked if they had been at a wedding, no doubt prompted by their formal attire, and they stayed only long enough to confirm before saying good night and heading for the stairs.

It had been a long day, one that contained considerable emotional upheaval, but Vivian felt exhilarated. She and Zack had exchanged their feelings for each other in a crowded setting, unable to affirm their love with even a kiss, but now they would be alone. Her body tingled in anticipation. She wanted to be naked in bed with him so badly that she couldn't get up the stairs fast enough.

When she was near the landing Zack, just a few steps behind her, said, "Wait a minute."

She turned. "What?" Then she gasped as he reached around her waist with one hand and under her hips with the other. "Zack! What are you doing?"

"Preparing to carry you over the threshold."

She linked clasped hands at the side of his neck to keep from falling, taking a moment to be thankful for all those "light" frozen entree she'd consumed. She said a silent apology for all the grumbling she'd done about the portions being too small to keep a cockroach alive, for now she was benefitting from all those 300-calorie meals. Zack couldn't have weighed a whole lot more than she did, but at least he didn't appear to be out of breath from carrying her. "Why? It was Desirée and Austin who got married, not us."

He shifted her weight as he unlocked the suite

door. "I know. But I was hoping just the same that we could make like we're on a honeymoon."

It was incredible. To be in bed with him, kissing him with such intensity and abandon, feeling the taut muscles beneath his naked skin, his hands squeezing her breasts and the firm skin of her thighs . . . When his exploration by touch became an oral one, she cried out, unable and unwilling to stifle the lust he brought out in her.

In spite of their wild cravings for each other they took their time, as if recognizing the significance of the occasion; and by the time they lay back exhausted they had both experienced fulfillment like they had never had before.

"Hi, Glenda!"

"Hi! When did you get in?"

"About an hour ago. I just finished unpacking. Did I interrupt you?"

"No, I'm not doing anything but looking at a magazine, and I'm about to put the damn thing down because it's so ridiculous. They've got an article on a lot of black female celebrities talking about their dress sizes. You know these people are lying through their teeth. Hardly none of them will admit to being bigger than a size six. And you wouldn't believe who claimed to be an eight." She named a statuesque performer. "It makes me wish I could show up on her doorstep with a size eight and say, 'Here, let me see you get into *this.*' I guess they don't call them actresses for nothing. But enough about that. Tell me all about Denver and the wedding."

"It was wonderful, Glenda."

"The wedding, or the city?"

"Both."

"Ooo-ee. Some-thing must have hap-pened!" Glenda spoke in a singsong pattern.

"Something did. Zack and I are in love."

"I *knew* it!"

"Well, I wish you'd shared your foresight with me before. You could have spared me a lot of unnecessary worrying. Just a few weeks ago I was thinking he wasn't even going to call."

"You know what I mean, Viv. I didn't know way back when. I distinctly remember thinking that each time you saw him it was going to be the last. But when you hooked up in Africa and arranged to go to Colorado together . . . it's like that feeling you get just before something happens that it's going to happen, like when you're at the jewelry store and a woman with skin-tight leopard print pants, two-inch nails and cranberry-colored hair comes in. You just know she's going to ask the clerk to see the cubic zirconia."

"I know."

"I'm so happy for you, honey. It's only July, and you're reeled in your Mr. Right. You do think he's Mr. Right, don't you?"

Vivian rocked her upper body from side to side. "I think this is it, but we'll just have to see. So tell me, how's Pete?"

"We went out again last night."

"Really? Is something happening that I should know about?"

"I'll tell you this much. Remember what I said about it not taking long to know you've got something special?" She paused just for a second. "Well,

I know this is special, and I've got a feeling he knows it, too."

Vivian squealed. "Both of us finding love at the same time! It's amazing."

"Just remember that I like September for a wedding month."

"Yeah, well, *you* just remember not to let him write any checks."

Zack called at ten-thirty from the hospital. "They're killing me, making me come in the same day I get back into town. Now that I'm done with mine, I think they ought to bar people from taking vacations."

"Now that you're done with yours, of course," she repeated with a giggle. "But next month it'll probably get worse. More people go on vacation in August than any other time."

"I'll be all right. I'm off Tuesday and Wednesday—I'll be up to take you to a two-hour lunch, so be prepared—and on Thursday I go on days." He paused. "I hope my schedule isn't going to be a problem for you. I have to work next weekend too, but since I get off at three at least we'll be able to go to dinner on a Saturday night like normal people."

"I think it would be very selfish of me to not want you to share those healing hands of yours with those who need them." She chose her next words carefully. "Believe me, I learned a long time ago that if you can't accept people for what they are you have no chance for happiness. But the hospital isn't going to beep you in the middle of the salad course and tell you to come in, are they?"

"Doubtful. It sounds like you're planning on being a part of my life for a while, I hope."

"Yes, because I'm happy, Zack. I hope you are, too."

"More than you know." His next words were spoken softly. "I love you, Vivling."

"I know."

Zack sounded playfully indignant. "How do you know?"

"I just know. I can feel it. It's like this, Zack. When you're in a jewelry store and this woman comes in dressed in skin tight leopard print pants—"

Dear Reader:

I hope this book made you smile. For this story I drew on many personal experiences I had during my former life as a single professional in New York. Years after I've changed both my marital status and the way I make my living, I'd forgotten how funny my former life could be.

Next up for me is a story I'm calling FROM THIS DAY FORWARD. It features TV newsman Schuyler Audsley from LOVE AFFAIR—a character I knew I hadn't seen the last of (to be quite honest, I just really liked his name). Look for books in stores in late summer 2002.

Keep romance alive!

Bettye

bunderw170@aol.com

or

P.O. Box 20354
Jacksonville FL 32225

ABOUT THE AUTHOR

Bettye Griffin wrote two dozen romantic short stories during the 1980s and early 1990s, most of them published by the Sterling/McFadden group of "confession" magazines. She spent four frustrated years in Florida before getting her first book published in 1998.

When not writing, Bettye works as a freelance medical transcriptionist. Originally from Yonkers, New York, she now makes her home in Jacksonville, Florida, with her husband and is stepmother to one adolescent, one teen, and one young adult. PRELUDE TO A KISS is her fourth Arabesque title.

More Sizzling Romance from
Jacquelin Thomas

__Undeniably Yours	1-58314-131-6	$5.99US/$7.99CAN
__Love's Miracle	1-58314-126-X	$5.99US/$7.99CAN
__Family Ties	1-58314-114-6	$5.99US/$7.99CAN
__Hidden Blessings	1-58314-160-X	$5.99US/$7.99CAN
__Someone Like You	1-58314-041-7	$4.99US/$6.50CAN
__Forever Always	1-58314-007-7	$4.99US/$6.50CAN
__Resolution of Love	0-7860-0604-8	$4.99US/$6.50CAN

Call toll free **1-888-345-BOOK** to order by phone or use this coupon to order by mail.

Name_____

Address_____

City_____ State_____ Zip_____

Please send me the books that I checked above.

I am enclosing	$_____
Plus postage and handling*	$_____
Sales tax (in NY, TN, and DC)	$_____
Total amount enclosed	$_____

*Add $2.50 for the first book and $.50 for each additional book.
Send check or money order (no cash or CODs) to: **Arabesque Books, Dept. C.O., 850 Third Avenue 16th Floor, New York, NY 10022**
Prices and numbers subject to change without notice.
All orders subject to availability.
Visit our website at **www.arabesquebooks.com**.